NURSING HOMES ARE MURDER

A PAUL JACOBSON GEEZER-LIT MYSTERY

NURSING HOMES ARE MURDER

MIKE BEFELER

FIVE STAR

A part of Gale, Cengage Learning

GALE
CENGAGE Learning®

Farmington Hills, Mich • San Francisco • New York • Waterville, Maine
Meriden, Conn • Mason, Ohio • Chicago

GALE
CENGAGE Learning®

LIBRARY OF CONGRESS CATALOGING-IN-PUBLICATION DATA

Befeler, Mike.
  Nursing homes are murder : a Paul Jacobson geezer-lit mystery / Mike Befeler. — First edition.
    pages cm
    ISBN-13: 978-1-4328-2816-5 (hardcover)
    ISBN-10: 1-4328-2816-9 (hardcover)
    1. Murder—Investigation—Fiction. 2. Retirement communities—Fiction. 3. Memory disorders in old age—Fiction. 4. Retirees—Fiction. I. Title.
  PS3602.E37R47 2014
  813'.6—dc23   2013050380

Find us on Facebook– https://www.facebook.com/FiveStarCengage
Visit our website– http://www.gale.cengage.com/fivestar/
Contact Five Star™ Publishing at FiveStar@cengage.com

Printed in the United States of America
2 3 4 5 6 7 18 17 16 15 14

For Wendy, Roger, Dennis, Laura, Kim, Kasey, Paige,
Asher, Kaden, and Adam.

ACKNOWLEDGMENTS

Many thanks for the assistance from Wendy Befeler and my online critique groups and the editorial support from Deni Dietz and Alice Duncan.

CHAPTER 1

Deep in contemplation over how much longer my eighty-five-year-old body and soggy mind would last, I sat on the balcony of our Hibiscus Hotel room overlooking the Honolulu Ala Wai Yacht Harbor. I felt a surge of gratitude that my limbs moved and my organs did what they were supposed to, but I did have this one little problem—overnight my short-term memory disappeared like a mosquito being zapped in one of those electric traps. Getting old was a pisser, but I counted my blessings to be here in this tropical paradise with my family.

Behind me I heard running footsteps, a thump, and hands covered my eyes.

"Guess who?"

I could see daylight through the fingers. "Let's see. No ring on the finger, so it's not Marion. Fingers too small to belong to Denny or Allison. That leaves Jennifer."

My twelve-year-old granddaughter removed her hands and plopped down in the chair beside me. "Well done, Grandpa. Your deductive reasoning figured it out."

"That, and you're the only one young enough to have been galumphing around behind me."

Jennifer set her elbows on her knees and rested her chin in the palms of her hands as she stared out to sea. "Good waves today. Are you going to come watch me surf one more time before we fly home tonight?"

"Wouldn't miss it."

There was a knock on the hotel room door. I turned to see my wife, Marion, usher in a short man in a crumpled suit. He seemed out of place since the rest of us wore shorts. I watched as he strode directly to me with Marion following.

A shiver ran down my spine. I didn't recognize him, but his pursed lips and scrunched eyebrows didn't look like he was here to give me a ukulele lesson.

"Mr. Jacobson, may I speak with you for a moment?"

I scooted my chair around to face him. "I think you have a captive audience since you're blocking my escape route unless I want to fly over the balcony." *Whoops. I shouldn't give ideas like that to a stranger.* "And who the hell are you?" I added in my most welcoming manner.

"Paul, this is Detective Chun," Marion said.

The name clicked with what I had read in my journal earlier this morning. Marion had shown me a diary entry I had written the day before. She had also reminded me that we were newlyweds, and that she had picked me out as a used husband after my first wife had died. "Got it. What brings you to our humble abode, Detective?"

"I have a favor to ask you."

"Well, well. What can I do to help the fraternal order of police on this fine day?"

Chun looked to Marion, Jennifer, and back at me. "This is an unusual request, but you may be the perfect person to help with a police investigation."

I opened my hands toward him. "I think you have the wrong guy. I'm a retired auto parts store owner with no experience in law enforcement."

"Oh, Grandpa, you've forgotten all the times you've helped the police solve cases," Jennifer said.

I stared at my granddaughter, and my mouth must have dropped open because I found myself snapping it shut.

"Jennifer's right," Marion said. "Paul, you've helped the police in Hawaii, Colorado, California, Seattle, and on a cruise ship."

"Well shut my mouth," I replied, opening my mouth.

"But Detective Chun," Marion said. "We're all heading back to the mainland tonight."

"That's why I came as soon as possible to speak with you. Mr. Jacobson, would you be willing to extend your stay in Honolulu? We'll cover expenses for you and your wife as well as any rebooking fees for the airlines."

"I'll be happy to stay and help, too," Jennifer volunteered, bouncing up and down in her chair.

My son, Denny, who had come into the room through the adjoining door, said, "No dice, young lady. You have to get back to school."

"Aw, Dad. I've helped Grandpa before with solving crimes. He needs me."

"I haven't agreed to anything yet, anyway," I said. "What's this all about, Detective Chun?"

"Last night, someone sexually assaulted a resident of the Pacific Vista Nursing Home here in Honolulu. We have an initiative in the police department to crack down on elder-abuse crimes. We haven't been able to figure out who the perpetrator is yet, but I thought you might be able to help."

"I applaud your efforts to catch criminals harming old farts, but I don't know what I can do to assist."

For the first time Chun smiled. "With you, Mr. Jacobson, there's one thing I've learned. You may forget things overnight, but during the day you have an excellent memory."

"Yeah, that's true. I could repeat our conversation so far word-for-word, but I can't remember yesterday from yams. How could I possibly contribute to your investigation?"

Detective Chun's intense eyes bore in on me. "I'm hoping I

can convince you to go to the nursing home as a resident, undercover."

I waved my arms in a crossing motion. "Whoa. I'm not sure I want to be in a nursing home above covers or under covers. The last thing people my age want to do is go to a nursing home. No sense rushing things. A nursing home should be the last resort when my memory really goes in the crapper and I can't control my pee anymore."

"Please watch your language in front of Jennifer," my daughter-in-law, Allison, who had joined the confab, said.

"Sorry. I got carried away."

"It's all right, Mom. Grandpa was only venting."

Out of the mouths of babes. "That's it. Like a volcano, I was venting." I turned my attention back to the detective. "Let me get this straight. You want me to go to this nursing home, pretend I'm even more mentally dysfunctional than I already am, and snoop around?"

"I wouldn't have worded it exactly that way, but yes."

I pictured myself surrounded by drooling, slobbering old people. Wait a minute. That could be me in a few years. "Don't you have a police officer you can send in undercover?"

Chun nodded. "We have. We convinced the nursing home to add a night security man and made a recommendation for that position that they've accepted. You've even met him. Officer Benny Makoku goes on duty this evening as an undercover member of the security team."

"That's my friend Hina's dad," Jennifer said, "Grandpa, you saw him yesterday."

"I don't remember him." I regarded Detective Chun. "What can I do that your undercover guy can't?"

"Good question. Officer Makoku won't be there around the clock. I thought it would aid the investigation to have a resident who can observe what's going on at the nursing home. You notice things, and as long as we find a way to get your information during the day before you fall asleep, I figure you'll help us nail the perp."

"But why Paul?" Marion asked. "And won't it be dangerous for him?"

"We don't have anyone in the police department who looks old enough to be a resident in the nursing home. Also, by having officer Makoku there, someone will be keeping an eye on Mr. Jacobson."

"Do it," Jennifer urged. She looked toward her mom. "Can't I please stay to help Grandpa?"

"No!" her parents said in unison.

Jennifer rolled her eyes upward. "The parental unit won't let me have any fun."

Chun turned to Marion. "Mrs. Jacobson, we're prepared to put you up in a condo near the nursing home. That way you'll be able to visit Mr. Jacobson whenever you want."

Marion bit her lip. "It's not like we have to rush back to California for anything. I'd like to see my grandson, Austin, but I could defer that a week or so. Can you give Paul and me a moment together to discuss this?"

The others adjourned to the adjoining room, and Marion sat down next to me. "What do you think, Paul?"

"I'm trying to put this all together. You and Jennifer indicated I've helped with police investigations before."

"Yes. You have a knack for being in the wrong place at the wrong time and have been implicated in several murders. Along the way you cleared yourself and helped the police catch the real killers."

I searched my leaky brain and found no evidence of this. "Really?"

Marion gave a resigned sigh. She held up her index finger. "The time I first met you at the Kina Nani Retirement Home

13

in Kaneohe." She held up a second finger. "Then in Boulder where you lived with Denny, Allison, and Jennifer." She raised a third finger. "When we got married in Venice Beach." Her pinky went up. "On our Alaskan honeymoon cruise." She added her thumb. "And here on this vacation over the last two weeks."

I put my hands to my temples but couldn't squeeze out any recollection. *Nada.* Zip. Zilch. "Okay, so I've somehow been around people committing crimes. Do you think I could really help in this nursing home?"

"Just like you have a knack for getting in trouble, you also have the ability to figure out who really perpetrated crimes." She looked out toward the ocean. "I wouldn't mind staying in Honolulu for another week or so." She turned to look at me. "But only if Detective Chun can assure your safety."

"I can't say the idea of being in a nursing home ahead of schedule appeals to me that much, but if I could really help get the bad guy locked up, I guess I'd do it."

Marion clasped my hand. "You're a good man, Paul Jacobson."

"Or completely wacko."

Marion went to invite the others back to our room. I stood and stretched my legs. I guessed I'd have to get used to being immobile for a while.

When Detective Chun returned, I said, "I'll do it."

Jennifer gave me a high five.

I sucked on my lip. "But first I have several questions."

"Fire away."

"Won't the staff be suspicious of my suddenly showing up?"

"There are several openings at the nursing home," Chun said. "We can have your name added today, and you can move in tomorrow. No problem."

"How am I going to communicate what I find?" I asked.

Jennifer danced around and waved her hand. "Ooh. Ooh. I

can answer that. Grandpa keeps a journal. It's his way of reading every morning what happened to him recently. At the end of every day, he can document the results of his investigation."

I had only skimmed yesterday's entry in my journal this morning. "I suppose that will work."

"Do you have any suspects?" Marion asked.

"Not yet. The victim described a man, average build and height. No further information. We think it may be someone on the staff or a visitor."

"Could it be a resident?" Marion asked.

Chun raised an eyebrow. "That's possible, but I think it's more likely to be someone else. We're running a background check on all residents and staff."

"And although my parents won't let me stay to help"—Jennifer paused to give Denny and Allison her preteen evil eye—"I can be Grandpa's consultant over the telephone."

"How will that do any good?" I asked.

"We can brainstorm on what you're learning. I've helped you before, and I can do it again." Jennifer gave her head a determined nod. She leaned close and whispered in my ear. "And we can continue to tell geezer jokes as well."

I winked at her.

Jennifer skipped away, a conspiratorial grin on her face.

I sat there thinking over our discussion. I pictured myself skulking around dark hallways, trying not to trip over walkers and wheelchairs. A shudder ran through me. Did I really want to do this? Questionable, but I had committed myself, and Paul Jacobson kept his word. I certainly hoped I'd be able to do something useful and not end up doing more harm than good with the police investigation.

CHAPTER 2

Detective Chun pulled out a folded document from the inside pocket of his suit coat and handed it to me. "Here's a release form you'll need to sign, Mr. Jacobson."

I eyed the document as if I'd been given a live hand grenade. "Some lawyer's gobbledygook I assume."

He gave me a wan smile. "Yes. Our attorneys require it."

"You should have a lawyer look at it, Dad," Denny said.

"I don't need any stinking attorney laying his mitts on this," I replied in my most legal manner. "I've read a few contracts in my day."

"And I'll be happy to check it over as well," Jennifer said.

"There you go. I have all the legal representation I need."

Jennifer and I read the document that said I agreed of my own free will (who else's would it be?) to help the police department, and they would not be held liable if I ended up with so much as a hangnail. I had to hold them harmless (police never seemed very harmless to me), and my only recourse was for expenses incurred. The document indicated every precaution would be taken to assure my safety, but that I acknowledged the risk of the situation.

"Damn lawyers," I muttered.

"Grandpa, don't be so negative. One of your best friends, Meyer Ohana, is a retired judge and lawyer."

"I don't remember him, but if he's retired he can't be all bad."

"He's nice and has helped you several times."

"That's good to know. Any suggested changes to the law-yerese in this document, young lady?"

Jennifer gave me her most lawyerly crinkled nose. "Nope. It's good to go."

I affixed my Paul Jacobson, added the date after being reminded what century I was in, and handed the papers back to Detective Chun. "I'm ready to rock and roll."

"Thank you. Mr. Jacobson, I have one more document for you to sign."

Uh-oh. Now what?

He pulled out another set of papers. "Here's your application to be admitted to the Pacific Vista Nursing Home."

Jennifer and I scanned through this one. I read that I was agreeing to reside in a facility with skilled nurses on duty at all times, that I would divulge preexisting medical conditions, and that Pacific Vista was not responsible for the loss of any valuables, which I was advised to leave elsewhere. I couldn't argue with anything there, so I affixed my name with a flourish. "Okay. I've signed my life away. Anything else?"

Chun reached in his pocket and pulled out a third document. I imagined one of those little circus cars from which more and more clowns kept climbing out. He handed it to Marion. "This is a release form indicating you will be in residence at the condo the police department is paying for."

"Is this like a safe house?" Marion asked.

"I certainly hope it's safe," I said.

Detective Chun eyed me warily. "We have a building with several apartments used by mainland visitors such as consultants that come periodically to aid an investigation. It's in a good neighborhood, and we've never had any problems there."

Marion and Jennifer read through the document, and Marion signed.

I pointed at Chun. "You prepared these papers before I even agreed to do this crazy thing."

He gave a sheepish grin. "I hoped I could convince you to do it."

"I should tear up the documents, but what the hell. If you need my assistance, who am I to object?"

Chun pulled out one more thing from his bottomless pocket. "Mr. and Mrs. Jacobson, you can move into the condo any time this afternoon. Here's a map."

"Dad can drive us over, and I'll help you unpack," Jennifer said, bouncing around in pogo stick mode. "After my last surfing expedition."

"When do I start my new career as a bedridden vegetable?" I asked.

Marion glared at me and punched me on the arm.

I rubbed the spot. "Ow. Did you see that, Detective? Spousal abuse."

"I hardly tapped you." Marion grabbed my chin between her hands and gave me a kiss. "Does this make up for it?"

"I guess I can stand the pain for the reward."

"Tomorrow morning you can check in at the nursing home," Chun said. "It's two blocks from the condo. Do you have any other questions?"

My mind raced with a thousand questions, but I didn't think Detective Chun could answer any of them. The prime one being: what was I getting myself into?

After Chun departed, we changed into our swimming togs to accompany Jennifer down to the beach while she surfed. Marion, Denny, Allison, and I plunked down on the sand while Jennifer paddled out to the line of other surfers waiting to catch the perfect wave. The sun sparkled on the crests of waves, a sailboat tacked in the distance, two kids splashed each other in the shallows, and I contemplated my near-term future.

The next day I'd be a resident of a nursing home, the type of place I had spent my whole life avoiding. I was voluntarily giving up my freedom to spend nights in a hospital-style bed, eat baby food again, and be treated like an addled old fool. Well, the old and addled part applied, but in order to help the police I would need to be no fool.

Marion and Jennifer had said I'd assisted the police in the past. Couldn't remember squat about that. I'd have to use my observation skills to figure out what was what and who did what and why the sun always rose in the east. I slapped my cheek. I would need to stay focused.

I returned my attention to Jennifer, who caught a wave and headed into shore. Amazing. I hated the ocean, and my offspring loved it. There was no explanation for this turn of events.

Marion stood and took my hand. "Come on. We need to take one last swim."

"Last as in for today or forever?"

She swatted me. "Come on."

I raised my old body and joined my bride in sticking my toes into the dangerous waters of Waikiki. When no creatures attacked, I allowed myself to be dragged in knee-deep. Bracing myself, I ventured in up to my waist.

"There, that isn't so bad," Marion said.

"I guess you're right. If I'm going to be in a nursing home, I might as well get used to being wet."

Marion punched my shoulder.

"Please, no more violence." I rubbed the tender spot. "When the nurses check me, they're going to detect all this bruising from spousal abuse."

Marion cocked her fist at me, and I pictured Jackie Gleason as Ralph Kramden saying, "To the moon, Alice."

Instead she reached down and splashed water in my face.

I spluttered and returned the favor. We engaged in a good old-fashioned water fight, and I felt positively young again—not a day over eighty.

We returned to the sand to watch Jennifer catch a few more waves while I caught a few sand fleas before Denny signaled to her to come in.

Like a true kid, she ignored him for a while, but then he gave a piercing whistle that couldn't be disregarded. When she paddled to shore, a girl her age accompanied her. We met them in the shallows.

"My friend Hina was out there surfing," Jennifer said.

Her companion, sporting sparkling black hair, waved.

"Can't I surf another half hour?" Jennifer asked.

"No," Denny said. "We have to shower, pack, check out, and take your grandfather and Marion to their new condo."

"Aw, Dad."

But the universal kid appeal produced no results from my hard-hearted son who, with his arms crossed, stared down Jennifer.

Jennifer gave a resigned sigh. She and Hina exchanged a goodbye hug and promised to email, friend, and tweet each other, whatever that meant.

Jennifer dragged her surfboard to the rental booth, and we headed back to the hotel.

After everyone showered, I stopped by the adjoining room to find Jennifer reading an electronics magazine.

"Hi, Grandpa. I'm looking at things to get for my next birthday. There are all kinds of cool gadgets I want. Check it out." She handed the magazine to me.

I took it as if she'd handed me a live snake. Bracing myself for the horrors of the electronic age, I opened it and began scanning through. I thought I'd landed on another planet.

"What is all this crapola?"

"Paul," Allison said in her protector-mother voice. "Watch your language."

"Sorry." I hung my head. "What is all this strange and unusual stuff?"

"It's the latest and greatest," Jennifer said.

I began reading. "Okay, here's one I understand. A laptop. That's where the cat sits."

Jennifer rolled her eyes.

I tapped the magazine. "And a smartphone. That's a telephone that tells jokes."

Jennifer put her finger in her mouth and made gagging sounds.

I was on a roll. "An iPhone. You put it to your eye rather than your ear. iPad—a soft eye patch. An iBook—large print."

Jennifer grabbed the magazine. "Enough. You're impossible, Grandpa."

"That's one of my best traits."

Jennifer motioned to me and led me out to the balcony where we sat down. "Since you insist on dumb jokes, do you have any geezer jokes for me?"

"Why did you drag me out here to ask that?"

Jennifer looked over her shoulder and whispered. "Mom doesn't think it's politically correct to tell geezer jokes, but you and I both enjoy them."

I couldn't remember the details but her words made sense to me. "And I suppose she wouldn't appreciate me calling them old fart jokes either."

"Nope." She leaned closer. "Here's one for you. What's the difference between a pirate and a geezer?"

"I give."

"One's bold and one's old."

"Jennifer!" Allison shouted. "Cut that out."

I elbowed Jennifer and whispered in her ear. "I notice your mom waited for the punch line before yelling at you."

"Yeah. She wanted to overhear the joke before she censored me."

I returned to my room and packed.

"It's a good thing we brought two suitcases," Marion said. "You'll be able to take one with you to your new home tomorrow."

"You're kicking me out and sending me to a nursing home." I sniffled and stuck out my lower lip in an exaggerated pout.

"Don't give me that. I'll be two blocks away and coming to visit you all the time. I can also spring you for walks and excursions once in a while."

I waggled my eyebrows. "How about conjugal visits?"

Her lips curled in an enigmatic smile. "That might be arranged."

"Good. I have something to look forward to."

CHAPTER 3

Waiting to the very last minute to check out of the Hibiscus Hotel before being forcibly evicted, we lugged our suitcases down to Denny's SUV. My son drove us to a food store to buy some provisions for Marion. Next stop, the condo along the side of Punchbowl, the inactive volcano that rested above downtown Honolulu. As long as it remained inactive for the next few weeks or until I graduated from the nursing home, I would be a happy camper.

Marion's new abode had a view of the ocean. The compact one-bedroom apartment was furnished with utilitarian but clean furniture: in the living room a couch, easy chair, desk, and bookshelf; in the bedroom a double bed, dresser, nightstands, and reading lamps; in the bathroom a commode that sparkled; and in the kitchenette a fridge, stove, microwave, and the necessary pots and pans. Nothing but the best for my bride while I was off catching criminals in the world of decrepit old fogies.

Jennifer pointed toward the ocean. "I can see a cruise ship. Is that like the one you went on for your Alaskan cruise, Grandpa?"

"Can't say as I remember."

Marion squinted. "It looks approximately the same size. Paul managed to cause all kinds of commotion on that trip."

"Me?" I thumped my aging chest.

"Yes, you. Fortunately, everything worked out fine, and you even saw a whale at the end of the cruise."

"It must have been a whale of a trip," I said, immediately

ducking before my wife could swat me.

Denny unloaded the luggage into the living room so it wouldn't attract any interested felons who might break into the back of the SUV.

"We have time for one excursion before our dinner reservation," Denny said. "Any suggestions?"

"I want to see the cemetery in the center of Punchbowl," Jennifer said.

"You want to check out dead people?" I asked.

Jennifer put her hands on her hips and gave me her almost-teenage withering glare. "It's a famous place—the National Memorial Cemetery of the Pacific. I studied it when doing research for my school paper that's due next week."

With no one dissenting, we clambered back in our magic chariot, and Denny drove into the center of the volcano, so to speak. And what a view—a sweeping vista of closely cropped grass and granite markers for over thirty thousand men and women who had served in four wars. As we stood looking toward a flagpole with Old Glory waving in the trade winds, I thought back to my friends who had died during World War II. I had been fortunate. I served in the European theater, but as a logistics swabbie, arranging provisions for the fighting men who landed at Normandy. I was never at risk, but I did my part to support the incredible supply chain that fed and fueled the troops.

"Maybe you can be buried here someday, Grandpa."

"Let's not rush things, kiddo."

Jennifer stomped her foot. "I want you around for a good long time. I'm only suggesting you consider it."

I gave my granddaughter a hug. "Don't get so indignant. I'm joshing you."

Jennifer gave me a huge smile. "Back at you, Grandpa."

Grandkids. You couldn't put anything over on them.

We strolled around and came to one spot that overlooked Manoa Valley to the east or, as the Kama'ainas said, the Diamond Head direction. So much green, lush scenery. I guessed this wasn't so bad a place to be laid to rest, as long as the volcano stayed extinct.

Afterwards, at Jennifer's insistence, we drove past the Pacific Vista Nursing Home where I would take up residence the next day. It was an institutional white two-story building that reminded me of the hospital I had been in during my tour of duty in England. My one war wound—a broken leg while cavorting around London on leave.

Jennifer craned her neck. "You can barely see the ocean from here, Grandpa."

"That's okay. I didn't sign up on this tour for the view."

Jennifer punched her right fist into her left palm. "That's right. You're going to nail the bad guy."

I only hoped I could do something constructive before anyone nailed me.

After a brief stop at the condo to freshen up, we hit the road again to go to dinner. Jennifer sat between Marion and me in the backseat, bouncing around as if she had ingested Mexican jumping beans.

"You don't sit in one place much, do you?" I commented.

"Nope. I leave that to you ah-dults."

I regarded Jennifer out of the corner of my eye. She grinned.

As we entered rush hour traffic, Jennifer leaned close to me and whispered in my ear. "Want to tell geezer jokes?"

I whispered back, "Sure. I have one for you. Why is a geezer like a buggy whip?"

Jennifer shrugged. "I dunno."

"They're both antiques."

"Stop it, you two," Allison shouted.

"Busted," Jennifer said.

"And I thought telling geezer jokes was a prerequisite for being admitted to a nursing home," I added helpfully.

"We're trying to teach Jennifer to respect people of all ages," Allison said. "Geezer jokes are disrespectful of older people."

"I don't know," I replied. "I'm an older person, and I get a kick out of geezer jokes. They don't offend me one iota."

"Paul, stay out of it," Marion warned.

Taking the advice of my good wife, I zipped my lips. I knew when I was outnumbered, so I changed the subject. "Denny, where are you taking us for our last supper?"

"If we can get through this traffic, we're going to Michel's at the Colony Surf. One of the best restaurants in Waikiki."

I regarded the bumper-to-bumper traffic. "Honolulu has all the trappings of a major city. Next there will be smog."

"You have that right, Dad. Without the trade winds this would be like Los Angeles."

We finally arrived, and a hostess wearing an elegant, flowing holoku led us to a table for five, replete with a crisp white tablecloth and peaked napkins resting on china plates. Strategically placed pots of fresh flowers gave off tropical aromas as we enjoyed a view over the beach to the gentle waves of the Pacific Ocean. Several coconut trees lined the sand. My stomach rumbled. I was ready to decimate some seafood.

Jennifer ordered Mahi Mahi Almondine; Allison chose Wellington of Wild Sugpiaq Salmon; Marion, Oven-roasted Rack of Lamb; Denny, Filet Mignon Madagascar; and I selected Michel's Seafood Sampler providing tastes of fish, abalone, scallop, crab, lobster, and shrimp. I was an equal-opportunity eater of ocean creatures.

Marion and Allison adjourned to the powder room, and Denny went to get a closer look at the view. I leaned toward Jennifer. "We're unchaperoned, so I can corrupt you. Ready for a geezer joke?"

She leaned closer as well and in a conspiratorial tone replied, "You bet, Grandpa. Give me your best shot."

"What's the difference between the devil and a geezer?"

"You got me."

"One promotes sin and the other is older than sin."

Jennifer gagged.

I smiled, happy to be able to contribute to the delinquency of my granddaughter. Ah, the small delights as we aged.

Everyone returned, and the wait staff immediately delivered our salads. After I masticated my greens, our main courses arrived, and we dug in. Every one of my sea creatures was delectable. I figured this might be my last gourmet meal for some time. I hated to imagine what I would be eating the next day.

For dessert Marion and I shared cherries jubilee; Denny and Allison indulged in the tableside crepes suzettes for two; and Jennifer scarfed down white and dark chocolate mousse. Thus sated, we staggered back to the car.

Denny drove us to the condo without having to suffer through much traffic. While he and Allison loaded their suitcases in the SUV for their trip to the airport, I had Jennifer to myself for a moment. "Here's one last geezer joke for you. What does the hundred-year-old geezer say to the ninety-five-year-old geezer when they part?"

"I give."

"Bye, youngster."

Jennifer gave a ten point—on a scale of one to ten—preteen eye roll, and I knew I had been successful.

We all went outside and exchanged hugs.

"When will I see you next, Grandpa?"

"Don't rightly know."

Jennifer regarded me with pursed lips. "You'll have to call me and report on your investigation."

"If Marion will remind me, I'll be sure to do it."

They climbed in the SUV, and Jennifer rolled down the window. As they drove away she shouted, "Get the bad guy!"

"Bye, youngster." I waved as they drove out of sight.

A sense of sadness trickled through my insides. I was going to miss my family and, in particular, the dynamo named Jennifer.

Sensing the slump of my shoulders, Marion gave me a hug. "We'll have to either go to Colorado or invite them to come to Venice Beach over Jennifer's spring break."

That lightened my spirits as we strolled arm-in-arm back to the condo. Below, I saw the twinkling lights of Honolulu, and as I craned my neck upward, I spotted a sliver of moon off to the west. That old moon had been around for a long time. I wondered how much longer I would be on this revolving orb. I'd keep on truckin', enjoy times with Marion, and see what was in store for me.

I helped Marion unpack, but left my suitcase largely intact since I would be moving on to the great nursing home in the sky the next morning. I pictured me as a cowboy sitting around a lonely campfire, playing a harmonica and serenading the prairie dogs. I slapped my cheek. No sense getting maudlin. Besides I'd never been able to play a harmonica worth spit.

"Now you have an important task to complete," Marion reminded me.

"Brush my teeth?"

"Not yet, silly. You need to take your pills."

"I hate taking pills."

Marion gave an exaggerated sigh. "We go through this twice a day. Take your medicine."

"Yes, ma'am."

Somehow I managed to swallow the rocks disguised as pills.

"One other activity for you, Paul."

"Now what?"

"You have to write in your journal." Marion handed me a brand-new spiral-bound notebook. "You filled up the previous one, so you can start fresh tonight."

For the next thirty minutes I documented the life and times of one Paul Jacobson, corrupter of youth and soon-to-be undercover operative. What the hell? As a great philosopher once said, when life gives you heartburn, you can always burp.

CHAPTER 4

I awoke in a room I didn't recognize and had no clue where I was. A woman lay in bed beside me. She had silver hair, a cute nose, and seemed to be here of her own free will. This wasn't my wife, Rhonda, who had died. At that moment my bed companion awoke, identified herself as my new wife, Marion, and indicated I was a recycled husband. Wonder of wonders.

Marion insisted that I read the journal lying on the table beside my bed. After going through it, I realized that I'd seen my son, daughter-in-law, and granddaughter the day before and agreed to some crazy scheme to help the police find a sexual predator at a nursing home. It's amazing what my right hand had signed me up for without my brain being aware of it.

After a solid breakfast of scrambled eggs, toast, orange juice, and coffee, I repacked my suitcase, and Marion led me two blocks to my new abode, the Pacific Vista Nursing Home. I found no banners proclaiming, "Welcome, Paul Jacobson." The door was locked. Marion pushed a button, and we were buzzed inside to a reception counter where a woman in a white nurse's uniform greeted us. She wore her hair bunched in a bun, had reading glasses dangling from a chain around her neck, and pinched her lips together as she concentrated on a list in front of her. She informed Marion that I was expected.

I patted my stomach. "That's a relief. At least I'm not expecting."

The nurse stared at me as if I had tracked dog poop on the

rug and said to Marion, "Is this a symptom of his dementia?"

Marion nodded vigorously. "Oh, yes. He says the strangest things. I don't know what will come out of his mouth."

The nurse scribbled vehemently on a chart and looked up at Marion. "Does he swear?"

Marion put a finger to her cheek and looked thoughtful. "Oh, let me see."

"Hey," I said. "I'm right here. You can talk to me, damn it."

"There's your answer," Marion said with a glint in her eye.

The nurse wrote some more. "Does he exhibit any signs of violence?"

Marion grinned, having way too much fun with this. "He has a temper and gets in arguments but not anything physical."

"Is he at risk of wandering away?" the receptionist asked.

I tapped the counter. "Hey, you can ask me. I like to take walks."

She made a mark on the sheet and raised her eyes to Marion. "Besides inappropriate comments, bad language, and the risk of wandering off, is there any other behavior we should be aware of?"

I stepped in front of Marion so the receptionist would have to look at me. "I like to tell geezer jokes."

She made another check on her sheet, and I backed away before they put me in a padded cell with a straitjacket.

She continued to question Marion, so I took the opportunity to look around the lobby. Two women sat in wheelchairs against one wall. One was knitting, and the other slept with her head lolling to the side, drool running from the side of her mouth. A man with a walker clomped along a hallway. A nurse pushed another woman in a wheelchair toward a room partway down the hall, and they disappeared inside. A large pot containing Bird of Paradise flowers stood in the entryway. I sniffed a strange aroma that seemed to be a blend of pine cleaner and pikake.

Behind the nurses' station I spotted a large dining room. Three hallways merged to form a T.

I turned my attention back to the discussion as Ms. Nurse announced I would be in semiprivate room one-forty-two on this floor.

"I don't know if I qualify for a semiprivate or even a private room since I wasn't in the army but the navy," I said.

She made another check on her list, and Marion elbowed me.

"Okay, okay, I'll behave," I said. Then I whispered in Marion's ear, "Have I done enough to give the appearance of deserving to be here?"

"More than enough," Marion whispered back.

The nurse picked up her phone, made a few curt comments, and in moments a certified nurse assistant the size of Godzilla appeared. He picked up my suitcase as if flicking a toothpick and led us into the hall to the right. I decided he was not a guy to mess with, so kept my smart remarks to myself.

We went through a doorway that led to a room with a curtain down the middle. Godzilla placed my suitcase on the top of a dresser. I looked around my new accommodations. A clean hospital-style bed, a nightstand with lamp and telephone, a mounted television, an easy chair, a wooden chair, and a bookshelf rounded out the furniture. An open closet displayed metal hangers on a wooden dowel. The walls were off-white and bare. A small adjoining room had a potty and sink. All the comforts of home.

"Can I put pictures on the wall?" I asked.

"You can decorate any way you want, but no holes in the walls. We have special tape you can use. By the way, my name is Puna Koloa." He held out a huge mitt.

"Paul Jacobson." I gingerly shook his hand without getting any fingers crushed.

"Do you have any questions, Mr. Jacobson?"

I thought of asking where to find the nearest bar, but instead posed a different question. "When do we eat around this joint?"

Puna grinned. "Breakfast from seven to eight, lunch twelve to one, and dinner five-thirty to six-thirty."

"What happens if my stomach is on a different schedule?"

He leaned close to me and whispered. "You call for me. I have a cupboard full of snacks. Cracked seed, potato chips, cookies, candy, you name it."

I figured he required a lot of calories to keep his large engine going.

Puna pointed to a call button by the bed. "Push that if you need anything. I'll let you get settled in." He gave me a departing wave and lumbered into the hallway.

I took the opportunity to further scrutinize my new domain. Only one window, and it looked out over Honolulu. I spotted a few specks of blue ocean between the buildings. I could live with this.

Marion helped me unpack, which took all of five minutes. She looked around the room. "I'll have to buy you some posters to put on the walls."

"No dancing girls, but I wouldn't mind some pictures of lush mountains."

"I need to get some more provisions for the condo, so I'll pick out something for you later today."

A shout came from the other part of the room, "Hey, do I have a new roommate?"

I stepped over and pulled the curtain aside. A crinkled old man lay in bed. A vase of yellow hibiscus stood on his nightstand, the only bit of color against the bare walls.

Marion and I went to his bedside.

"I'm Paul Jacobson."

"Ralph Hirata." He held up a twisted hand. "I'm blind and

riddled with arthritis but have all my marbles."

I carefully took his hand, so as not to further damage the bent fingers. "I have good eyesight and working limbs, but my marbles have fallen down a gopher hole."

Ralph chuckled. "Sounds like we'll make a good pair."

"My wife, Marion, is here with me, Ralph."

"I heard two sets of footsteps after that huge clunker Puna left the room. Pleased to meet you, Marion."

Marion took his hand. "I need to mention one aspect of Paul's dementia since you'll be getting to know each other. When he wakes up, he'll have forgotten everything that happened to him the day before. He won't remember who you are."

Ralph waved a crooked finger generally in our direction. "I can live with that, but it must make things pretty difficult for you, Marion."

I regarded Ralph. He was sharp.

Marion hugged my arm. "You have that right. Almost every morning I have to remind him who I am. It's like starting over on the dawn of a new day."

"You said *almost* every morning," Ralph replied.

Nothing got past this guy.

"Yes, Ralph. There's one circumstance when Paul remembers when he wakes up, but after a day he's back to his usual forgetfulness."

This piqued my interest. "What causes me to remember on the special occasions?"

Marion patted my hand. "It's a surprise. You'll know when it happens."

It was obvious she didn't intend to give any further clarification.

"How long have you been held prisoner here, Ralph?" I asked.

He laughed. "You have an interesting way of saying things,

Paul. Going on two years."

"Yeah, my mouth has a way of getting me in trouble. When we checked in, the attending nurse kept making check marks every time I mouthed off."

"I'm going to run some errands today," Marion said. "Anything I can get for you, Ralph?"

A watery glint showed in his clouded eyes. "Licorice. I love licorice."

"Puna told me he keeps lots of snacks," I said. "Doesn't he carry licorice for you?"

"Yeah, but I finished off his stash," Ralph said.

"I'll add that to my shopping list," Marion said. "Now I'll leave the two of you to get better acquainted. I'll be back this afternoon."

"Look at the service I get." I gave Marion a peck on the cheek.

After Marion left, I pulled over the wooden chair from my side of the room and sat. "Tell me your whole life history, not that I'll remember it tomorrow."

"The highlights. I'm Nisei, second generation, born in Waipahu. My parents came from Japan to work the pineapple fields, met here and married. After high school I enlisted in the army and served in the Four-Forty-Second Regiment in Europe."

"Wow. You were in the Four-Forty-Second, the most decorated regiment in US history."

"I thought you couldn't remember things, Paul."

"Man, nothing gets by you. I have great long-term memory and have a photographic memory during the day. I can picture everything that's happened to me so far today. But yesterday or anything from the recent past, forget it. I was in the navy in the war but didn't see action. You must have been involved in some serious fighting."

Ralph bit his lip and remained silent for a good thirty seconds. "Yes, as you probably know we suffered tremendous losses. Many of my friends and fellow soldiers died. I was with the Hundredth Infantry Battalion trained at Camp Shelby in Mississippi. We went into battle near Belvedere in Italy. I was wounded at Castellina but returned to action before we took Bruyères. I received another wound in the fight to rescue the Lost Battalion near Biffontaine. That took me out of the war while I recuperated for a year. Probably why my eyes went bad and my limbs gave out."

"Man, you had quite a war experience compared to my behind-the-lines logistics support."

"Tell you what, Paul. There's a shoebox up in my closet. I haven't had it brought down for a long while. Would you mind retrieving it?"

"No problem." I scampered over, found an old dusty box, and brought it to Ralph.

He opened it and rummaged around with his hand, extracting a metal five-pointed star with a red, white, and blue ribbon attached. "Here's the Bronze Star I was awarded for gallantry in action."

"It's good to know I have such a gallant roommate."

Ralph chuckled. "I'm going to like bunking next to you, Paul. Here, take a close look."

I held it and turned it over in my hand. "I've never seen one of these. The closest I got were my honorable discharge papers after the war."

"I have my discharge papers in this box as well, although I can't read them anymore. Four thousand Bronze Stars were awarded to the Four-Forty-Second, as well as five hundred Silver Stars, fifty-two Distinguished Service Crosses, twenty-one Medals of Honor, and more than nine thousand Purple Hearts."

"Quite a set of accomplishments." I grabbed his hand. "It's

an honor to be in the same room with you, Ralph."

He closed the box. "Would you put it back in the closet?"

"Sure." I took it and reached up to put it back on the closet shelf. The box slipped out of my hand and dropped to the floor. "Damn. Clumsy me." Only an old ration book from World War II seemed to have fallen out. I picked it up, put it back in the box, and carefully placed the box back on the shelf.

I returned to Ralph and dusted my hands together. "Everything's shipshape again. Tell me what you did after the war."

Ralph smiled. "Life was good. I went to the University of Hawaii, met Lily, got married, started selling insurance, raised three kids. Did pretty well for a shot-up kid from the Islands. How'd you like to buy some long-term-care insurance, Paul?"

"Huh?"

"Just joshing you. Probably too late if you don't have it already, and I'm retired anyway."

I thought of a bumper sticker I'd seen many years ago, back before my memory went on the fritz. It read: "I'm retired. Yesterday I was tired, today I'm tired again."

"Tell me your background, Paul."

"I grew up in San Mateo, California, and, like you, enlisted. I provided logistics support to the allies landing in France. After the war, I worked at an auto parts supply outfit in Southern California and eventually became owner. I ran the store until I retired and moved to Hawaii with my first wife. After she died, it's kind of hazy, but somewhere in there I met Marion, and she agreed to put up with my defective brain and signed up for a secondhand husband."

"You do have a unique way of describing things."

"Hey, it's the way my remaining brain cells work."

"What time is it?" Ralph asked.

I looked at my watch. "Twelve-o-five."

"Good. Soup's on. You ready for lunch?"

I patted my stomach. "Sure. At least they didn't ring a bell."

Ralph chuckled. "Then like Pavlov's dogs we could start salivating."

"No thanks. I already saw an inmate drooling out in the reception area."

Godzilla, now known as Puna, appeared and lifted Ralph out of bed and into a wheelchair.

"I can push Ralph to lunch," I volunteered.

"Okay by me. I have plenty to do." Puna smiled at me, revealing a large gold front tooth. Then he left the room.

I moved behind the wheelchair and began pushing. "How many gears does this baby have?"

"Two. Stop and go."

"Anything I should know about mealtime here?"

"Yeah. No food fights."

I was going to enjoy rooming with Ralph. I steered him into the hallway and followed the line of wheelchairs and walkers converging on the dining area. The staff had prepared tables for two, four, or six, covered with white tablecloths. It reminded me of the dining tables from the night before as described in my journal, although I'm sure the average age of clientele here was fifty years greater than at the restaurant where I'd eaten with my family.

I wheeled Ralph into place at a two-person table and sat across from him. A young woman in a white apron put plates in front of us. I sniffed the aroma of rice and boiled broccoli. Some kind of mystery meat quivered in front of me as well.

"Do you want me to cut your meat for you, Ralph?" I asked.

"That's kind of you, Paul. That would help."

I stood and cut the meat into bite-sized chunks. I couldn't tell what it was. Possibly chicken-fried steak, maybe chicken, or who knows what. I returned to my chair and cut a piece for myself. I chewed and tasted but still couldn't determine if it was tender beef, tough dark chicken, or something else. Oh, well, I'd live.

I decided to do my first detective work. "How safe is this place, Ralph? Residents ever have any problems?"

He put his fork down and leaned toward me. "Things have been pretty good until the night before last. The administration is trying to keep it quiet, but someone attacked Mrs. Rodriguez in her room."

"How did you learn that?" I asked.

Ralph pulled his earlobe. "I overheard two CNAs talking. I've compensated for my lack of sight with excellent hearing."

"I'll have to remember not to whisper any secrets near you."

"I'm not worried. You'll forget any secrets anyway."

I laughed. "You have me pegged. Tell you what. I'll be your eyes if you'll be my memory."

"It's a deal."

I whispered, "Now tell me more about what you overheard."

CHAPTER 5

Ralph filled me in on the assault on Mrs. Rodriguez, but I didn't learn anything more than what Detective Chun had previously related. After finishing my lunch dessert, which turned out to be green Jell-O with an embedded piece of pear, I wiped my mouth and tossed the napkin down on the table. The food was nothing to write home about but filled my tummy.

"You ready for the trip back to the room?" I asked Ralph.

"You bet. I have to get rested up for the big event this afternoon."

"You have a belly dancer coming to visit?"

"Almost as good. We play bingo."

I rolled my eyes. "That sounds as exciting as watching a cockroach race."

"Hey, that's not a bad idea. We have some pretty good-sized cockroaches around here."

I stuck out my tongue. "Yuck. You trying to convince me to move out of here?"

"Nah. Only giving you the skinny on what to expect. They keep this place pretty clean, but in Hawaii you can't avoid cockroaches. Besides I like having you for a roommate. The last guy didn't talk much."

I decided not to ask what had happened to his last room-mate.

I pushed Ralph into the hallway where we came alongside a skinny woman sitting in a wheelchair with Puna behind her.

She turned to Ralph and winked. "You want to drag race, Ralphie?" I noticed a bumper sticker on her wheelchair that read "Hell On Wheels."

"Not today, Alice. I don't think my engine can keep up with Puna."

Puna grinned. "She's right, Mr. Hirata. I think I provide a little more strength than Mr. Jacobson can."

I was tempted to accept the challenge but reconsidered after recognizing the muscle power behind the other vehicle. "You must do a lot of weight work, Puna," I said.

He shrugged. "I'm in training to become a sumo wrestler."

"Really?"

"Nah. Just kidding you, Mr. Jacobson. I like working at Pacific Vista. I have great residents like Mrs. Teng here and you and Mr. Hirata."

Everyone was a comedian around this place.

Alice Teng reached out and rapped her knuckles on Ralph's wheelchair. "I'm ready to rumble. Don't listen to this malarkey."

"You don't have much of an island accent, Mrs. Teng," I said.

"It's Alice, buster. I was born in San Francisco and came to Hawaii after my husband retired. He kicked the bucket while surfing."

"I'm sorry," I said.

She gave a dismissive wave. "He caught a perfect wave and died of a heart attack with a big smile on his face."

"I guess that's as good a way to go as any," I said. "I grew up in San Mateo."

"A peninsula brat. Okay, you going to yak all day or are you ready for a little friendly competition?"

In spite of my misgivings, I couldn't let the challenge go unanswered. "What do you say we show these people what Paul and Ralph are made of? You up for it, Ralph?"

Ralph waved a shaky hand. "Let's clean their clocks."

Alice Teng rubbed her hands together. "First one to the shower and bathroom gets an extra serving of tapioca pudding tonight. Let's move, Puna."

I looked down the hall. "Is that the room with the green light above it?"

"That's the one," Ralph replied. "Green means no one is taking a shower or bath. Red indicates someone is in there."

"How do you know?" I asked. "You can't see it."

"It's been described to me."

Puna started pushing Mrs. Hirata down the hall. I grasped the handles and shoved Ralph ahead.

Puna sped up and passed us.

With my competitive juices flowing, I engaged a higher gear and shot past them.

"Now we're cooking!" Mrs. Teng shouted. "Floor it, Puna!"

Puna raced past us. I made a valiant attempt to keep up, but he was too much for me. They beat us to the finish line by a wheel and a half. I came to a stop with my heart pounding and my breath coming in gasps. "Phew. I'm too old for this."

"Looks like you need to get a refurbished engine, Ralphie," Mrs. Teng said.

Puna looked over his shoulder. "Don't tell anyone what I did. My boss wouldn't approve."

"Don't worry," Mrs. Teng said. "This is between us race car enthusiasts. See you in Indianapolis. I'm ready for my nap, Puna."

"I'm set for a nap as well," Ralph said.

"I'll be back to your room in a moment to help you into bed, Mr. Hirata." Puna pushed Mrs. Teng away, and they entered a room two doors down the hall from ours.

"I think I'm going to have to change my opinion of nursing homes," I said.

Ralph chuckled. "We're not all drooling vegetables."

"You can say that again."

"We're not all drooling vegetables."

"Cut it out or I'll whap you alongside the head."

"You want to knock some sense into me, Paul?"

I wheeled Ralph into our room. "No. I don't think it will work. You might try it on me sometime, though. Maybe it would loosen up some of my errant brain cells. What time is this bingo extravaganza?"

"Three o'clock."

Puna appeared and lifted Ralph into his bed.

"You don't have to pump iron with the workout you get around here," I said.

"I still have to lift weights. Mrs. Teng and Mr. Hirata don't weigh much."

An image formed in my mind of Puna juggling old people as if they were tennis balls. I pinched my cheek. No, I was really here in this crazy place.

Once Ralph settled in, I said to Puna, "Ralph mentioned the attack on Mrs. Rodriguez. How's she doing?"

Tears formed in Puna's large eyes. "Poor lady. She's so nice, and to have something that awful happen to her. She's at the hospital for observation. Should be back here later this afternoon."

I didn't think Puna was involved in the sexual assault. He seemed genuinely concerned with what had happened to Mrs. Rodriquez. Besides, he didn't fit the description of the attacker in my journal. No one could mistake Puna for someone of average build and height.

After Puna left the room, I told Ralph I intended to explore around while he took his nap. I certainly didn't want to risk a nap and forget everything that had happened to me today.

I felt a little twinge in my left calf from the race and wanted to stretch my legs. I walked to the end of our hallway, where I spotted an emergency exit with a large sign warning that an alarm would sound if the door was opened. I retraced my steps and sauntered to the nurses' station. Puna was helping two female nurses by stashing some boxes on a high shelf. He was a handy guy to have around. The dining area tables had been re-arranged. I saw a stack of bingo cards. Bingo. I knew where the big event would be taking place.

I explored the other two halls and found them identical to mine except my hallway was beige; one other hall, light blue; and the third, a purplish tint. Color-coded to help those of us with eyesight to keep from getting lost. I found a stairwell and went upstairs. There I noticed an almost identical setup with three halls, nursing station, and dining area. Right above the downstairs entryway was a small lounge. Two women sat in wheelchairs watching a soap opera on TV. I had never gotten hooked on daytime television. I had enough drama in my life without resorting to soaps. One of the women, a rotund lady in a bright blue muumuu, looked up at me with rheumy eyes. "You got a smoke?"

"Nope, and I'm sure they don't allow it in here anyway."

"Tarnation. You can't get any service in this hotel." She turned back to the tube. "Don't go with him, Marisa. He's a scumbag."

I watched a twenty-something man and woman arguing on the television program, shook my head, and wandered away. Satisfied with the lay of the land, I returned to my room to read a few short stories before it was time to rouse Ralph for bingo. With my memory, it didn't work for me to read novels anymore since I'd have to start over every day. Short stories were the ticket for me. I could finish one or more in a sitting, and it didn't matter if I reread the same stories the next day.

I pushed the call button, and Puna came to help Ralph to the bathroom and assisted my roomie into his wheelchair.

"I can take it from here," I said. "That will free you up to go retrieve Mrs. Teng. But no racing this time."

"Thanks, Mr. Jacobson. You're the best." He galumphed out of the room.

I pushed Ralph to the dining area and up to a table with two open spaces for wheelchairs. Puna wheeled Mrs. Teng into the other spot, and I sat on one of the two wooden chairs.

Mrs. Teng rubbed her two hands together. "I'm going to whup you two gents."

"You have quite a competitive spirit, Alice," I said.

"I love to win." She turned to a woman who stood next to a cage with bingo balls inside. "Hey, where are my cards? I'm ready to kick butt."

"Be patient, Mrs. Teng," the young woman answered. "We'll distribute the cards when everyone is here."

"Patience, my patootie. Let's get this show on the road."

I decided to use the time to ask a few questions. "Alice, do you know Mrs. Rodriguez?"

"Darn tootin'. It's a shame what happened to her. No one better try to mess with me if they know what's good for them." She reached into her lap, fiddled with something, and brought her right hand out. She wore brass knuckles.

I gawked.

"Anyone shows up in my room unannounced, pow!" She punched toward me, missing my chin by inches.

No one would mess with Alice Teng.

The young woman passed through the tables and gave each of us two bingo cards. In the center of our table rested a dish filled with little cardboard discs. After everyone had received cards, she returned to the front of the room and announced that we would be playing a regular bingo game to begin, first to fill any row, column or diagonal.

"What's the prize?" Alice shouted.

"A jar of macadamia nuts."

"Aw, nuts," Alice said. "They get stuck in my choppers."

I put my hand on Ralph's arm. "How are you going to play bingo?"

He tapped the table. "I have Braille cards."

I looked carefully. Sure enough, each square on his two cards contained little bumps. It amazed me how people read using their fingertips.

Our hostess spun the cage and took out a ball. "B-nine."

"That's not me," Alice said.

I agreed that she wasn't the mild, harmless type.

"I-eight."

"I'm glad you've already eaten, but why don't you pick something on my card?" Alice yelled.

The activity lady glared at her.

I leaned toward Ralph and whispered in his ear. "Is Alice always like this?"

He nodded.

We continued, and I filled in a few spaces but nothing close to completing a row, column or diagonal. Finally, a woman in the back of the room shouted, "Bingo!"

Alice slammed her hand on the table. "This game is rigged. I demand a recount."

The activity lady went and checked the winning card. "We have a winner." She handed over the jar of macadamia nuts. "Next a blackout game. You have to fill every square on your card."

"Good," Alice said. "I'm going to kick some serious heiny this time."

I was curious. "Alice, what did you do before you retired?"

"I hosted a radio talk show program. Why do you ask?"

As the game continued, my card looked more like a whiteout

than a blackout. I wondered if they offered a booby prize for the person with the fewest squares covered. Our table was shut out again when a geezerette at a table near us won.

"Preferential treatment," Alice grumbled.

"You don't seem to be having much fun," I said.

"What do you mean?" A glint came into her eyes. "I love this."

Back in my room late in the afternoon, Puna and a small woman in a white nurse's uniform came up to me. The woman stood a foot and a half shorter than Puna at a third of his weight. "Time for your medication, Mr. Jacobson." She handed me a cup of water and three pills the size of the bingo balls used earlier.

"I hate taking pills. I can't swallow these."

"Your wife warned us you might give me guff. Be brave and take your medicine."

"Is Puna here to push them down my throat?"

Puna crossed his arms. "Whatever it takes, Mr. Jacobson."

I opened my mouth in surprise, and the nurse popped the first pill in. Before I knew it, I swallowed. With Puna distracting me, I downed the second and third pills.

Puna grinned and dusted his hands together. "Works every time."

Marion stopped by with some posters for me and a supply of licorice for Ralph.

"I'll be back this evening to bring your journal and to hang your posters," she said.

"I get such special treatment."

"Good licorice," Ralph called out, having already popped the first piece in his mouth.

"Marion, you're now a dealer, having delivered Ralph his drug of choice."

After dinner that evening, a CNA appeared. He stood approximately five-foot-ten and was probably in his thirties with neatly combed hair and a twinkle in his eyes. "I'm Ken Yamamoto. Time for your shower, Mr. Jacobson."

"I can do that on my own."

"I'm here to help you so there will be no accidents. Nursing home rules."

I'd showered and bathed myself for the last eighty years but didn't intend to get in an argument over the procedures around this place.

"I see you have a robe and slippers in the closet, Mr. Jacobson. Why don't you change into those, and I'll wait for you in the hall." Ken pulled the curtain between my part of the room and Ralph's. He went outside and closed the door.

I took off my clothes and put on the robe and slippers. I shuffled out into the hallway and found Ken in heated discussion with another CNA.

This guy had a similar build and stood an inch shorter. He sported thick eyebrows and dark, deep-set eyes. Giving me a smile, he said, "I'm Sal Polahi."

"Where's Puna?" I asked.

"He's off duty," Ken said. "We're the night shift."

"You guys don't look that shifty to me," I said.

Ken's eyes lit up. "Good one, Mr. Jacobson. You'll have to come audition at the playhouse."

"What playhouse?"

"Besides working here, I'm an actor at the Aiea Community Theater. We're always looking for comedians."

Sal groaned. "That's all he discusses. Sports and acting."

Ken elbowed his companion. "I told you to come audition

any time you want. We're looking for people who can play grouchy roles."

Sal rolled his eyes. "Give me a break."

"What was your big argument a moment ago?" I asked.

Sal smiled. "We're both sports fans. We're discussing who was the best athlete of all time. I say Bo Jackson, and Ken insists it's Michael Jordan. What's your vote, Mr. Jacobson?"

"Hmmm. Two good candidates. Let me hear your pitches for each."

Ken poked Sal in the chest. "Michael Jordan had speed, agility, and precision. No one could stop him on the basketball court. The greatest basketball player of all time."

"I agree," Sal said. "But our topic is the greatest athlete. Bo Jackson excelled in football, baseball, and track. At college he was a Bowl MVP twice, All-American, and Heisman winner. First person to play in an All-Star game in both professional baseball and football. He also qualified twice while in college as an Olympic sprinter. There's no telling how many records he would have set if his hips hadn't given out. What do you think, Mr. Jacobson? Care to settle the debate?"

"I'd probably go for someone way back when I was a kid. Jesse Owens."

They both stared at me. "Why him?" Ken asked.

"Your two candidates are both excellent choices. But Jesse Owens ran and jumped like no one before him. He won four gold medals at the nineteen thirty-six Olympics and shoved the Fickle Finger of Fate right up Hitler's nose, dispelling the fanatical Aryan propaganda crap. Under the pressure of the Third Reich, Jesse showed what Americans and people of all races could achieve."

"Not a bad argument," Ken said. "We'll rule it a three-way tie. Time for your shower."

I guessed I wasn't going to be able to distract them any longer.

"I read on your chart that you have . . . um . . . some memory problems, Mr. Jacobson?" Ken said.

"Yup. That's me."

"But you recited some facts from nineteen thirty-six," Ken said.

I grinned. "You were paying attention. I have a great long-term memory, but don't ask me anything from yesterday."

"You aren't going to wander away on us, are you?" Sal asked.

"Not planning to. Is that why both of you are here?"

Ken gave a sheepish grin. "Yeah. Rules again."

They led me to the room with the green light, flipped a switch, and the light changed to red. Inside stood a high-technology walk-in metal tube that looked like a still to brew hooch. They guided me to the walk-in shower. I turned on the water but found no soap.

I called out to my two guardians, "Hey, I need a bar of soap."

"Oh, yeah," Sal said. "Let me unlock the cupboard." He took out a key and opened a door and handed me a bar of white soap and a tube of shampoo.

I proceeded to wash and shampoo. After toweling off and putting on my robe, I said, "I may have dementia, but I can move around fine. I don't think you have to accompany me in the future."

"Rules is rules," Sal said.

They led me out of the room, and Ken flipped the switch turning the indicator light green.

As we started to my room, I happened to turn back for a moment and noticed a small, wiry woman duck into the shower and bathroom. I came to a halt and pretended to tighten the cord on my robe. In a moment the woman came out of the room. In her hand she held the bar of soap and nibbled on it. Her gray hair spiked up as if she had stuck her finger in an electric socket, and she darted her head from side to side, her pale eyes making contact with mine.

I waved.

"Uh-oh," she said.

Sal and Ken turned at the sound.

"Oh, no, Mrs. Wilkins is at it again," Sal said.

Mrs. Wilkins scampered in the other direction along the hall and disappeared into a room. Ken raced after her.

"What happened?" I asked Sal.

He tsked. "Mrs. Wilkins has a condition called pica. She likes to eat soap."

I stuck out my tongue. "Yuck. Why does she do that?"

Sal shrugged. "No one knows for sure. Some people think nutrient deficiencies cause the condition, or it might be a chemical imbalance in her brain."

"I'm an expert on imbalances in the brain," I said.

Sal ignored my comment. "Whatever the reason, she says she likes the taste of soap."

Ken returned holding the bar of soap. "I took it away from her, but she almost bit me."

"Maybe you taste like soap, too," I said.

Ken glared at me. "She's a gentle woman unless you try to get between her and a bar of soap. I forgot to lock it up after your shower, Mr. Jacobson."

"Jeez. This is some place if you lock up soap."

"We have to," Sal said. "Otherwise, Mrs. Wilkins will steal it."

"What's the big deal?" I said. "Is soap dangerous for her?"

"No," Ken said. "We use pure white soap with no additives, so it's not dangerous to eat. But it wouldn't look good for visitors to see one of our residents eating soap. They'd think we're starving people."

I chuckled. "I get it. You have to keep up appearances." This place was starting to grow on me—like a malignant mole.

"How long have you guys worked here?" I asked.

"Ken's the old timer," Sal said. "He's been here over a year. I'm the new kid on the block. I came here from a nursing home in Maunalani Heights two weeks ago."

I decided to do a little interrogation while I had a captive audience. "Did you guys hear what happened to Mrs. Rodriguez?"

Sal shook his head. "That was awful."

Ken let out a deep sigh. "She's a nice lady. She just came back from the hospital. Everyone will be checking to make sure nothing happens to her again."

They both appeared duly contrite. The good news, I now had an opportunity to speak with her.

"I need to go help Mrs. Teng," Sal said. "See you again, Mr. Jacobson."

I waved as he disappeared down the hall. Ken accompanied me to the door to my room and left me on my lonesome. I changed into slacks, a Hawaiian shirt, and tennis shoes. Time for a little reconnaissance.

CHAPTER 6

Before leaving my room, I called over to my roommate. "Hey, Ralph. Do you know Mrs. Rodriguez's room number?"

"Yeah, one-eighty. Blue corridor."

"For someone with no eyesight, you sure are good on the visual cues."

He tapped his temple. "Nothing to it. I ask lots of questions and remember what I'm told."

I regarded him. Ralph might aid my investigation. I thought it was too soon to level with him, but I'd see how things progressed. "I'll remember that. Well, if you remind me, that is, I'll remember it. I didn't think you could hear the difference between beige, blue, and purple tint."

"No, not even I can do that, although I pick up things with my hearing that others miss. Plus, I'm a nosy old cuss. You want to know anything that goes on around here, I'm your guy."

Perfect.

Ralph squirmed in bed and adjusted his pillow. "I can tell you've already checked out the three hallways."

Nothing got by Ralph. He should be the one going under-cover. Oh, yeah. That would be kind of difficult with his lack of eyesight. Still, he could certainly play a useful role. "I noticed the color-coded halls when I wandered around earlier. That would be ideal for finding my way around, except tomorrow I won't remember what I learned today."

"You should write things down, Paul."

Once again he was right on top of it. "Good suggestion. Right now, I'm going to take another constitutional. I'll be back in a little while."

He chuckled. "Don't do anything I wouldn't do, Paul."

"Wouldn't think of it."

I moseyed down the hall to the nurses' station. One nurse eyed me suspiciously, but when I didn't make a dash for the door and instead entered the blue hallway, she looked away. It would be difficult to escape if I wanted to. I'd have to learn the code to open the door or quickly tailgate someone leaving the building.

I checked room numbers until I found 180, a private room. I knocked on the open door. "May I come in?"

A creaky voice announced. "Sure. I'm presentable."

I entered to find a room full of posies. There must have been twenty vases on her dresser, nightstand, bookshelf, and even on the floor.

"Wow, this reminds me of a field full of wildflowers. I think you've put all the florists in Honolulu out of business."

She gave a gentle laugh. "People have been so kind to me. Can you imagine all these flowers?"

"By the way, I'm Paul Jacobson. The newest inmate. I was admitted today." And that was all I intended to admit.

She held out a withered hand. "Linda Rodriguez."

I carefully shook it, not wanting to do any damage, but she surprised me with a firm grip. Never underestimate little old ladies.

"As a newbie, I'm trying to meet people here. My memory's not so hot, but my legs allow me to wander around."

"Well, pull up a chair, Paul, and tell me your life story."

I did as requested and gave the *Reader's Digest* version of my life. "That's pretty much me except I can't account for the last half-dozen years or so. Somewhere in there I got married again, and my wife, Marion, lives in a condo near here. For whatever reason, she puts up with me."

"I'm glad she's close by so she can come visit you regularly."

That reminded me that I should be seeing Marion this evening. She'd told me she would be by with my journal for me to write my account of the day.

"Yeah, it's nice having someone who checks on me."

She cupped her hand. "I have a secret."

"And you're going to tell me?"

"You seem like a dependable gentleman."

"That's the nicest thing anyone has said to me today."

Linda grinned. "I have a boyfriend."

I flinched. Where was this conversation going?

"Don't look so surprised. He came to visit me two nights ago." She giggled. "We were intimate."

Uh-oh. "Uh . . . what does your boyfriend look like?"

"He's close to your height, young and handsome."

"How young?"

She winked at me. "Very young. In his sixties. He has a cute mustache and beard. His mustache reminds me of Errol Flynn."

"What's his name?"

She giggled. "We haven't told each other our names. That would take all the mystery away."

"How did you two meet?"

"He showed up in my room. It was love at first sight."

Crapola. She was in la-la land. I needed to keep her talking to see if I might learn anything useful.

"I understand you just came back from the hospital."

"Yes. For some reason, the doctor and nurses checked me down there." She patted her lap. "I think they were trying to find out if I was pregnant, but I think I'm past that."

Yeah, by a good thirty years.

"A very strange hospital visit," she continued. "I'm not sure what was going on, but it's nice to be back here. I don't like hospitals. Have you ever spent time in a hospital, Paul?"

I couldn't imagine ever being to the point of considering it nice to be back in a nursing home.

"I went in a few times for operations. I don't enjoy hospitals either, Linda."

"Places to be avoided." She gave her head a vigorous nod. "You can get infections in hospitals."

"Didn't the police speak with you as well?" I asked.

"Yes, a detective even interviewed me." She leaned toward me and whispered. "I think they're trying to find my boyfriend. They believe he committed some crime. It adds to his mystery."

"Are you sure he's your boyfriend?"

"Oh, yes."

"When did he first show up in your room?"

She bit her lip. "I'm not sure. Things are kind of fuzzy."

That's an understatement.

Linda's eyes lit up. "My daughter gave me a coming-home present today." She held out her left wrist.

"That's a mighty fine diamond bracelet."

She jangled her wrist. "She thought I'd like something sparkly."

I wondered if it was a good idea to have such an expensive-looking piece of jewelry in a nursing home.

"What does your daughter think of your boyfriend?"

She gave a dismissive wave of her hand. "Oh, she hasn't met him yet. She always nags me. That's why I'm keeping him a secret."

I figured her daughter was going nuts over this situation.

"Do you have other relatives who visit you?"

"No. My son and his family live on the mainland."

A female nurse stuck her head in the door. "Is everything all right, Mrs. Rodriguez?"

"Yes. I'm making the acquaintance of a new resident, Paul Jacobson."

The nurse glared at me. "Mrs. Rodriguez shouldn't be disturbed."

I waved to the nurse. "I'll be leaving in a moment."

She pursed her lips, turned on her heels, and left.

"What else can you tell me about your boyfriend?"

She scrunched up her nose in concentration. "Hmmm. He's haole and has a nice soothing voice. I need some sleep, if you don't mind, Paul."

"It was good meeting you, Linda." I stood and left.

As I walked back to my hallway, I thought over what had happened. Linda Rodriguez obviously possessed some errant brain cells. Hers, rather than affecting her memory, had turned a sexual assault into a romantic encounter with a mysterious man. If the police apprehended the culprit, her testimony would be dicey.

Rather than immediately returning to my room, I decided to go meet Mrs. Wilkins, the soap eater, in person.

I spotted the room I had seen her duck into and knocked on the open door.

"Come in."

I stepped inside to see her sitting in a chair reading a book.

"Mrs. Wilkins, I'm Paul Jacobson. I'm new to the joint and want to introduce myself to other residents."

She shook a finger at me. "I recognize you. You're the stinker who gave me away to the cops."

"I didn't mean to. I was only curious, and then Ken and Sal spotted you."

She put her book down. "Not as fast as I used to be. That kid cop ran me down. My name's Louise. Have a seat."

I pulled up a chair and sat facing her. "Louise, I've never met anyone who eats soap. Why do you do it?"

"I dunno. I'm a little uptight right now. When I get nervous, I have this craving for soap. The darn coppers around here lock it up. I saw my chance after you came out of the shower room and took it."

"Why are you nervous?"

"Something bad happened to nice Mrs. Rodriquez." She leaned toward me, cupped her hand, and whispered, "This place isn't safe anymore." She straightened her back. "But no one better mess with me. I have good choppers, and I'll bite anyone who messes with me."

"Ken said you tried to bite him when he took away the soap."

"Darn right. How'd you like someone steal your snack?"

"Have you always liked eating soap?"

She gave me a conspiratorial wink. "Yeah. I discovered I liked it when I was a little girl. The first time I swore, my mother washed my mouth out with soap. It was supposed to be a punishment, but I liked the taste. I made a point of cussing in front of my mother at least once a week so I'd get my mouth washed out again. She eventually wised up and made my father take out his belt instead. That cured me of swearing, but I licked the bar of soap in our bathroom every chance I got. It was like having a lollipop sitting there—tempting me."

"What are you reading?" I asked.

She held up her book. "It's *The Dirt Eaters*. Can you imagine anyone doing something as disgusting as eating dirt?"

Back in my room, I found Marion hanging posters on the wall.

"My interior decorator is here." I went over and gave her a hug.

"I found some perfect pictures for you, Paul." She had already attached a mountain scene of rolling hills and snow-capped peaks. She held another in her hand of an island with sandy beaches and coconut trees.

"What's all the noise over there?" Ralph asked.

"Marion is beautifying my room."

"Ralph, do you want some scenic posters for your walls as well?" Marion asked.

"Sure. As long as you describe them to me."

Marion went to his side of the room and attached a poster. "Here's a picture of an underwater scene with brightly colored fish."

"Perfect. I used to snorkel before I lost my eyesight."

"And since I don't like the ocean, that's a better choice for Ralph," I said.

"Oh, Paul," Marion said. "You and your prejudices."

"Hey, I like most things excluding lawyers, pills, computers, and the ocean." I waggled my eyebrows at Marion. "And you certainly make my list of likes."

"That's a relief." Marion gave me a kiss.

With our habitat in perfect décor, Marion handed me my journal and pen. "Time for your writing, Paul."

"You an author, Paul?" Ralph asked.

"It's what you suggested earlier. I write what happens to me during the day. Since I'll forget everything overnight, Marion can bring it back in the morning for me to read first thing. Then I'll be able to recount the previous day's activities."

"So you'll be mentioning me in your writing," Ralph said.

I stepped over and patted him on the arm. "Absolutely. You're one of the highlights of my stay here so far. I'm hoping you'll also help remind me what happens."

"How about that?" Ralph said. "I'm a memory device."

"Exactly. The two of us combined make a pretty complete old codger."

"While you write, I think I'll read from your O. Henry short story book," Marion said. "I'd ask for a recommendation, but you wouldn't remember."

"That way I won't influence your choice."

Wondering if I would be able to do any good here, I sat down to document the adventures of Paul Jacobson, undercover detective and memory defective.

Chapter 7

I awoke to the sound of voices and running feet. My eyes popped opened, but I didn't know where I was. I lay on my side in a hospital bed facing a drawn curtain that spanned the room. Crap. Had I been admitted to a hospital? Had my ticker gone on the fritz? I couldn't remember diddly. I plunked my feet onto the floor and drew the curtain. Another geezer lay in a bed, staring at the ceiling.

"Good morning, Paul."

I did a double take. "I hate to be impolite, but who the hell are you, and where am I?"

He chuckled. "Marion warned me you wouldn't recognize me when you woke up. I'm your roommate at the Pacific Vista Nursing Home, Ralph Hirata."

I slapped my forehead. "Nursing home." This wasn't the kind of news to wake up to. "How long have I been here?"

"You were admitted yesterday."

"I don't admit anything. I've been framed."

"Stay calm. Marion will be here soon to explain everything."

Now I really didn't know what to think. "Who's Marion?"

"Your wife."

"You've got to be joshing me. I don't know any Marion. My wife, Rhonda, died." I looked at my left hand. It bore a wedding ring I'd never seen before. I dropped onto the bed. "Maybe I do belong in a nursing home. My brain has been French-fried."

At that moment an attractive young chick in her seventies

strolled in and gave me a kiss on the cheek. I wiggled my eyebrows. "I like the service in this nursing home."

She handed me a notebook. "Paul, I'm your wife, Marion. Before you make any faulty assumptions, sit down and read your journal."

"Journal?"

"Yes. You wrote this last night. It will give you a rundown on what you did yesterday."

I followed the instructions and read the diary. One good piece of news: I didn't end up in a nursing home because I needed additional care. That was a relief. I whispered to Marion. "Does my roommate, Ralph, know why I'm here?"

She whispered back. "No."

"I can tell you're sharing some secrets," Ralph said. "I can't see the two of you, but there's suspicious whispering going on."

"Sorry, Ralph," I said. "I'm trying to get some clarification on this strange new world I've awakened to."

"There's something going on here," Marion said. "When I arrived half an hour ago, the building was in lockdown. They wouldn't let me in. After the door opened, I came right here."

"Maybe one of the inmates had a seizure," I said.

I looked up to see a man in a crumpled suit standing in the doorway. He had a major scowl on his face. "It's worse than that, Mr. Jacobson. I need to speak with you and your wife."

I pinched my cheek. "I don't think I'm ready for an undertaker yet."

He motioned with his finger. "Follow me."

"In my pajamas?"

"I don't care what you're wearing," he said.

"We better do as asked," Marion said. She took my hand and led me out of the room. We followed the suit to an empty office. He motioned to two chairs and closed the door. We sat, Marion and I scrunched together on one side of a desk and the scowling man on the other side of the desk.

"Cozy place," I said.

"What's happening, Detective Chun?" Marion asked.

"That's a relief," I said. "You're not the mortician."

"This is no time for jokes, Mr. Jacobson."

"I'll be good. I recognize your name from my journal. You're the guy who recruited me to spy on people in this place."

"I wouldn't put it in those words, but yes. The reason for bringing both of you to have a private conversation—one of the nurses found Mrs. Rodriquez dead this morning."

I winced. "I read that I spoke with her last night."

The detective tapped the desk with a twitching digit. "And that's the problem. I hate to tell you this, Mr. Jacobson, but the staff here suspects you. You were the last person to see Mrs. Rodriguez alive. One of the nursing staff recognized you from last night. Mrs. Rodriquez died of asphyxiation. Someone smothered her."

My stomach tightened. "And the staff doesn't know that I'm here undercover?"

Chun gritted his teeth. "No, Mr. Jacobson. We didn't divulge that since the perpetrator might be a staff member. Let's review exactly what transpired last night."

"Okay. I can't remember any of it, but I can recount what I read in my journal."

"Let's start with that."

"There wasn't much to it. I visited Mrs. Rodriguez and chatted with her. Then I spoke with another resident, Mrs. Wilkins. Afterwards, I went back to my room and found Marion there. I wrote in my journal and went to bed."

"I think it's best if I take the two of you and your journal to police headquarters for additional questioning."

"You don't suspect Paul, do you, Detective Chun?"

He stared at me for a moment. "No, but we need to go over

anything you may have observed while with Mrs. Rodriguez."

"Do I have to go in my PJs?"

"Why don't you go back to your room to change and meet us back here? I want to talk to Mrs. Jacobson a little longer."

I scooted out of the room and headed back to throw on slacks, a Hawaiian shirt, and sneakers.

"What's going on?" Ralph asked.

"Mrs. Rodriguez died last night. The police want to speak to me because I was the last one to see her alive."

"Holy moly. I'll be happy to be a character witness."

"I'm sure they've witnessed a lot of characters besides me. I'll fill you in when I get back."

I returned to the office, and the three of us headed to the lobby where a nurse punched in the magic code to let us escape the building. Marion and I sat in the backseat of an unmarked police car.

"What did Detective Chun have to say while I was changing?" I whispered in my bride's ear.

"He wanted to tell me that all precautions would be taken to assure your safety," she whispered back. "I'm still concerned."

Chun drove us to Beretania Street where we entered a parking lot for a huge three-story building with pillars in front and a red roof.

The detective escorted us inside to a bright conference room rather than an interrogation room. A man with a ponytail waited for us.

"This is Officer Makoku."

"I've read his name but don't recognize him," I said.

"He's working as the night security man at the Pacific Vista Nursing Home. He called me when Mrs. Rodriguez's body was discovered. Let's start with going through in detail what you wrote in your journal, Mr. Jacobson. Care to read it to us?"

"That won't be necessary. You can look at the journal. I can recite it word-for-word."

Benny Makoku arched an eyebrow high enough to make him look lopsided. "Are you kidding me? With your memory?"

I tapped my temple. "My weird wiring doesn't prevent my photographic memory from working during the day." I proceeded to recount what I had written.

Detective Chun looked at Officer Makoku. "There's some new information. When we interviewed Mrs. Rodriguez in the hospital, she wasn't able to give any description of her 'boyfriend' other than average height and build. Now we know he's a haole guy in his sixties with a mustache and beard."

"Might be fake facial hair," Officer Makoku said.

"That's possible," Chun replied.

"And the diamond bracelet?" I asked. "Was that found on her?"

"No jewelry on the body," Chun said. "Looks like we have a robbery as well as a murder here."

"How do you know it's a murder?" I asked.

"The nurse who entered the room found a pillow covering Mrs. Rodriguez's face. The odds favor the same person who sexually assaulted her came back and killed her and stole the bracelet. I'm having our administrator correlate a list from the night of the assault with a list made this morning of everyone in the nursing home last night—staff, visitors, and residents."

"I was in the blue hall around midnight," Makoku said. "The place was deserted."

"We'll have to see if the coroner can give us a probable time range of death."

A woman knocked on the door. Chun stepped over and took several sheets of paper. "I want each of you to go through this list and put your initials next to any names you recognize."

We did as instructed. From names I had read in my journal, my list ended up being pretty short: Ralph Hirata, Alice Teng,

Sal Polahi, Ken Yamamoto, Louise Wilkins, and Puna Koloa (my fellow race car engine).

"Anything from the background checks?" Makoku asked.

"Nothing that jumps out," Chun replied. "Next I'm going to have a list run of haole men fifty to seventy."

"Whew," I said. "That rules me out. I can do the haole part, but can't fit in the young age group you've defined."

"And you weren't there the night of the sexual assault either," Chun said.

"That too."

"Do you think it's safe for Paul to remain in the nursing home?" Marion asked.

"A murder does step up the urgency of solving this case but also the risk. It's entirely up to you, Mr. Jacobson. You've already provided important information. We can use your ongoing assistance but can also pull you out any time."

I looked from Chun to Makoku. I didn't want to let them down. I had to help find who killed poor Mrs. Rodriguez. No way I'd duck out. "I'll stay there for the time being."

Smiles appeared on both of the men's faces. Marion didn't change her expression.

My stomach rumbled. "Hey, I haven't had any breakfast. Do you think you might rustle up some of those special police donuts for me?"

"I'll find something," Makoku said, "even if I have to raid the chief's special stash of malasadas." He left the room and returned with a pot of coffee, a bunch of cups, and a box of the soft, deep-fried Portuguese confections covered in granulated sugar.

I poured cups of coffee for Marion and me and downed a malasada in swift bites.

"For someone who can't swallow pills, you sure can put away the malasadas," Marion said.

"Mmffgg," was all I could answer with the second malasada in my mouth.

Chapter 8

My gullet stuffed with malasadas, I returned to my new home and admired the thin slice of pacific vista visible from the nursing home. At least there was some truth in advertising here. Marion reattached one of the posters to my wall where the tape had come undone and informed me she would be leaving me on my lonesome for an hour or so while she went to a store down the block to replenish a few food items for her larder at the condo. I couldn't begrudge her time for food shopping. Fortunately, a kitchen staff now took care of my every need, except when I missed breakfast and had to settle for police malasadas.

Now fully interior decorated and abandoned, I went into the bathroom to scrape off my whiskers, brush the malasada sugar off my moldy teeth, and wash my puss.

I rubbed my now smooth chin and stared at the face in the mirror. The wrinkled visage of a geezer stared back at me. Where had my youth gone? For that matter, where had my brain cells gone? But I needed to count my blessings. I possessed most of my hair, all my original teeth, no organs on the fritz, well, other than the one in my head. And Marion had actually hitched up with me. Amazing.

Having seen enough of my face, I left the bathroom and turned my attention to my roommate.

"Howzit going, Ralph?"

"To be honest, I'm bored out of my skull. How was your visit with the police?"

I thought of involving him in the sexual assault turned murder investigation but reconsidered since I knew Detective Chun wouldn't approve of me blowing my cover. I waggled my hand. "Not much happened. They asked about my visit to Linda Rodriguez's room last night." Then an idea to distract Ralph occurred to me. "I bet you were once an avid reader."

Ralph gave a long sigh. "You bet. That's the thing I miss most with the loss of my eyesight. I resigned myself to giving up driving, even no longer watching sunsets. But I sure miss curling up with a good book."

"I can't bring back your vision, but I can certainly supplement it. How'd you like me to read to you?"

His clouded eyes widened. "For real?"

"Sure. I have a book of O. Henry short stories. I'll read you one." I retrieved my book from the nightstand, pulled my wooden chair over to Ralph's bedside, and plopped down.

"Any particular types of stories you like?" I asked.

"It doesn't matter. Pick something."

"I'm not that picky. Hmmm, in the table of contents I see one called 'A Cosmopolite in a Café.' "

"Go for it."

I licked my fingers, thumbed forward to the beginning of the story, and settled in to read of a man who says he's a citizen of the world and not bound to any one locale. He pontificates on how he has traveled so much that he prefers no one location over another. At the conclusion of the story, he gets in a fight with a man who insults the town the cosmopolite was born in.

"Just goes to show that everyone has emotional ties to their roots," Ralph said.

"Whereas I've never rooted for wearing ties," I replied.

Ralph groaned. "Do you always tell dumb jokes, Paul?"

"Yeah. It's one of my most endearing qualities, although I

read in my journal that Marion usually smacks me upside the head when I mouth off with one of my jokes."

"Justly deserved. Thanks for the story."

"I can read to you on a regular basis if you remind me."

"Perfect. I'll provide the memory and you can contribute the eyes."

I patted his arm. "Sounds like a good division of responsibility."

Marion sauntered into the room. "What are you two up to?"

"Paul's been reading to me."

Marion smiled. "Paul, you used to read to your friend Meyer Ohana who has macular degeneration."

"You mean I'm a serial reader?"

"Is that like a tea leaf reader who sees signs in a cereal bowl?" Ralph asked.

I groaned. "Everyone wants to be a comedian."

"Only trying to keep up with you, Paul."

"I can tell the level of discussion here has descended to Jennifer's age range. Too bad she isn't here to appreciate it."

"My twelve-year-old granddaughter has a good sense of humor. I read in my journal that we tell each other geezer jokes."

Marion rolled her eyes.

"What's a geezer joke?" Ralph asked.

"It's a highly sophisticated type of joke about old farts like us. Here's one I remember from the old days before my memory went in the crapper. 'What happened to the old man who sat on Old Faithful at Yellowstone Park?' "

"What?" Ralph asked.

"He became a geezer geyser."

Ralph groaned.

"Don't give him any response, Ralph," Marion said. "Groaning at one of Paul's dumb jokes or puns only encourages him."

A nurse appeared to take Ralph's blood pressure, interrupting our intellectual discussion. She asked me to move my chair back to my side of the room. I obliged, and she pulled the curtain.

"Care to accompany me on a stroll outside?" I asked Marion.

"Sure."

"Good. Since they won't let me escape on my own, you can be my chaperone."

We headed to the lobby, Marion signed us out, and the attending nurse pushed a button to release the locked door.

Once outside I said to Marion. "I'll have to remember that. In addition to the code pad by the door, there's a door release behind the receptionist's desk."

"I'm not worried," Marion said. "You won't remember it, but you are quite the observant one."

I took Marion's hand. "That's why Detective Chun pays me the big bucks. And speaking of Chun, what am I going to do to help this investigation so I can soon bail out of the nursing home? I like Ralph, but I'd prefer rooming with you."

"Aren't you the romantic?"

We took a walk for several blocks along the side of Punchbowl discussing the weather (sunny with intermittent showers), the state of the world (disastrous as usual), and our future (we were both alive so no need to knock it).

When we returned, Marion led me safely inside, kissed me on the cheek, and said she was going back to the condo to read and take a nap. The nap sounded like a good idea, but I didn't want to forget the morning discussion with Detective Chun. I headed back to my room.

"There you are," Ralph said. "You disappeared, and I thought aliens might have abducted you."

"Nah. Only Marion accompanying me on a promenade."

"It's lunch time. You ready to grab a bite to eat?"

"You bet. My malasada breakfast has worn off."

Ralph pushed his call button, and Puna came to load him in the wheelchair. I volunteered to push him to the dining room.

"No racing today," Puna said. "Mrs. Teng has gone out to lunch with her daughter." He actually looked sad.

"Cheer up. We can race at dinner time."

He gave me a wan smile before leaving the room.

We headed along the hall at normal speed and situated ourselves at a table in the corner of the room. In a moment a pleasant young woman placed plates with tuna sandwiches and potato salad in front of us. Ralph patted around on the table and found a fork. He placed his hand on the plate and began poking with the fork.

"Can I help?" I asked.

"That's okay. I've located everything."

After he took a bite of potato salad, he waved his fork in my general direction. "I have a question for you, Paul."

"Shoot."

"To this day, a lot of white folks from our World War II era hold a grudge or are prejudiced against people of Japanese extraction. You don't seem to be that way. How come?"

"Hmmm. I've never been asked that. I guess I held the German and Japanese governments responsible for the atrocities and conflict, not the people themselves. I suppose it also has something to do with the way I was brought up. My parents were open-minded and encouraged me to have friends of all backgrounds."

"Whereas my parents only wanted me to associate with Japanese. They had a cow when I dated a Chinese girl in high school."

I realized I got along with nearly everyone. The only citizens I didn't cotton to were rapists, diamond thieves, and murderers.

★　★　★　★　★

After lunch, who should turn up but Detective Chun. He asked me to join him in an administrative office for a one-on-one chat. We were seeing entirely too much of each other. I hoped Marion wasn't getting jealous.

"To what do I owe the honor of your visit, Detective?"

"I received the results back from correlating all the names of people in this facility the nights of the sexual attack and murder, with haoles in the age range of fifty to seventy. We ended up with three names."

I rubbed my hands together. "That's good. The suspect list narrows."

He eyed me as if I were an amateur at this business, which I was.

"The first is Dr. Burber, a physician who made calls both evenings to attend to patients with the flu. The second, Fred Langley, the son of a resident. His name was in the visitors' log both times. And third, Hugh Talbert. He's night supervisor of the cleaning crew."

"And Officer Makoku is on the night shift, so he should be able to keep tabs on Hugh Talbert."

"Up to a point," Chun said. "He can't be watching Talbert the whole time. I want you to see what you can learn about each of these persons of interest."

"You're not calling them suspects."

"No. We have no evidence yet that they're linked to the crimes."

"Okay."

"Find a way to meet them casually so they won't question your interest in them. Your insights and observations will be very helpful."

I saluted. "I'll start poking around today."

"Evening will be your best bet. Dr. Burber only makes calls

after his regular daytime scheduled patients. Langley visits his mom when he's finished with his day job as a stockbroker, and Talbert comes on duty for the night shift."

"Got it."

"And be careful. One of these men could be dangerous."

CHAPTER 9

After eating dinner with Ralph and finishing what I was ninety percent certain was chicken, I wheeled my roomie back home. The sound of the clicking wheels reverberated along the hallway. I sniffed the antiseptic aroma, glad that I didn't have to live here permanently. The real residents knew they had little chance of returning to a house or another, less-dependent environment. That would be hard to deal with, whereas with my little charade, it was all pretend.

I pushed the call button on Ralph's side of the room, and a female CNA came to help him into his bed.

"That must be Sandy Sechrest," Ralph said.

I, of course, couldn't recognize Sandy from curried rice, but my blind friend knew exactly who entered the room. "How the hell do you figure out who's here, Ralph?"

"I'm a good listener."

Sandy maneuvered Ralph into his bed and straightened the sheet. "There. Anything else for you, Mr. Hirata?"

"I'm fine until I need to pee," Ralph said.

"Push the call button any time you want help." Sandy turned and headed out of the room.

"You certainly get the deluxe treatment," I said.

"Hey, since I can't move and can't see, I provide employment for CNAs. I'm their job security."

I left the room to do a little reconnoitering. When I reached the nurses' station, a young man was on duty.

"Good evening, Mr. Jacobson."

"I hate to be impolite, but I don't remember who you are."

He grinned. "I'm Ken Yamamoto."

I remembered his name from my journal. "How's the acting business?"

He wiggled his hand. *"Comme ci, comme ça.* I have a small part in the community theater's next play. I'm the butler in *Sound of Music."*

"Too bad you aren't in a murder mystery," I replied. "Then I could say the butler did it."

"I wouldn't mind being in a mystery," Ken said. "Maybe some time we can perform *Mousetrap."*

"If you work the night shift, how do you participate in plays?"

"Good question. Pacific Vista management has been very flexible in scheduling my responsibilities. When rehearsing and performing, I work a split shift—start in the afternoon, leave for the theater, and return afterwards."

I figured I might as well start on my investigation. "Do you know if Dr. Burber will be here this evening?"

"Not tonight. He'll probably come tomorrow evening to look in on Mrs. Chu, who has a bad back."

A thought occurred to me. "I've been having some back spasms. Put in a request for Dr. Burber to stop by to see me as well?"

"Sure, no problem. I could also help you with a hot bath in a few minutes. That might loosen things up."

"Nah. I don't want to turn into a prune. I'll get by and wait to see the doctor tomorrow night."

"Up to you. This evening we have a dentist making rounds who was also here last night and three nights ago. Do you want your teeth checked?"

I intended to say not only no, but hell no, when an idea struck me. "How old is this dentist?

Ken shrugged. "Probably early sixties. Why do you ask?"

"I don't want any young kid messing with my teeth. Sure, add me to the poke and probe list."

"Be in your room in an hour," Ken said.

I walked away thinking that I might have uncovered something the police had missed. Here was another visitor in the right age range from the nights of the sexual assault and murder of Linda Rodriquez. I'd have to check out this interloper.

I cruised the halls for a few minutes to stretch my legs, and then another idea occurred to me. I returned to my room and asked Ralph, "Do you know Mrs. Langley?"

"Yeah, she's upstairs in room two-one-seven."

"Damn, how do you know so much?"

"I memorize useless things since I have nothing better to do."

"Whereas I memorize things, and they disappear like balloons in the wind."

"You do have a colorful way of describing your short-term memory loss, Paul."

"Okay, Mister Memory, who are all the people residing on our hallway?"

He proceeded to reel off a whole series of names.

"Damnation. Since I don't know any of those names except Alice Teng and Louise Wilkins, I'll assume you're accurate."

"One hundred percent." Ralph patted around on his night-stand and found his TV remote. "I think I'll listen to the evening news."

"Have at it. It will only depress you. I'm going to wander around for a while."

"Don't get in trouble."

"I wouldn't think of it." *Right.*

I headed upstairs and found semiprivate room two-seventeen. On the right side I spotted a wrinkled Asian woman and on the left an equally wrinkled haole lady. I chose the left. "Mrs. Langley?"

"No, she's on the other side."

I slapped my cheek. *Never make assumptions.* I entered the other side of the curtain and tried again. "Mrs. Langley?"

The woman sat up in bed. "That's me."

I went up to her. "My name is Paul Jacobson. I'm a new resident. I'm going around to meet people."

She held out a hand. "Pleased to make your acquaintance. I'm Aiko Langley."

I decided to get right to the point since I didn't know how much longer either she or I would live. "I understand your son visits you periodically."

She smiled broadly. "That's right. Fred often comes by after work. He's quite the successful young man. Inherited his logical ability from my haole husband and his inscrutability from me." She winked at me.

"Is Fred coming tonight?"

A frown crossed her face. "No, he's taking an important client out to dinner." Her smile returned. "But he promised to visit tomorrow night."

I was zero for two so far.

We chitchatted for a few minutes, and then I excused myself. Next on my list: the cleaning supervisor, Hugh Talbert. I didn't see anyone in the halls other than nurses so returned to the first floor. I spotted a CNA with a name tag I remembered from my journal, Sal Polahi.

I collared him. "Sal, do you know if the cleaning supervisor, Hugh Talbert, is here tonight?"

He eyed me warily. "Why do you want to know?"

Uh-oh, improvise. "Well . . . uh . . . I want to thank him for the good job his people are doing."

Now Sal really stared at me as if inspecting a weird bug under a microscope. "Residents don't give many attaboys around here."

I opened my hands and gave what I hoped was a disarming grin. "No time like the present to start. So where can I find him?"

"He's not here. This is his night off. You should be able to catch up with him tomorrow night."

"Thanks." I hightailed it back to my room feeling like he was staring daggers into my back. Strike three for tonight's investigation. Amateur snoop Paul Jacobson retiring for the night with no success.

When I strode into the room, Ralph said, "Welcome back, Paul. Why are you so upset?"

I came to a dead stop. "Huh? How did you know it was me, much less that I'm pissed off?"

He tapped his right ear. "I've learned your footfalls. And you usually walk calmly, but you came into the room as if you wanted to stomp something into the floor."

"Damn. I better watch myself around you. What's new on the news?"

Ralph groaned. "As you predicted. All depressing. Fires, floods, homicides, politicians mouthing off."

"If you want a break from disasters, I can read you another story."

Before you could say "News anchors away," he grabbed the remote and clicked off the television. "I'm ready."

I retrieved the book from my nightstand and pulled up my chair to read O. Henry's "Man About Town." The protagonist has heard the saying *Man About Town* and wants to meet one. Everyone he talks to can define it, but can't show him one. The protagonist is knocked unconscious, and when he awakens in the hospital and asks the doctor what happened, the doctor gives him a newspaper that describes the incident, indicating the injuries weren't serious, and the victim appeared to be a typical Man About Town.

After I closed the book, Ralph said, "Sounds like you, Paul. With all your cavorting around here, I'm going to call you the Man About the Nursing Home."

"As long as no one knocks me unconscious."

With nothing better to do, I returned to my side of the room when a thought occurred to me. "Ralph, are you seeing the dentist tonight?"

"No, I took care of that three nights ago."

"I don't cotton to dentists but thought I should have my teeth checked," I said.

"You won't have a problem with Dr. Fujita. She's very gentle."

"She? A woman dentist?"

"Of course. She's excellent."

Oops. Another bad assumption. "Excuse me for a moment, Ralph." I raced out of the room as fast as my old legs could churn. At the nurses' station I found Sal Polahi studying a clipboard.

"Excuse me. I spoke with Ken Yamamoto a little while ago. Said I needed to see the dentist tonight."

"Yes, Mr. Jacobson. It's noted right on this list. Dr. Fujita will be here any minute."

"You can strike my name. I need to go to sleep early tonight."

Sal gave me a half smile. "Get cold feet?"

"Nah, my feet are warm. We'll try it another time."

I skedaddled before I got my old body in any more trouble.

Back in the room I changed into my PJs, brushed my choppers, and lay in bed to read to myself a bit before Marion showed up. Halfway through a story, my eyes fluttered closed. I felt myself fading into sleep, when I sensed someone watching me. My eyes shot open to find an old woman's face six inches from mine. She stared at me intently.

"Are you ready for me to tuck you in?" she asked.

I blinked twice. "Is this some new kind of nursing home service?"

Ralph chuckled from across the room.

"What's so funny, Ralph?"

"Paul, you need to meet Evelyn Newberry."

The woman hadn't budged. I couldn't even sit up or I would have bonked my head into hers. "Hello, Evelyn."

"It's Mom to you, Junior. I'll be right back after I tuck your brother in." She shuffled over to Ralph's bed and adjusted his covers. "Now, it's time for my two boys to get some sleep. Lights out."

"Aren't you going to sing to us first?" Ralph said.

"Oh, all right." She launched into a liberal rendition of the ABC song. After she finished, she said, "And you know, of course, letters are pastels. A is aqua, B is marigold, and C is fuchsia pink."

"Huh?" was all I could say. This whole scene left me wondering if I had been sent to the nuthouse rather than a nursing home.

"I never understood that book we read in high school," Evelyn said. "The teacher kept harping on this scarlet A. She obviously had her colors wrong."

I wondered if Evelyn or I had landed on the entirely wrong planet.

Evelyn came over, adjusted my blanket, ruffled my hair, kissed me on the cheek, and left the room.

I lay there in a state of shock, until I heard Ralph laugh again. "Man, the tone of your voice, Paul. You don't know what to make of Evelyn, do you?"

"I don't know how you can tell that from me only saying, 'Huh?' but you're absolutely correct. What was all that?"

"Evelyn is one of our resident characters. She has dementia and thinks I'm her son. She comes in several times a week to tuck me in. Tonight she thought you were her son as well. Welcome to the brotherhood."

"Okay, so her brain is wired even worse than mine. What's with the colors of the alphabet?"

"That's another interesting thing with Evelyn. She has synesthesia."

"Sin-what-ia? What the hell is that?"

"It's a condition that a small percentage of the population experiences. Evelyn sees colors for letters and numbers."

"Damn. I've never heard of it."

"She sees a color for every digit and each letter of the alphabet. Apparently, it's a quite pleasant condition to have. She's enthusiastic about the colors she sees."

"Is this part of her dementia?"

"Nope. She's always experienced seeing these colors."

"This place is something else. My roomie can't see squat, and Evelyn sees colors for letters and numbers. What a world."

Marion pranced into the room, rescuing me from my contemplation. "Sorry I'm late. I was on the phone with your friend Meyer Ohana. Your other friend, Henry Palmer, is due back from his honeymoon in two days, and Meyer will arrange for them to come visit you."

"I don't remember either of them, but if you say so."

"You'll enjoy seeing them." She handed me my journal. "Now it's time for your evening writing."

Whereas others might have nothing exciting to write in a diary, I duly sat down to document my adventures of being a misidentified son of some wacko lady who saw colors everywhere.

CHAPTER 10

Someone shook my shoulders, and my eyes shot open.

An old wrinkled woman thrust her face inches from mine. "Time to get up, Junior."

I shot up, cracking my forehead into hers.

She rubbed her head. "Ow. That's no way to treat your mother."

"I don't know who you are, lady, but I can assure you you're not my mother."

She wagged a finger at me. "Don't be difficult, Junior. Why can't you behave like your brother, Sonny, over there?"

"I don't have a brother."

"Now, now. I know you wanted to be an only child, but you have to learn to get along with everyone in the family."

I took a moment to try to get my bearings. I was in a hospital bed, but homey posters hung on the wall. I spotted another geezer lying in bed across the room. I wondered if I had ended up in an infirmary like the one during World War II.

"I hate to be impolite, but where the hell am I?"

The codger said in a gravelly voice, "Paul, you're in the Pacific Vista Nursing Home in Honolulu."

That caught my attention. "I don't remember becoming decrepit enough to be in a nursing home. And who are you and this crazy lady?"

"Watch your tongue, Junior."

The old guy chuckled. "You and Evelyn make quite a pair,

Paul. I'm your roommate, Ralph Hirata, and the woman is Evelyn Newberry. She's another resident who thinks we're her sons. You're Junior and I'm Sonny."

None of this made any sense. Obviously I had lost my marbles and that's why I'd ended up here. I smacked my right palm against my temple. Didn't knock any sense into me, though.

Evelyn tapped her watch. "Seven o'clock. The seven is glowing bright purple. Rise and shine."

I put my hand to my forehead to make sure I was awake and not running a high fever, causing me to hallucinate. *Ouch*. It hurt from the collision. Everything continued to become more and more confusing. "What do you mean, seven is purple?"

She thrust her wristwatch in front of my face. "See. Five is blue, six is orange, and seven is purple. Sometimes the colors are so bright I can't see the numbers."

I stared at her watch. I saw black numerals on a white background. "Ralph, help. I'm in the loony bin."

Evelyn wagged her index finger at me again. "I'll be on my way, but you get dressed, Junior." She harrumphed and marched away.

I lumbered out of bed. "Care to tell me what's going on around this asylum?"

"Let me give you a recap," Ralph said. "Your wife, Marion, told me to remind you of recent events when you wake up in the morning."

"My wife, Marion? I don't remember having a wife named Marion." I rubbed my tender forehead. "Maybe I have a concussion."

"Nope. You have short-term memory loss and wake up every morning in this state of confusion. This is your third day in the nursing home."

"And the woman claiming to be my mother who sees numbers as colors?"

"Evelyn thinks we're her sons. She's a synesthete who sees letters and numbers as colors. It's a unique condition. Her brain is wired differently than ours."

"Whereas mine seems to be missing a section of wiring altogether."

Ralph laughed. "You have a very interesting way of describing things, Paul."

"Yeah, but I see numbers as black and white, not colors."

"One other thing with Evelyn Newberry," Ralph said. "She's always trying to escape from the nursing home."

"Can't say as I blame her."

"She likes to wander around. She's very sneaky at finding ways to get outside. The staff has hunted for her half a dozen times."

"A regular escape artist."

"That she is."

At that moment a fetching young woman in her seventies strolled into my room and gave me a kiss on the cheek.

An old organ in my chest went pitter-patter. "I think I like this room service better than with my last visitor."

This earned me a hug.

"Your wife, Marion, is here, Paul."

Marion looked toward Ralph. "How did you know it was me? You can't see."

"You have distinctive footsteps, Marion. I heard you arriving."

"This place is really something," I said. "A blind guy who can distinguish people by footfalls."

Marion handed me a journal and told me to read it.

After I finished, some things became clearer, and I realized I had come to the nursing home under false pretenses. That was a relief.

I whispered to Marion, "Does Ralph know why I'm really here?"

"No," she whispered back. "Detective Chun doesn't want anyone to know."

"I can hear you're exchanging secrets," Ralph said. "It's not polite to whisper in front of a blind guy. I could only make out my name being mentioned."

I improvised. "I told her I'm grateful you've been helping me. I didn't want you to hear it and have it go to your head."

"Hey, at my age and in my condition, I appreciate any compliments. Who's ready for breakfast?"

"I'll let you two gentlemen go eat and get reacquainted. Paul, I'll be back later in the day."

Marion picked up the journal and left. Ralph pushed his call button. Soon, a hulking CNA appeared. I figured this was Puna, the guy named in my diary. He loaded Ralph in his wheelchair, and I offered to push him to the dining area.

"Thanks, Mr. Jacobson," Puna said. "I'll go help Mrs. Teng."

I steered Ralph's contraption into the hallway. "Which way?"

"Turn left."

I pointed him in the correct direction, and Puna pulled up alongside with a woman in a similar wheelchair.

"Good morning, Alice," Ralph said.

"How in tarnation did you know it was me?" she asked.

"Alice, your wheelchair has a distinctive squeak."

"Ready to race?" Alice Teng asked.

"Not this morning," Puna replied. "The hall's too crowded."

I looked ahead and agreed. Two other wheelchairs and three walkers blocked our path. It looked like a geriatric conveyance convention.

Since we would have to proceed at a slow pace, I decided to use the time to query my companions. "Do any of you know

Dr. Burber? I'm supposed to see him this evening for back pain."

"He's visited me several times," Ralph said. "Gave me some medication for my arthritis. Seemed like a competent fellow."

"I don't believe in doctors," Alice said. "They always want to give you pills or operate. No, siree. Chamomile tea, ginger, and turmeric. That's all an old body needs."

"I don't see Dr. Burber around here much since I'm usually off shift by the time he arrives," Puna said. "Residents like him."

"And what does the staff think of him?" I asked.

"We get a kick out of him. He tells good jokes."

I would find out more that evening.

After we ate, Puna appeared to retrieve Alice. He pushed her alongside Ralph's wheelchair.

"Time for the exercise class," Alice said. "You wimps ready to pump iron?"

"Good idea," Ralph replied. "I need to stretch my arms. Paul, you up for it?"

I shrugged. "I guess so. Couldn't hurt."

But I was wrong. We gathered in the open area by the lobby. Twenty oldsters, most in walkers and wheelchairs, and a few like me, free of an apparatus, faced a young woman in tight leotards. She had a blond ponytail and wore a whistle around her neck. I thought of an army drill sergeant, minus the uniform.

"Ain't she a sight for sore eyes," Ralph said.

I elbowed him. "You can't even see her."

"I know, but I have a good imagination."

Ms. Drill Sergeant blew her whistle. "Let's get started. Arms out."

Elbows creaked, and groans emanated as the members of the group held their arms out. I did the same but without moaning.

That was saved for later.

"Now twirl your hands." She made exaggerated circles, and we imitated her with varying degrees of success.

"Hands over your heads. Shake those fingers."

We obeyed like good little lemmings.

"Now lean over as far as you can, touch your knees or toes."

I bent over and heard creaks as my back stretched.

"Hold it there for thirty seconds."

My back began to ache. Now I really had something for Dr. Burber to check tonight.

"Sit or stand straight."

I pulled myself upright with a new creaking sound.

"Now twist your waist to the left and hold for thirty seconds."

I did as instructed.

"Same to the right."

I followed the instructions and felt a twinge in my right side.

This continued for another twenty minutes until every muscle in my body burned.

Afterwards I pushed Ralph back to our room.

"That was good," he said. "I feel much more limber."

"Easy for you to say. I feel like a piece of pulverized meat." I was ready to take a nap but knew that would only cause me further problems. After Ralph called to have Puna come help him into his bed, I lay down but made sure I didn't close my eyes.

"What else is there to do around here besides going through torture exercises?" I called out to Ralph.

"This afternoon there's an arts and crafts class. You willing to give it a try?"

"Sure. I'm a crafty fellow."

Ralph stared vaguely in my direction. "That's what I suspect. You're up to something here that you haven't told me, Paul. I'm not going to press you, but when you decide, you can level with me."

CHAPTER 11

So, my roommate suspected I was up to no good. Should I fess up to my hidden agenda? I thought Ralph was a straight shooter, but I didn't want to go against what I had read in my journal—Detective Chun wanted to keep my mission under wraps. Rather than elucidating, I made my excuses to Ralph and scurried out of the room to wander around the facility.

A few inmates were clunking around with their walkers, and I navigated past, careful to not get impaled. I stopped at the nurses' station to see who was on duty. Of course I didn't recognize any of the staff, but no one looked suspicious. I noticed Evelyn Newberry hanging out near the door. She stood there casually, watching the proceedings nearby. Maybe she had a roommate bugging her as well.

A large woman approached the outside of the main door, and I heard a buzzing sound at the nurses' station. A CNA on duty reached under the counter, and the door clicked. The woman came through the door and thundered up to the duty nurse, who immediately pointed to the visitors' sign-in log. Like a rabbit, Evelyn Newberry scooted out the door. It happened so quickly, no one besides me noticed her escape. I was close enough that I caught the door before it closed completely. What the hell? I might as well participate in the jailbreak.

I loped outside before you could say "Paul Jacobson, escapee."

Evelyn must have had her track shoes on. She had already scampered halfway down the block. I raced after her as fast as

90

my old legs could pump, catching up with her as she started across a crosswalk.

"Hold on, Evelyn," I gasped.

Her head jerked toward me. "It's Mom to you, Junior. You aren't going to send me back to the pen, are you?"

"I wouldn't think of it. Slow down so we can walk together."

She darted across the street but came to a stop on the opposite side.

"Phew." She wiped her forehead with the back of her hand. "I'm safe now that I'm across the Jordan."

"Huh?"

"Junior, how many times do I have to tell you to pay attention?" She pointed to the street. "We've crossed the bridge over the river to safety. The prison guards aren't going to catch us. We're free."

"If you say so."

"Besides, it's such a nice day that we need to stroll around the gardens."

Looking to my left and right, I only saw houses and buildings. Oh, well. I'd go with the flow in her imaginary world. "Do you wander around here often?"

"Any chance I get." She turned onto a street that sloped down toward town, and I walked with her until we came to a small park. She selected a bench and sat down. I joined her.

"Look at all the colors today." She waved her hand toward a storefront that displayed a sign reading: Hanada Store. "Like a rainbow."

"You're the first person I've met who sees colors for numbers and letters."

"Everyone should. It's beautiful."

"Do you see colors when you dream?" I asked.

"Hmmm. Good question, Junior. I think so. I remember dreaming of a big clock on a tower. Yes. It had bright colors."

"I have to tell you, I'm not really your son."

"Sure you are, Junior. You and Sonny are my kids."

"Haven't you noticed that Ralph . . . er . . . Sonny and I don't look anything alike?"

"That's okay. I love both of you, even though you're troublemakers." She chuckled. "Of course you look different. You're both adopted."

Jeez. She came up with an answer for everything. I decided to play along. "Where's Dad?"

She swatted a fly off her arm. "He kicked the bucket a number of years ago. Old ticker gave out. Couldn't keep up with me."

I wasn't sure I could keep up with her either.

"You live in Honolulu long?"

"Came here in nineteen forty-six. Right after the war. Never looked back."

"Tell me what I was like as a kid."

She looked at me askance. "You should remember. You were hell on wheels, getting into everything as soon as you started crawling. Ate the dog's food if I so much as turned my back on you."

"Woof," I said.

"There you go. I think you're part schnauzer. You and Sonny loved baseball. Played it every chance you got. I thought you were going to be a pro player but you decided to become a lawyer instead."

"Hold yours horses," I said. "You can have me be anything you want except a lawyer. I hate attorneys."

"Oh, pshaw. You loved the law. Sued the pants off one of those big insurance companies."

"Maybe I wasn't so bad after all."

"Unfortunate you never married and had kids. Good thing Sonny made me a grandma. Three darling little tykes."

I sniffed. "You always favored him."

She patted my hand. "Now, now. I love both of you. You were very smart and energetic. Kept the whole neighborhood entertained."

I felt much better. *Wait a minute.* I slapped my cheek. If this kept up, I'd become a fellow dingbat as well.

A bus came by with a large number two on its side.

"What color do you see for that number two?" I pointed.

"Two is yellow. You should know that, Junior."

"Now I do."

"Say, Junior, I'm getting hungry."

I looked at my watch. Noon. "I know a place that's serving lunch." I stood, took her hand and led her back to the nursing home. I pushed the button by the door, and a nurse came running to let us in. She practically dragged us into the lobby. "Where have you two been? We were all worried."

"No problem," I said. "Evelyn ducked out the door. She wanted a little outing, and after a stroll and chat, I brought her back."

The nurse put her hands on her ample hips. "You aren't allowed outside the facility, Mr. Jacobson. We know Evelyn tries to get out, but we're going to have to watch you as well."

"Hey, I retrieved her, didn't I?"

She wagged her finger at me like I was a naughty little boy. "No unaccompanied trips outside the facility."

"No one was unaccompanied. We went together."

She pulled herself up to her five-foot-six and stared me in the eyes. "You can't leave without a supervising adult."

I thought I was back in kindergarten. As my cheeks became warm, I opened my mouth to argue but thought better of it. "Yes, ma'am."

"I'm hungry," Evelyn said. "Are we going to this restaurant or not?"

"First, let's go get your face washed, Mrs. Newberry." The nurse took Evelyn's arm to lead her away. She paused and shot me one last glare. "And you behave yourself, Mr. Jacobson."

Damn. I wondered if I would have to sit in the corner or be sent to the principal's office.

I returned to my room and found Puna helping Ralph into his wheelchair. Puna looked at me with wide eyes. "There you are, Mr. Jacobson. We've been looking all over for you. We thought you were lost."

"Nope. I knew exactly where I was. Now that I'm back, I can wheel Ralph to lunch."

"Thanks, Mr. Jacobson." Puna tramped out of the room.

"Where did you go, Paul?" Ralph asked.

I pushed the wheelchair into the hallway and toward the dining area. "Evelyn Newberry and I decided to explore the great outdoors."

"She made a break for it again," Ralph said. "Third time this month."

"Next time we can take you along for a ride on the wild side, Ralph. We rolled two elementary school kids for their lunch money, started a crap game, and stole a package of gum from the local store."

"Over lunch you can tell me what really happened, Paul."

"Damn. I can't put over anything on you."

"Other than what you're really doing here."

Oops. He gave no indication of letting up on that subject. "I'll make a deal with you. I can't discuss it right now, but I promise I'll give you the whole skinny when I can but don't bug me in the meantime."

"It's a deal."

We settled in for a halfway decent meal of spaghetti, peas, and chocolate pudding. After I licked the last dab of chocolate out of the cup, I asked Ralph, "What time's the arts and crafts class you mentioned earlier?"

"One-thirty."

I checked my watch. "We have half an hour."

"I don't want to go back to the room. Find a place to plunk me down with the other vegetables."

"Attitude check, Ralph."

"Just kidding. Find a place with sun so I can work on my tan."

"You got it."

I wheeled him to a window off the lobby where sun streamed in so he could risk skin cancer. "I need to go pee, but I'll come retrieve you at one-thirty."

I returned and pushed Ralph back to the rearranged dining area; a collection of crêpe paper, finger-paints, children's scissors, paste, crayons, and drawing pads covered the tables. Holy moly. I *was* back in kindergarten.

One of the nurses introduced Moonbeam Rainbow, a new volunteer here today to lead the arts and crafts class. We applauded to welcome Moonbeam, a glowing young woman in her sixties with a plumeria blossom in her long brown hair. She wore a tie-dye muumuu and waved her hands at us. Gold and silver rings covered every finger, and multiple bracelets jangled from both wrists. She gave us a lecture on the importance of tactile feel in art. She encouraged us to dive in, get our fingers gooey, and make creations.

"Ah, my kind of art," Ralph said. "I can do it by touch rather than sight."

I helped him locate the different paraphernalia and started my own work of art. I pasted colorful squares of crêpe paper to a background sheet. I doodled with the crayons to make swirls and added some streaks with finger-paints. I admired the result. The only thing missing: a gold star. I could tape my creation to the wall in my room. Maybe I'd change my name to Paul Picasso. I felt oh, so artistic.

Moonbeam circled the room oohing and aahing at all the creations. When she came to mine she made a sound like a cat ready to regurgitate a hairball. Then she held up Ralph's artwork and rhapsodized on the exquisite combination of colors and the artistic eye exhibited by the creator. I didn't have the heart to tell her that Ralph couldn't distinguish a color swatch from sasquatch.

CHAPTER 12

After my artsy-fartsy experience, I wheeled Ralph back to our room, and he used his push button to call Puna for bedside assistance. Ralph said he was tired and wanted to take a nap, so I read to myself for a while. After finishing one short story, I became restless, pulled myself out of the chair, and explored the hallowed halls to see if I could scare up any clues or scare the staff by hanging out near the front door—a good way to make people at the nurses' station nervous. I hunched near the door as Evelyn had done earlier in the day. Every time someone entered or left the building, the person on duty watched me like a circling raptor. I found it so easy to entertain the nursing staff.

With nothing fruitful accomplished, I returned to my room. As a reality check, I splashed some water on my face. No, I was awake and still here. I had hoped to come out of a dream and find myself under a palm tree on a sunny beach with a tropical drink in my hand. A nursing home was a pretty boring place except for sexual assault, murder, prison escapes, and wheelchair races.

Late that afternoon, Marion stopped by and suggested we go to the lobby so as not to disturb Ralph.

"I have something you need to do, Paul."

I wiggled my eyebrows. "My stud service?"

She swatted me. "Not now. I promised Jennifer I'd have you

call her." She took out her cell phone thingy and set it up for me.

"I'm going to get a drink of water while you talk with Jennifer," Marion said.

Marion disappeared. I pushed the button she had shown me. After some ringing and a click, I heard Allison say hello.

"This is your long-lost father-in-law, held in captivity in remote Hawaii."

"Paul, can't you identify yourself like anyone else does?"

"Nope. I'm not anyone else. Is my illustrious granddaughter around?"

"I'll have to pry her off her computer. Just a minute."

I imagined Allison taking a crowbar and separating Jennifer from a metal box adorned with flashing lights.

"Grandpa, how's the investigation going?"

"Not too much happening, other than a murder."

"Did you find a dead body?"

"No, someone else did. But the woman who had been assaulted was found suffocated."

"And you're hot on the trail of the perpetrator, right, Grandpa?"

"Detective Chun has given me three people to check out. I'm hoping to have a friendly chat with each of them tonight."

"Be careful, Grandpa."

"I will. How are things in Boulder, Colorado?"

"I'm back in school, and it snowed yesterday. Dad and I will be hitting the slopes a lot this winter. I love snowboarding."

"I went skiing a few times back in the days I can remember. It never stuck with me. I was a better snowballer than skier."

"I love the black slopes. I swoosh down."

"I never swooshed. But when I fell, I wooshed I hadn't fallen."

Jennifer groaned. "I have a geezer joke for you."

"I'm all ears."

"Why did the vampire only drink blood from complaining geezers?"

"I give."

"He preferred aged whine."

Now I groaned. "I hope your mother didn't hear you."

"No, she and Dad are watching TV."

"That's good. I read in my journal that she doesn't approve of geezer jokes. I bet she isn't a vampire fan either."

"No. She got upset when I read the *Twilight* series, but I assured her all my friends were reading them. She wasn't convinced, but my dad said it was good to read rather than play video games all the time."

"Father knows best. I have a piece of trivia for you. I met a woman here in the nursing home who has a strange condition called synesthesia. Ever hear of it?"

"Nope."

"This is something new for your education. She sees colors when she looks at numbers and letters. It's not a problem or anything, and she enjoys the kaleidoscope of colors."

"I'll have to Google it. Maybe she can help you solve the crime."

"I don't know about that, but I have a very sharp roommate named Ralph Hirata. He's suspicious of why I'm at the nursing home. I haven't told him because Detective Chun doesn't want anyone to know my real mission."

"But if you found some allies, they might be eyes and ears for you, Grandpa."

"Ralph could be half of that. He has super hearing, but he's blind. I've even read to him several times."

"Like you used to do for your friend Meyer Ohana who has macular degeneration. You're great, Grandpa. Always willing to help someone."

"Don't tell anyone. Otherwise, I'll have to turn in my

curmudgeon badge." I looked up to see Marion had returned.

"I wish I were there," Jennifer said. "I'd help you track down the bad guy."

"You're in charge of school and snowboarding. I'll see what I can figure out on the nursing home front."

We signed off. I handed the phone to Marion, who gave me a kiss on the cheek and said she'd be back later before I went to bed.

Back in my room after dinner that night, I had settled in when a man my height, probably in his early sixties, sauntered in like he owned the place. He had graying hair and a matching neat mustache and beard. He pulled the curtain between Ralph's half of the room and mine.

"How are you feeling, Mr. Jacobson?"

"Mighty fine. Who the heck are you?"

A twinkle shone in his eyes. "I'm Doctor Burber. I understand you want to see me because of back pain."

"That's right. I've been told I'm a pain in the butt, but right now it's more in the small of my back. I figured I'd start with you, and if this doesn't work, I'll try a pretty young massage therapist."

"Nothing wrong with following both courses of treatment. Take off your shirt and lie on the bed face down." He adjusted the bed to a flat position.

I removed my shirt and hopped . . . well, more like slid, onto the bed and lay on my tummy. He prodded and jabbed my back. Although this originally had been a bogus request to see him, after the exercises that morning I now had a sore lower back. He kneaded one spot, and I flinched. "Ouch! That's the place, Doc."

He poked around a little more and told me to sit up.

"Will I live?"

He chuckled. "I'm glad to see you have a good sense of humor, Mr. Jacobson."

"Although I've been told it's more senseless humor. What's the diagnosis?"

"Nothing more than a slightly strained muscle. Have you been overexerting lately?"

"No somersaults or anything, but I may have bent the wrong way."

"You need to strengthen your lower back and keep it flexible. I have two exercises to recommend."

Uh-oh. "Are you sure exercises are called for in my condition?"

"Definitely. Two easy types of muscle stretches. First, lie on your stomach while putting weight on your forearms, holding your stomach down and stretching your back. Give it a try."

I brought my elbows in and lifted my head and torso. He adjusted my arm position.

"Stay like that for a minute."

I counted to sixty. It actually helped.

"We call the second exercise a Cat Pose. Get up on your hands and knees. Align your hands beneath your shoulders and extend your arms. Position your knees beneath your hips."

I did as instructed without even a groan.

"Now arch your back like a cat does and then let it sag. Do this fifteen times."

I performed my new trick and heard a few crackling sounds but was no worse for wear. "That's easy."

"Do these exercises once a day. You can also try a hot bath to see if it helps you. Other than that, you're good to go."

"Whew. No surgery." I sat up. "Thanks, Doc. Say, did you ever treat Linda Rodriguez?" I watched him carefully to catch his reaction.

He frowned. "No. She was the woman who died recently.

What an awful thing to happen."

I decided to press a little. "I met her once. She certainly had a tough last week of her life. Since you're here in the evenings, did you ever notice anyone suspicious?"

He shook his head. "I was as surprised as the staff members here. There have never been any problems before at Pacific Vista. I also attend to residents at a care home in Nu'uanu. Nothing like this has ever occurred before."

"It's kind of scary to be in a nursing home where an assault and murder have taken place. Who do you think could have done such a thing?" I continued to scrutinize his reactions.

"I have no idea. I share your concern, Mr. Jacobson. Anything else before I attend to other patients?"

"No, you've been very helpful."

"Good. I can also arrange for that massage therapist. One of the CNAs, Puna Koloa, is a licensed massage therapist and could give you a massage."

I noticed the twinkle in his eyes again.

"That's okay. I think I'll give the exercises a try for the next few days." I didn't welcome the idea of Puna pummeling me. I imagined him jumping on my back and performing a Hawaiian war dance.

I watched as Dr. Burber left the room. He seemed like a nice fellow. No indication that he was the perpetrator. Maybe he had learned to be a good actor, but my gut told me he didn't assault or kill Linda Rodriguez.

From behind the curtain, Ralph shouted, "Hey Paul, why don't you open the barrier so we can talk?"

"You got it, Roomie." I stepped over and pulled the curtain. "Let the show begin. What's on your mind?"

"Sore back, huh?"

"Yeah. Your little exercise program did me in."

"Was that the only reason you wanted to see the doctor?

Seems like you had some other questions for him as well."

My roommate was a super sleuth.

"I'm concerned about what happened to Linda Rodriquez. I figured a doctor might know more of what's going on."

"I'd pursue this question, but I agreed not to bug you, Paul."

"Good. If you'll excuse me, I think I'll wander around a little before my bedtime."

I quickly escaped. One suspect down, two more to go.

CHAPTER 13

Next stop on my agenda, room two-seventeen, a number I remembered from my journal. I climbed the stairs, which caused no problems given my now loosened back muscles. I stuck my head in Aiko Langley's side of the room and knocked on the door jamb. "Okay for a visitor?"

"Come on in."

A skinny woman was propped up in bed gazing at a *Popular Mechanics* magazine with a cover picture of some sort of robotic doohickey on tank treads.

I did a double take. "You into reading about gadgets?"

"Sure enough. Taught my boys a thing or too. We flew model airplanes together, constructed train sets, and shot off rockets. I also used to rebuild cars."

"The closest I came to that was running an auto parts supply store. But speaking of sons, is Fred coming to visit you this evening?"

Aiko tapped her watch. "He should be here in five minutes. Punctuality is another thing I taught my kids. He'll arrive right on the dot at eight."

I pulled up a chair and sat next to her bed. "Did your husband share your interest in mechanical devices?"

"Nah, Hubert was into cooking. He kept us well fed." She wagged a finger at me. "Best advice I can give anyone. Marry a gourmet chef."

"My first wife was a good cook. I can't say how my second

wife cooks because I have short-term memory loss."

Aiko stared at me intently. "That surprises me. You remem-bered me, and Fred's name, from our last conversation."

"I have a memory trick. I write things in a journal at night and read it every morning to figure out what I've been up to."

She chuckled. "Good approach. I'll remember that if I lose my marbles. Whoops. I guess I'll have to write it down to *read* if I lose my memory."

"Now you understand the system. How long have you been here at Pacific Vista, Aiko?"

"A little over a year. I lived in a care home but needed more nursing assistance. The old body doesn't function the way it used to."

"Your brain seems to be working fine."

"Other than controlling the rest of my body. Oh, good. Here's Fred."

A knock-kneed gentleman in his late fifties or early sixties waddled into the room. He had no facial hair but sported a comb-over of gray hair. He wore a white sweatshirt with large letters proclaiming, "Mother Is Number One."

Aiko laughed and pointed, "Fred always wears that sweatshirt for me when he comes to visit."

"Hi, Mother. I brought you a box of dark chocolate-covered macadamia nuts."

"Hot damn. Break open the box."

He took off the plastic covering and handed the box to Aiko.

"We can share them with Mr. Jacobson here. Paul, meet my son, Fred." She popped a piece of candy in her mouth.

I stood and shook hands. Fred pulled over another chair, and we settled in to munch the treats.

By the time I finished two pieces of candy, mother and son had demolished the rest of the box.

"I don't understand it," Aiko said. "Those darn things never last long. I swear they're making the boxes smaller. Don't you think so, Fred?"

"Yes, Moffer," Fred said with his stuffed chipmunk cheeks.

I took this opportunity to scrutinize Fred Langley. Was he a sexual predator and murderer? He looked more like a teddy bear. But appearances could be deceiving. I needed to poke at things a little.

"Fred, are you worried over your mother's safety here at Pacific Vista?"

He wiped a dab of chocolate off his lower lip. "No, should I be?"

I put a finger to my cheek to feign thoughtfulness. "There have been several disturbing events in the last week. A woman was assaulted and murdered."

Fred sighed and looked wistfully at the empty candy box. I thought he might pick it up and lick the insert. Then a glower crossed his face. "Awful business. I hope they catch the bastard."

"You might have been here the nights of the two dreadful events. Did you notice anything?"

"Can't say as I did. I spend my whole time in Mother's room."

"And when you left?"

"At the end of every visit, I help Mother get out of bed and to her walker. We take the elevator down, and she accompanies me to the front door. I don't recall anything unusual on any of those treks. Mother, do you remember seeing anyone suspicious recently?"

"No, most of the residents were in their rooms. Usually there are only one or two nurses at their station in front. I have one of them buzz the door open for Fred, and then I hobble back to the elevator and my room."

I looked at Fred one more time. He didn't appear to have had an opportunity to attack Linda Rodriguez and, I was convinced, would only have done so if he thought she was a giant piece of chocolate. With one more dead end, I excused myself and headed into the hall.

Next on the Paul Jacobson investigation docket: find cleaning staff night supervisor, Hugh Talbert. I checked the three upstairs halls and didn't see any cleaning types hanging out, so I headed downstairs. I found one guy with long straggly hair and a dangling earring mopping the floor in the purple wing. He wore a faded, gray sweatshirt, the type you see in a boxing gym. I noticed a tattoo of a surfboard on his right hand that grasped the mop handle.

"Is your supervisor on duty tonight?" I asked.

Earring Guy looked up with wide eyes. "You have a problem?"

"No, actually I wanted to thank him for the good cleaning job you people are doing."

Earring Guy's mouth dropped open. "No kidding. No one does anything but complain around here. You can find Mr. Talbert in the first floor break room behind the nurses' station."

"Thanks." I trotted . . . well, more like walked fast, to the nurses' station and spotted a little room with a man at a corner table reading a newspaper. I scooted in before anyone questioned where I was going. The guy had his back to me. He appeared average build with gray hair and wore a blue work shirt.

I cleared my throat. "Mr. Talbert?"

He dropped the newspaper on a table and turned to me. "Yes?"

He had dark piercing eyes and a gray mustache and beard. I surmised he was in the acceptable age range for our suspect.

"One of the members of your cleaning crew told me I'd find you here. I'm a resident of the first floor."

Talbert clicked his tongue. "Whatever your problem is, I'm sure we can fix it."

I held up my hand. "I have no complaints. I actually wanted to thank you for the way your people keep things clean at night.

When I get up in the morning it's nice to see the floors scrubbed and everything tidy."

His mouth dropped open, and I thought I heard his jaw popping. "Did I understand you correctly? You're not complaining but complimenting what we do?"

"That's correct. May I join you for a moment?"

Talbert waved toward an empty chair. "Please. You can spend the night."

"I won't keep you long. I know you have a busy schedule but in addition to mentioning the good work your staff is doing, I want to ask you one other thing."

"I knew this was too good to be true."

I gave him my best innocent smile. "It's no big deal, but I'm concerned about security at Pacific Vista."

"Whoa." Talbert held up his hand in traffic cop fashion. "That isn't my department. Nope. I only handle the cleaning, not security."

"I'm not asking you to fix anything. I'm concerned that a woman was assaulted and murdered. Since you head up the cleaning night shift, I thought you might have seen something the two nights the crimes were committed."

"You some sort of undercover cop?"

I gulped. "No, only a nosy old coot. Since I'm not sleepy, I wander around and talk to people. I thought you might have come across something to prevent another occurrence of these dastardly deeds."

"Now you sound like an actor in a melodrama. Who exactly are you?"

I forced a smile. "Paul Jacobson. I suffer from short-term memory loss. I won't even remember you tomorrow."

"That so. If I insulted you, you'd never recall what I said in the morning?"

"Nope. But I wouldn't suggest doing it. I keep a journal and write a summary of what happens to me."

Talbert chuckled. "Just testing you. No, Mr. Jacobson, the police questioned me after both events. I was here those nights but didn't notice anything out of the ordinary."

"No one skulking around and looking suspicious?"

"Only Mrs. Newberry, who tried to escape out the front door in the early morning when the first shift people started to arrive. That woman is sneaky. She almost slipped through, but one of the CNAs caught her."

"Any men wandering around who shouldn't have been?"

"I only saw the regular nurses and my crew. And I can assure you that we've screened any employees we hire. We do a background check and follow up on three or more references before we hire a new employee."

"Sounds thorough."

"Yeah, I don't think any member of my night shift caused the problems. I work them hard and keep an eye on them."

At that moment I gazed out of the break room toward the nurses' station. I saw Earring Guy. He quickly looked from side to side, picked up a pen on the counter, and disappeared out of my view. Hmm. Did Earring Guy have sticky fingers?

"I saw one of your people mopping the floor tonight. He wore a dangly earring. Who's that?"

"You must mean Dan Aukina. New on the crew. Only been here a month. Hard worker. Since you live on this floor, he's the one you should thank."

"I'll be sure to do that." With nothing further to ask, I excused myself.

Nothing Hugh Talbert said made me suspicious of him. He had been here the nights of the crimes and met the age range and description given by Linda Rodriguez of her "boyfriend." But the only one acting suspicious was Dan Aukina. He appeared much too young to be the "boyfriend," but he swiped a pen and might be into stealing larger items, such as a diamond bracelet. He was worth checking out.

As I walked past the nurses' station I spotted Dan Aukina, AKA Earring Guy, at the end of my hall. He pushed the mop as vigorously as some of the swabbies did on the navy transport ships I'd been on during World War II.

I ambled along until I reached Dan. "Thanks for the heads up. I found Hugh Talbert in the break room as you suggested."

He didn't look up. "That's good."

"Do you by any chance have a pen?" I asked.

"No. I had one a few minutes ago. A nurse with a resident asked me to get one from the counter at the nurses' station. You should be able to find another one there."

"Thanks."

So much for the great pen heist.

CHAPTER 14

I meandered back to my room and found Ralph snoring to beat the band. He was a good roommate, in spite of his tendency to be suspicious of my activities. I couldn't imagine what it would be like to lose my sight. Losing brain cells was bad enough. So here I was in the land of decrepit old people trying to find a bad guy when I wasn't able to find my memories of yesterday. What a pisser. I couldn't curl up in a ball and suck my thumb. I needed to keep working on this, but I didn't know what my next step would be.

I didn't have to make a decision, because who should walk in with a big smile on her puss but my bride.

"You look like the canary that swallowed a cat," I said.

"Yes. I have a surprise for you."

"You found some of my errant brain cells in the mop closet?"

"Even better than that. I've arranged to take you out of here for part of the night."

"Hot damn. Does that mean conjugal visit?"

"You play your cards right and good things might happen, Mr. Jacobson."

After a day with walkers and wheelchairs I looked forward to a change of scenery, and anything else that unfolded would be a bonus.

"When do we start?"

"Any time."

"Do I need to pack an overnight bag?"

111

"Although I have permission to kidnap you, you have to be back before midnight. The nursing home takes a headcount every night to meet Federal Medicare regulations, and they can lose payments if someone isn't in his or her designated bed."

"I'll promise to be back in time and be in the head so they can do the headcount," I said.

This didn't even earn a groan but instead a cold shoulder.

"Forget what I said. I'll go along with it. I don't want the place going belly up because I went AWOL."

"Go get ready." Marion tapped the toe of her shoe on the floor.

"Okay, okay." I grabbed my light jacket. "I'm ready to boogie."

We went to the nurses' station, and Marion signed a list on the counter.

"I feel like I'm in preschool where a parent has to sign me in and out," I said.

Marion gave me a Cheshire-cat grin. "Almost the same thing, except there might be some side benefits."

I rubbed my hands together. "Oh, boy."

We strolled outside, arm-in-arm, where a quarter moon shone. The gentle trade wind ruffled my hair, and I sniffed the aroma of steaks being grilled. The background noise of traffic was far enough away that it provided a soft hum, reminding me of swarming insects.

"Are you enjoying being abandoned in a condo?" I asked.

"It's not bad. I'm getting a lot of reading done. I've made some shopping trips to buy presents to give to my daughter and her family when we return to Venice Beach. By the way, I spoke to them earlier, and Austin says hello."

I remembered the name from my journal. "How is my step-grandson doing?"

"He and Jennifer are emailing and texting each other."

"I don't know how email is any different from a, b, c, or d-mail, and I hope texting isn't anything dirty—"

I was interrupted by a swat on my arm. "Paul, those are merely means of electronic communications."

"I like communication, whether it's electronic, magnetic, or in person."

Marion groaned. "As Jennifer says, you're impossible."

"I wouldn't go that far. I'd settle for improbable." I put my hand over my mouth. I decided to clam up before alienating the beautiful woman standing with me.

She clicked her tongue. "I love you, however impossible and improbable that might be."

I stopped and gave her a hug. "Thank you for putting up with me. I only wish I could remember you from day to day."

"We'll see what we can do to address that problem."

I didn't know what she was referring to, but chose to keep my big yap closed. Who says an old fart can't learn?

We continued our promenade until we reached a building, and Marion led me up the stairs and into an apartment. It had the main accoutrements—a refrigerator and bed.

Marion put her key on the counter and went into the small kitchenette. "Would you like a piece of chocolate cake?"

My eyes lit up. That was the second best thing I wanted. "Damn right."

She cut a huge piece for me and a sliver for herself, adding a dollop of vanilla ice cream to mine to make sure I received my full ration of sugar to energize me for anything that might happen. With the plates in front of us, we stood at the counter.

After taking a first bite, I savored the rich chocolate and creamy a la mode. "Why the small piece for yourself?"

She pirouetted in front of me. "I have to maintain my youthful figure."

I whistled. "And a darn good one it is, I might add."

She gave me a peck on the cheek. "In spite of your strange sense of humor, you sometimes say the right thing."

I wiped my hand across my forehead. "Phew. Dodged another bullet."

After licking the last bit of chocolate off my fork, I took the plate to the sink and asked Marion, "Now what?"

She stepped over to me. "Don't give me your innocent act."

The next thing I knew, we wrapped our arms around each other, and our lips were playing patty-cake. A little-used part of my body perked up. Before you could say geezer heart-rate alert, we disposed of clothes and nestled between the sheets.

I snuggled up against Marion. "I like the accommodations better here. Much more friendly residents."

"I should hope so. No hanky-panky without me involved."

I kissed Marion deeply before coming up for air. "I can assure you that whatever happens is reserved for you and you alone."

At that point we each did some reconnaissance with our hands, and we matched the right parts with the right places. The old ticker beat at a frantic pace, we revved up the old engines, and the bed shook and squeaked. At the final moment, the bed crashed into the wall, but I was too occupied to worry.

As I lay gasping for breath, I heard pounding on the wall and a voice shouted, "Cut it out, you darn horny kids!"

"Well, that's a compliment," I said to Marion as we snuggled together. "You can write on my gravestone 'Darn horny kid, up until the end.' "

"No gravestones for you for a long time, Mr. Jacobson."

"Eew-whee. If you keep my blood circulating that vigorously on a regular basis, I may live to be a hundred and twenty."

We lay there, and I watched a kaleidoscope of colors whirl though my mind. I wondered if I had developed synesthesia.

I had almost fallen asleep when my bride elbowed me. "I

have to kick you out. Time for you to head back to Pacific Vista."

I emitted a deep sigh. "Just like a woman. A little loving and then she tells me to leave the house."

"I'll invite you back again."

"I wish I were half a dozen decades younger and up for that again, so to speak."

Rather than an elbow, I received a kiss. "When you're ready, I'll be waiting for you."

Damn. With an invitation like that, I had something to look forward to.

After dressing, I received my goodnight kiss and floated back toward the nursing home. Tilting my head back, I spotted a few stars bright enough to shine through the ambient city light. I zipped up my jacket as the breeze picked up. From a bush between the sidewalk and the side of a building came a meow. A gray tabby cat scampered out and rubbed against me. I bent over to scratch it under the chin and heard a loud crash. A fist-sized rock landed on the sidewalk.

I jerked erect and spotted a shadowy shape across the street.

"Hey!" I shouted.

The figure disappeared, and I heard running footsteps. I regarded the chipped stucco of the building where the rock had struck before bouncing on the sidewalk. The missile would have smacked right into the side of my head and turned my already mushy brain into pâté if I hadn't leaned over at the opportune time, thanks to the cat that had saved my bacon, ham, and sausage.

I shivered. My hands shook. I needed to get out of there.

I jogged the rest of the way to the nursing home and jabbed the button repeatedly. In a moment the door beeped. I pushed through, gasping for breath. I didn't know if I should have a call placed to the police or not. The nurse on duty was on the phone and turned her back to say something she didn't want me to overhear, so I found the log sheet and signed myself in, forging Marion's signature. When she finished the call and turned toward me, I decided to follow up on something from my journal entry.

"Do you know if the security guy with a ponytail is working tonight?" I asked the nurse.

"I saw him go upstairs fifteen minutes ago."

I headed up the steps and found Benny Makoku near the emergency exit at the end of one of the hallways. I approached him and whispered, "We need to talk."

"I'll meet you in your room in twenty minutes."

Still shaking, I returned to my room, changed into my pajamas, and brushed my teeth. I peeked around the end of the pulled curtain and ascertained that Ralph was sound asleep. *Oops.* I realized I had neglected to write in my journal. It was too late to call Marion to bring it over, and I didn't want her walking around with rock-throwing villains in the neighborhood. Oh, well. I'd have to go with a blank day.

As promised, Benny soon appeared. "I can't stay too long," he whispered. "What's up?"

I explained that someone had tried to remove my head with a rock.

"I'll let Detective Chun know in the morning when I'm off duty," Benny said. "I'll also check on your room whenever I can tonight."

"I'd appreciate the attention. Someone's out to get me."

CHAPTER 15

I was soaring around in a puffy pink and white cloud. I popped out of the cloud and turned my head downward to spot a rolling green meadow and a meandering stream. A flock of geese flew alongside me in the bright sunlight. One of them honked, and it sounded like an automobile horn. A breeze whooshed over my face. Up ahead I spotted a colorful, striped hot air balloon floating in my direction. Suddenly, the balloon crashed into me. The surface of the balloon covered my face. I couldn't breathe. I struggled, flapping my arms.

I awoke to find a pillow covering my face. I really couldn't breathe. My arms flailed for real. Someone held the pillow over my face. I bucked and kicked my feet. I heard an "oof." The pillow came off my face. I sat up as a figure ran out of my room. I blinked, not being able to make out the form in the darkness.

"Help!" I croaked.

I heard running footsteps.

"Help!" I shouted, louder this time.

A woman in a nurse's uniform turned on the light and came skidding to a stop at my bedside. "Are you having a bad dream, Mr. Jacobson?"

I gazed around the room. I recognized it as the Pacific Vista Nursing Home where I had been sent to help with a crime investigation. I opened my mouth to mention the assault when something else struck me. I remembered the day before—my abortive attempts to investigate the three suspects, going to the condo with Marion, almost having my skull bashed with a rock. My short-term memory was working better than a well-tuned engine. "I'm cured!" I shouted. I wanted to jump up on the bed and perform a victory dance.

The nurse crinkled her forehead as a look of worry crossed her face. "Are you all right, Mr. Jacobson?"

"I'm more than all right. Hot damn. I can remember yesterday." I wanted to give her a hug but thought better of it.

Reaching over, she placed her hand on my forehead. Her hand felt cool and soothing. My breathing returned to normal.

"You don't have a temperature," she informed me.

"Of course not. I feel as fit as a four-stringed musical instrument." Then I recalled what had happened to me. "Did you see someone running out of my room?"

She looked at me askance. "No, but I heard you shouting."

"What time is it anyway?"

She stared at her watch. "Five-thirty."

More people arrived, clucking their tongues and staring at me as if inspecting a specimen in a Petri dish.

Benny Makoku came into the room and took charge. "Everyone please leave. I need to speak with Mr. Jacobson." He pulled up a chair by the side of my bed. "What's all the commotion?"

"I didn't want to mention it to the other staff people, but someone tried to smother me with a pillow," I whispered

"First the rock and now this," he said in an equally soft voice. "Did you see the assailant?"

"No. I struggled to free myself. I think I may have kicked him in the *cojones*. He took off, but I didn't get a look at him. My only impression—a gloved hand when I knocked the pillow away."

"You said 'him.' Are you sure it was a man?"

"I'm sure from the reaction to my kick."

"How large a guy?"

"Can't say."

"Age?"

"Couldn't tell. Sorry. It happened so quickly, and in the dark I didn't notice much or think to chase the guy."

"That wouldn't have been a good idea anyway." Benny paused and tapped a finger on my nightstand. "Here's something to try. Close your eyes and recreate the scene. Sometimes that helps for remembering details."

I scrunched my eyes shut. I recalled the pleasant sensation of the flying dream until the hot air balloon attacked me. I recalled awakening to being smothered and lashing out, the shadowy figure. Nothing recognizable. Too dark.

I let out a burst of stale air. "Sorry. Can't bring up anything useful. The guy left my room in a hurry. Did you see anyone running?"

He bit his lip. "Unfortunately, I was upstairs at the time. I'll ask around. Is that the pillow?" He pointed to the floor.

"Yeah."

"Don't touch it. I'll call the police. A crime scene investigator can check for any evidence."

"Won't do much good if the guy wore gloves."

"You never know. He might have left hair or other evidence."

A concern nibbled at me regarding what happened. "Should I have mentioned the attack to the nursing staff?"

He regarded me thoughtfully. "No, you did the right thing to keep it quiet. This may work to our advantage if there isn't a general alert to the staff. I know Detective Chun will want to speak with you later this morning."

"Bring him on."

Benny looked at me out of the side of his eye. "You seem awfully chipper for someone who has been assaulted twice in one night."

"Hey, I'm alive. That's the important thing. And for some reason my memory is working fine this morning."

"I'll be back when the crime scene investigator arrives. We'll keep this under wraps, but see if we can learn anything more."

After Benny left my room, I heard rustling sounds on the other side of the curtain. "What was all the noise?" Ralph called out.

I went over and opened the curtain. "I had a bad dream and shouted. Everyone came to check on me."

"I must have been sleeping soundly. I heard you shout, followed by the footsteps of a bunch of people coming into your room."

"Yeah, I'm a popular guy."

"I'm going back to sleep. You can draw the curtain."

I obliged, turned off the light, and lay in bed thinking. I was too keyed up to sleep. I had nosed around last night. None of the three suspects seemed suspicious to me, yet afterwards I'd been attacked twice. I certainly had stirred up the hornet's nest. The three suspects had been here last night. One of them might have followed me to Marion's condo and waited for my return. But now the attack a little after five in the morning. Dr. Burber and Fred Langley wouldn't have spent the night in the nursing home. I'd check the sign-in register at the front counter to verify this. Only Hugh Talbert, cleaning staff supervisor, would have a reason to be here all night. My gut clenched. It was scary that he would be here at night with easy access to my room.

With that in mind, I put on my robe and padded to the nurses' station. The log book lay on the counter.

As I reached for it, the nurse from my earlier encounter saw me. "Are you doing better, Mr. Jacobson?"

"Yes. I'm hunky-dory."

"That's good. You had us worried."

"Sorry about that. Those bad dreams can seem so real

sometimes. I didn't mean to put you to any extra work."

She gave me a winning smile. "That's what we're here for. Any time there's a concern, shout or use the call button. I'm surprised you didn't push the button."

"I didn't think of it. I just yelled."

The phone rang, and she turned away from me.

I used the opportunity to review the visitors' log book. I ran my finger down the list of visitors from the night before and verified my supposition. Dr. Burber had signed out at nine-ten and Fred Langley at nine-forty-five. Either of them could have waited to throw a rock at me, but neither had signed in again to be in the facility around five-thirty a.m. That left Hugh Talbert as the only one in the vicinity at the time of my pillow attack.

I returned to my room to further cogitate, which is what codgers do. I thought how normal people woke up every morning remembering the day before. Would this be me from now on, or was there some anomaly that accounted for my unusually super memory today? If I had my memory back, I wouldn't have to keep writing in a journal. Best of all, I'd be able to recognize Marion when I woke up beside her—an unexpected treat. I put my hands behind my head and stared at the ceiling. I only needed to help catch the assailant and return to the life of a newlywed geezer.

In half an hour Benny returned, accompanied by a young woman wearing rubber gloves and carrying what looked like a doctor's bag. She wore dark slacks, a white blouse, and thick glasses and gave off vibes of a no-nonsense professional.

Benny made a shushing sound and directed the woman to the pillow. She spoke not a word, but went straight to her work, examining the pillow, running a swab over the cover, and removing something with tweezers. She continued to work on the pillow for another ten minutes as I watched. Then she turned with a jerk and, laying her finger aside of her nose and giving a nod, out into the hallway she went. Clement Clarke Moore would have been oh, so proud of my observations.

Benny gave a departing wave and followed her.

Left on my own and having done what I could to assist the local law enforcement cabal, I dressed for the day, selecting a pair of Bermuda shorts, a T-shirt that proclaimed, "Geezer and proud of it," and a pair of tennis shoes. I was prepared for my next adventure.

CHAPTER 16

I had no time to speculate on what to do next with my decrepit old self, because who should arrive but my beautiful bride. She wore a bright orange muumuu, complemented by a hibiscus flower pinned into her silver hair. My old ticker beat double time.

"You're a sight for sore eyes," I said.

Marion gave me the once-over as if inspecting a slab of beef. "You, on the other hand, look a little bedraggled, Paul."

And with good reason. I decided to defer the bad news and share something positive on this morning with me still alive.

"Guess what happened to me?" I asked in my most smug tone.

"With you, Paul, I wouldn't even hazard a guess."

I grinned. "I'm cured. I can remember everything that happened to me yesterday. You're not going to be stuck with an old poop who has a memory like a leaky faucet anymore." I practically clicked my heels. "My short-term memory works again."

A twinkle shone in Marion's eyes. "I wouldn't go that far. Let's just say that you'll have memories of yesterday until you go to sleep again."

Uh-oh. I frowned. "Are you raining on my parade?"

She patted my hand. "There is one circumstance when you do remember the next day. But it wears off."

"And what is that one circumstance?"

"Something that happened to you yesterday."

123

"Since I can remember clearly, let's see." I quickly reviewed the events of the previous day. "I went to an exercise class yesterday. I bet the physical stimulation rattled my brain cells into submission."

She gave me a Cheshire-cat grin. "It has something to do with exercise, but it wasn't your class."

"Aha. One of the residents escaped out the front door yesterday, and I followed her. We walked around and breathed the fresh air. Was that it?"

"No."

"Hmmm. I went to an arts and craft class in the afternoon. Maybe that did the trick and cleared the old noggin."

"Something later in the day."

"I wandered around and spoke with"—I lowered my voice—"three of the suspects. I don't think any of them committed the crimes. Did the investigative work jog my memory?"

"No, that wasn't it."

"After that I went back with you to your apartment . . . and then . . ."

"You're getting warmer."

And sure enough, heat coursed up my neck and into my cheeks. "You don't mean our conjugal visit?"

I received a kiss on the cheek. "Detective Jacobson, you've figured it out."

"I'll be hornswoggled. You mean I only have to engage in a little hanky-panky with you and the old brain cells connect again?"

"That's right."

"Hot damn. I'll be looking forward to a repeat performance."

Marion put her arms around my neck and planted a juicy kiss on my smacker. "I'll be ready when you are."

"Ooh, wee. With a promise like that, I'll be floating around for days."

"Unfortunately, you won't remember it tomorrow."

"I'll have to dedicate a whole page in my diary to this little idiosyncrasy of my mental dysfunction. By the way, I forgot to write in my journal last night. How about that? Me remembering what I forgot the day before."

She pulled my diary out of her tote and handed it to me. "No time like the present to catch up."

"And I don't need to review it because I remember everything I read yesterday morning. What a treat to be able to remember the day before."

I sat down and proceeded to recount my latest adventures, including the pillow attack. I still needed to mention that to Marion. When I finished writing, I handed the journal back to Marion for safekeeping, and she stashed it in her tote.

At the sound of footsteps, I looked up to see Evelyn Newberry padding into my room. She wagged a finger at me. "It's good to see you up, Junior. I thought I'd have to roust you from bed again." She turned to Marion. "Sis, what a pleasant surprise. It's been ages since you've visited."

Marion stared at Evelyn as if encountering an alien creature.

I decided to help clarify the situation. "Marion, meet Evelyn Newberry, one of the residents of Pacific Vista."

"This isn't Marion," Evelyn said. "It's my long lost sister, Bernice. She took a boat to Australia in nineteen sixty-one. Claimed she wanted to live in another country. You've finally returned, Sis."

Evelyn stepped over and gave Marion a hug.

Marion stood motionless, stiff as a board.

"Same old Bernice," Evelyn said. "Never one for affection. I remember as kids we snuck into the apartment with the big number four over the door. You couldn't see how emerald green the number was. I tried to hug you, and you only got mad."

Marion frowned.

"Now, I better go see if Sonny is up." She sauntered over to the curtain, found the opening, and disappeared into Ralph's side of the room.

"What was all that?" Marion asked.

"Let me decipher the code for you. Evelyn thinks I'm her son, Junior, for whatever reason. She checks on me in the evening and morning. She also imagines that Ralph is my brother, Sonny."

"You and Ralph look so much alike."

"Well, both of us are kind of wrinkled."

Marion crossed her arms. "I leave you alone, and you make friends with strange women. And what was that about four being green?"

"Evelyn has a condition called synesthesia where she sees colors with numbers and letters. Where you and I see black numbers, Evelyn sees colors. Four appears green to her. Like me, she has a good long-term memory and recounted something that happened with her sister long ago."

"I've never heard of synesthesia," Marion said.

"Me neither. Ralph explained it to me. It's not a problem to Evelyn. In fact, she seems to like the condition."

Marion's smile returned. "I was taken aback by her abrupt entrance. I'll try to be more understanding."

"She's harmless, although nutty as a fruitcake."

Evelyn groped her way through the curtain and returned to my side of the room. "Sonny is up as well. We have the whole family here. This is quite an occasion with Bernice coming to see us."

Marion went over to Evelyn and gave her a hug.

Evelyn's mouth dropped open. "Holy mackerel! I can't believe it." She hugged Marion back, tears in her eyes. "I can't remember the last time you actually hugged me, Bernice."

"I think we've had a successful family reunion, Evelyn," I said.

"It's Mom to you, Junior."

"Right. Mom, if you'll excuse us, I need to go speak with Aunt Bernice. I have a lot to tell her."

"I'll let you get reacquainted," Evelyn said. "I'll go make sure Sonny doesn't go back to sleep. He acts like he's awake, but if I don't keep after him, he tries to snooze a little while longer."

I led Marion from the room, down the hall, and into the lobby.

"I think you made Evelyn's day," I said.

"Everyone needs a hug now and then."

"I have some bad news." I looked around to make sure no one overheard me. "Someone tried to smother me with a pillow early this morning."

"What!"

"I'm fine, and the police came to investigate."

She clasped my arm tightly. "That's awful, Paul. We need to get you out of this place. It's not safe."

"Let's not jump to conclusions. I think we're getting closer to finding the person committing crimes around here."

She waved her arms in the air as if trying to catch low flying birds. "I don't care. It's not worth having you harmed to catch the culprit."

"I spoke with Benny Makoku. He's going to be keeping an eye on me to make sure there's no reoccurrence."

"That's not enough. I'm going to call Detective Chun." She pulled a cell phone thingy out of her tote, punched it a bunch of times, and put it to her ear, a scowl on her face. "Detective Chun, please."

She waited, tapping her foot.

"Detective Chun, this is Marion Jacobson. I want my husband pulled out of the nursing home immediately."

She twitched impatiently as she listened to his response.

"I don't care. We can't take the risk any longer."

She listened intently again, holding the phone so tightly, I thought she'd crush it into shards of plastic and metal.

"No, that's not acceptable."

I tried to imagine Chun convincing my spirited wife. I didn't think he'd be successful.

"Fine." She closed the phone and turned to me. "Detective Chun wants to speak with us, but I think we should head back to the mainland."

"We can't bail on the police now. We have to help find who is doing this. I can't have it on my conscience if someone else dies."

"That someone else could be you, Paul." She pursed her lips. "But we'll go to the police station and hear them out. Detective Chun is sending a car to pick us up."

"As long as I'm not being arrested," I said. "I'm not an arresting personality."

CHAPTER 17

Marion signed me out like a prisoner on parole, and we waited outside the Pacific Vista Nursing Home for our police escort. In the bright sunlight, I watched a puffy cloud drift over us from the mountains. A little spit of rain hit my face before the cloud continued its journey toward the ocean, obviously wanting to do a little sightseeing. Ah, yes. The famous Hawaiian liquid sunshine.

An unmarked car pulled up in front of us, and I checked to see a man in a police uniform driving. You can't be too careful. We climbed in the backseat and the driver introduced himself as Officer Kinau.

"I bet you never expected to have such a difficult detail as bringing us in," I said.

He chuckled. "I've heard of you, Mr. Jacobson. Detective Chun says you're to be given the royal treatment."

"I hope that's not like basting a turkey before it's roasted."

"Nope. But you have the comfort of a regular seat. That's why I didn't bring a patrol car with its very uncomfortable backseat."

"Ah, the luxuries we celebrities experience."

I looked toward Marion. She glared at me but refrained from any physical abuse of her husband.

After a short ride without any exciting chases of speeders or arrests of drug kingpins, we arrived at police headquarters. Officer Kinau escorted us into the building and left us in a conference room with a view out the window toward Beretania Street.

I watched cars whiz by, thankful that we hadn't ended up in a cramped and stuffy interrogation room.

Shortly, Benny Makoku appeared, followed by a man in a crumpled suit who I assumed was Detective Chun. Benny carried a tray with four full coffee cups.

"I like the service here," I said. "But where are the donuts or malasadas?"

Chun pulled a bag out from behind his back. "I remember you like malasadas, Mr. Jacobson."

I began salivating. "Let me at 'em. With all the excitement this morning, I haven't eaten any breakfast yet."

We settled in, and after a few minutes of slurping and chomping, Detective Chun cleared his throat. "The incident at the nursing home early this morning disturbs us. Officer Makoku filled me in on the details, but I'd like to hear your account, Mr. Jacobson."

I swallowed a last bite of malasada and wiped a dab of sugar off the side of my mouth with a napkin. "I awoke with a pillow crammed over my face. Fortunately, I had enough oxygen left to resist and cause the attacker to drop the pillow."

"And your description of the assailant?"

"As I told Officer Makoku, I didn't get a look at him. My main focus was staying alive. Afterwards, I tried Benny's suggestion to close my eyes and recreate the scene, but I couldn't dredge up any images of the intruder."

"I understand someone also threw a rock at you last night?"

"What!" Marion shouted. "Now I really want you out of the nursing home."

I held up a hand to stop the marital stampede. "Easy does it. No harm done. Someone launched a rock at me on my way home last night but missed. As they say, I didn't let it go to my head."

Marion groaned. "I never should have let you go alone." Then she put her hand to her mouth. "And I was supposed to sign you back in anyway."

"No problem. I forged your signature."

"Any description of the rock-thrower?" Chun asked.

"No. It was too dark. I'm zero for two on useful descriptions, I'm afraid. I can tell you I spoke with the three suspects last night, before the rock-throwing incident. Dr. Burber came to check my back and gave me some good exercises to do. I found nothing suspicious about him."

Chun made a note on his pad. "Go on."

"Next, I spoke with Fred Langley in his mother's room. He struck me as being an inoffensive type. No indication of guilt there. Finally, I tracked down Hugh Talbert in the break room and chatted with him. He also seemed like a nice fellow. So I have nothing useful to report on any of the three."

"And the log indicates that Burber and Langley signed out last night before the early morning attack on Mr. Jacobson," Benny added. "Of the three, only Talbert was in the facility at the time of the assault."

Chun pointed to Benny. "I want you to watch Talbert closely."

Benny nodded. "Yeah. And I also plan to stop by Mr. Jacobson's room regularly during the night. I know Mrs. Jacobson will want our assurance that we'll protect her husband."

"I think it's time for Paul to leave the nursing home," Marion said.

Chun gave me a steely stare. "If that's what you want to do, Mr. Jacobson, we'll honor your request. But your presence there is assisting our investigation. You may be instrumental in finding the perpetrator and preventing additional assaults."

I looked from Marion to Benny to Chun. Marion sat with her arms crossed. Benny smiled at me as if he'd found his long-lost brother. Chun's eyes bore in on me with an unflinching stare.

I let out a deep sigh. "I'm an old poop. I don't know how many more miles I have left on the odometer anyway. Assuring my safety is on Marion's mind, but I'm willing to give it a try a little longer."

Marion uncrossed her arms and leaned toward me. "Paul, I don't want you getting hurt or killed."

"I don't want me being harmed either, but I need to do everything I can to assist the police. Let's continue for a week, max."

Marion shook her head. "That's too long. A few days at most."

"I'll check on Mr. Jacobson every fifteen minutes at night," Benny said. "I'll make sure there are no reoccurrences."

"I can live with that." I only hoped that was the case. I held up five fingers. "Five days at most, and then we head back to the mainland."

Marion didn't argue, so with the negotiations completed, we prepared to leave.

"One other thing," Chun said. "Mr. Jacobson, I want you to have a cell phone to call me any time, day or night." He handed me a tiny electronic gadget. "This has my cell on speed dial."

I eyed it as if holding a stick of dynamite. "I don't know how to use these new-fangled gadgets."

"It's very easy. Here. Let me show you." He demonstrated and sure enough, I figured I could handle it.

"Keep it with you at all times."

I saluted. "I'll carry it even when I go pee."

"Too much information," the detective said. "Put it by your bedside at night and on your person during the day."

"My person will make sure to have it with him," I replied. "Now we need a ride back to my place of investigation."

"I'll drop them off on my way home," Benny said.

With that we departed.

As Benny drove us to the nursing home, he said, "By the way, my daughter has been in touch with your granddaughter, Mr. Jacobson."

I crinkled my brow at Marion.

She patted my hand. "You don't remember, but while Jennifer was here, she and Officer Makoku's daughter became surfing buddies. Officer Makoku, we also enjoyed meeting your wife."

"You can call me Benny."

I let them talk on while I considered my predicament. Had I been too cavalier in agreeing to stay at the nursing home? I knew Marion was worried. Should I have honored her desire to immediately return to the mainland? Fear niggled at my innards, but I pushed it away. I needed to help. I couldn't run off and leave a killer on the loose. I'd have to be careful and see what I might find out.

The sound of a buzzing phone interrupted my thoughts. Marion pulled her cell from her tote and answered it. She spoke for a moment and handed it to me. "It's your friend Meyer Ohana. He wants to talk to you."

"Hello?"

"Paul, it's good to hear your voice."

"I guess it's good to hear yours as well, even though I don't recognize it."

He chuckled. "Same old Paul. Are you up for visitors this evening?"

"Sure."

"Henry Palmer and his new wife, Madeline, are back in town after their honeymoon. We want to come take you and Marion out to dinner."

I wanted to dance a jig—a difficult activity in the backseat of Benny's car. "I'm up for something besides nursing home food.

The only thing that's kept me sane is eating police malasadas once in a while."

"I'm sure there's a story there that you can tell me when I see you. We'll be there at six. You can give us a tour, and we'll go grab a bite. Put Marion back on."

I handed the cell phone back to Marion, and she made the final arrangements. She clicked the phone shut and dropped it back in her tote.

"Help me remember all these people," I said.

"Meyer Ohana was your best friend when you lived in the Kina Nani Retirement Home in Kaneohe. He has macular degeneration. You used to read to him like you've been reading to Ralph Hirata. Henry Palmer also lived in the retirement home. He has Asperger's Syndrome, is very smart but has an obnoxious personality. You and he enjoy insulting each other."

"I better bone up on my best insults for this evening."

Marion hugged my arm. "I'm sure you'll handle it very well. Madeline and Henry got married in Kaneohe recently. You were the best man."

I blinked. "Imagine that. And I thought I was only a better man."

"Madeline is . . . different," Marion said. "She's a very commanding person. She also rescued you and helped catch a murderer."

"Maybe it's just as well I don't remember things. Sounds like too much for one brain to comprehend anyway."

"You'll enjoy becoming reacquainted with them tonight."

"Beats lolling around with the vegetables."

Marion swatted me. "Watch what you say. Your roommate, Ralph, is very with it."

"You're right. Also, he has a better memory than I do. And excellent hearing."

Benny pulled up in front of the nursing home. Marion and I

climbed out and waved goodbye as he took off to rejoin his family.

Marion looked at her watch. "It's almost lunch time. Before we go in, there's one other thing you should do. Give Jennifer a call."

"I called her yesterday." I tapped my temple. "See what I can recall with my amazing sex-fed memory."

"She'll want to know what's happened to you overnight."

"Should I give her all the bloody details?"

"Of course. She wants to hear everything."

Marion placed the call and handed me the cell phone.

Allison answered.

"Hello to Boulder from Hawaii," I announced.

"Paul, how much longer will you be there?"

"Another five days. Is Jennifer around?"

"Hold on. She just came home from school."

Good thing they lived in a time zone ahead of Hawaii. I waited a moment, and an enthusiastic voice said, "Grandpa. Have you caught the culprit yet?"

"No, but I'm becoming the scourge of the nursing home and meeting with the police regularly. Someone tried to take out your grandpa with a rock and a pillow."

"I don't understand."

I recounted the two assaults and my questioning the three suspects.

"You really caught someone's attention. Do you think one of the three is the bad guy?"

"That's the strange part. I can't picture any of them being the killer. They seemed like nice guys, not even wise guys."

Jennifer exhaled loudly. "Oh, Grandpa, what am I going to do with you?"

"Nothing. I can't do anything with me either."

"Maybe someone else noticed that you've been questioning

people. That person became concerned you were getting too close to solving the case and decided to eliminate you."

"Spoken like a true crime investigator."

Jennifer giggled. "I'm only speculating."

"You may have something there. I wasn't too subtle in asking around. Someone could have overheard. I'll have to give that some more thought."

"You work on it, Grandpa. I know you'll catch the killer."

Hopefully before he caught me.

CHAPTER 18

At five-forty-five p.m. I was sitting in my room ruminating, which was what you did in a room. I thought over life, the universe, and everything and thanked the stars to be still prancing around on this blue and green orb.

Ralph interrupted my reverie by calling out, "Paul, you ready for dinner? I've been sitting in this wheelchair for fifteen minutes."

I stepped into Ralph's side of the room. "I'm escaping to have dinner with Marion and some friends tonight, but I'll wheel you to the dining room."

Ralph sniffed. "Abandoning me to my sorrow."

I grabbed his wheelchair and gave it a gentle jerk. "Don't give me that."

Ralph chuckled. "Only trying to make you feel guilty. I'll have to go flirt with some of the old bats in your absence."

"Be careful you don't get rabies."

Ralph pounded on his armrest. "Let's get this carriage on the road."

I pushed him into the hall and found Puna wheeling Alice Teng toward the dining room.

"Pedal to the metal, Puna!" Alice shouted. "We have competition."

I revved up my engine, but Puna shot by us before I built up much speed.

"No fair!" I called out. "You had a running start."

"All's fair in love, war, and wheelchair racing," Alice's voice trailed behind as she and Puna outdistanced us by ten feet.

We reached the dining room in distant second. "Sorry, Ralph, I let you down."

"No problem. Set me at Alice's table. I'll let her brag a little and challenge her to an honest race next time. I'll have to put gum in her wheel bearings to sabotage her vehicle."

"That will gum up the works."

Ralph groaned. "Go to your dinner."

I left him at the table with Alice pumping her fist in the air over her victory. I shook my head as I sauntered back to my room. Who would have thought a nursing home could be like this?

Shortly, Marion arrived, decked out in a bright blue and green Hawaiian print dress.

"You look marvelous," I said. "Simply marvelous."

She pirouetted for me. "I thought I'd dress up for our visitors."

I gave a snuffle similar to the one Ralph had given me. "And here I thought it was all for me."

Marion planted a kiss on my cheek, and my spirits soared.

I heard the thumping of feet. Into the room burst a large woman resembling a valkyrie with long platinum blond braids, but dressed in a muumuu.

She stomped up to me. "Hello, jerk. How ya been?"

I stood there speechless. This had to be Madeline Palmer.

Two men followed, one with white hair and an equally white beard. I figured this was Meyer Ohana. The other guy looked like a bald, squat soccer ball. By the process of elimination I determined he was Henry Palmer.

Meyer came forward, searched around with his hand, and grasped my hand to give it a squeeze. "Good to see you, Paul." I knew he didn't see me very well because his eyes seemed to focus on my shoulders.

Henry stepped over. "Hey, jerk. There's sugar on your shoe."

I looked down. Sure enough there was a small splotch of granules probably left over from a malasada at the police department.

"How'd you notice that?" I asked.

Henry tapped his head. "I pay attention. Not like the rest of you dimwits."

This guy was starting to piss me off. "Okay, since you're so observant, I'm trying to find clues to track down a murderer who also tried to suffocate me with a pillow last night. Why don't you look around and find something useful?"

"I'll do that." He slowly turned three hundred sixty degrees, scanning the room. Then he pointed. "There. Under your bed. You'll want to check that out."

I stared where he pointed. The edge of something barely visible hid behind the leg of the bed. I went over and picked it up. It was a tube of face makeup.

My heart thumped. Maybe I'd found a clue. I'd have to show it to Benny Makoku when he came on duty tonight. I put it on my nightstand.

A nurse stuck her head in the room. "Is everything all right in here?"

Madeline strode over to the nurse. "Yes. Now straighten up. Your posture is bad. Stand at attention."

The nurse crossed her arms. "And who are you?"

Madeline put her face inches from the nurse's. "I'm someone who was in the WAVES, where we learned discipline and didn't argue with our officers."

The nurse shot up straight.

Madeline walked around her. "That's better. Smooth out your uniform."

The wide-eyed nurse did as ordered. "Yes, ma'am."

"Return to your station," Madeline bellowed.

The nurse ran off as if being attacked by wild dogs.

"What was all that?" I asked.

"Madeline is good at organizing people," Henry said. "Ain't she a beaut?"

That wasn't exactly how I would have described Madeline, but it was obvious Henry was smitten.

"Let's go grab some chow," Madeline said. "Everyone in line. Follow me. Let's go."

Before I knew what hit me, I was marching toward the front lobby with Madeline in the lead.

As we approached the front door, a nurse stepped in front of Madeline and wagged a finger at her. "You need to sign out."

"I'm taking responsibility for the prisoner," Madeline said. "Open the door for us."

The nurse visibly paled. With a trembling hand she entered the code to release the door.

"Stand at attention!" Madeline shouted.

The nurse did so. We proceeded out the door. I now knew what it was like to be struck by Hurricane Madeline.

"All you yahoos get into the van," Madeline ordered. "I'm driving."

"Ain't she something?" Henry had stars in his eyes.

None of us was going to argue, so we climbed into the white van parked in front of the building.

"Fasten seat belts," came the command from the driver's seat.

I never clicked one in place so fast. We roared away from the curb, my head bashing into the headrest. I figured I should have Madeline push Ralph's wheelchair. She'd beat Puna by a strong arm's worth.

In a short and fast drive with no police sirens behind us, we arrived at the Purple Orchid Palace. In moments Madeline rallied her troops out of the van and marched us into the restaurant.

"Reservation for Palmer, party of five," Madeline announced to the maître d'.

"Your table will be ready in twenty minutes." He lifted his nose in the air.

Madeline stuck her face inches from his. "Now."

Sweat rolled down the man's face. "Uh, let me see what I can do." He dashed off and returned in a minute with an obsequious smile on his face. "Right this way."

"Ain't she a beaut?" Henry said.

I had to admit, in getting results, she was a beaut.

We sat at a large table and opened menus. The waitress, a small Chinese woman, appeared and bowed.

Madeline began speaking to her in Chinese. The woman smiled, bowed again, took out a pad, and wrote furiously. Madeline kept going until the waitress filled up her sheet and flipped to a second page. Madeline spoke a few final words and sat back. The waitress smiled, bowed, and dashed off.

"No menus?" I asked.

"Not needed," Madeline replied. "Everything's ordered."

"Ain't she dynamite?" Henry said.

Moments later huge platters and bowls of food began to arrive until they covered the whole table. The waitress put plates and chopsticks in front of us.

"Dig in," Madeline said.

We all knew how to carry out that order.

After we began stuffing our faces, Marion asked, "How was your honeymoon?"

Madeline slurped in a long noodle and dabbed her mouth with a napkin. "Terrific. We stayed at the Pioneer Inn in Lahaina. Snookums and I had a grand time." She winked at Henry and elbowed him, almost knocking him out of his chair. "We didn't surface for two days."

A glazed look came over Henry's face. "She's some woman."

"And don't you forget it." Madeline picked up a shrimp in her chopsticks, tossed it in the air, and caught it in her mouth. She chewed for a moment and continued. "On the third morning we took a van to the top of Haleakalā and bicycled down at sunrise."

"Didn't that stress Henry's heart after his attack last year?" Meyer asked.

Madeline elbowed Henry again, this time causing him to expel a piece of chicken onto his plate. "I've whipped Snookums into shape. After two days of romance, his heart was strong and healthy."

That wasn't a picture I wanted to contemplate.

"We went swimming, snorkeling off Molokini, and more loving." She pitched her elbow, but this time Henry was prepared and ducked out of striking range.

"After the good times we sailed back to Kaneohe, and here we are."

"Sounds as exciting as our honeymoon cruise to Alaska." Marion hugged my arm, rather than elbowing me. I was thankful to have a calm bride.

"And along the way, we quizzed each other on baseball facts." Madeline winked. "That is, when we weren't otherwise occupied." She reached over and squeezed Henry's cheek, leaving a bright red mark.

"Baseball facts?" I asked.

"Henry's an expert on baseball," Meyer explained. "He can recite every imaginable fact and statistic."

"That's right," Madeline said, whacking Henry on the back and knocking his face into the chop suey. "He knows almost as much as I do."

I remembered something from my journal. "Okay, experts, I

heard two CNAs debating the best athlete of all time. One said Bo Jackson. Tell me what you know about him."

"I'll let Henry field that simple one." Madeline chortled.

"Vincent Edward Jackson," Henry said. "Definitely a top candidate for the best athlete of all time. Played in the major leagues from nineteen eighty-six through nineteen ninety-four, missing the nineteen ninety-two season due to his hip injury. He was in the nineteen eighty-nine All Star game and won MVP. Not bad in football either. Wore number thirty-four on his football uniform at Auburn, earning a Heisman trophy. Played pro football from nineteen eighty-seven to nineteen ninety with the Raiders, going to the Pro Bowl in nineteen ninety."

"As a baseball player, he struck out a lot, though," Madeline added. "Led the American League with a hundred seventy-two strikeouts in nineteen eighty-nine."

Henry shrugged. "You have to swing to play ball. Sometimes you connect and sometimes you miss."

"Kind of like my memory," I said. "Most mornings it definitely misses."

CHAPTER 19

In spite of the large amount of food, we managed to finish off every platter and bowl served. I patted my stomach. I was full but hadn't overeaten. Marion and Meyer had taken small portions. Madeline and Henry had consumed three-quarters of the food.

"Meyer, how's your friend Hattie Wilson?" Marion asked.

Meyer reddened. "She's . . . uh . . . fine."

"Even in spite of your beard, I can see there's something going on here," I said. "Who's Hattie Wilson?"

"She's Meyer's new squeeze," Henry said.

Meyer coughed. "We're just friends."

Marion patted my arm. "You don't remember, but Hattie Wilson lives in the same care home with Meyer. You met her."

I shrugged. "Don't recall her, but with my mental in-acuity, it's understandable."

Madeline reached across the table and poked Meyer in the chest, causing him to release a whoosh of air. "With the jerk and Henry having found brides, you should follow their lead."

Meyer scraped his chair back to stay out of reach. "As I said, Hattie and I are only friends."

"Have it your own way." Madeline snapped her fingers. "We're ready for fortune cookies."

Our waitress scurried over with a platter full of orange slices, almond cookies, and fortune cookies.

"Snookums, who should open the first fortune?" Madeline asked.

"The jerk can do it." Henry pointed to me.

"Since the bald, squat pissant asked so nicely, I'll oblige." I cracked it open. "Hmmm. My fortune is, 'You flirt with danger and will find happiness.' " I waggled my eyebrows at Marion. "I like flirting with this dangerous woman, and I'm happy."

Everyone else opened a cookie, resulting in innocuous fortunes, and then Madeline took her turn. She crushed the cookie in her fist, pulled out the strip of paper and read, "You are a born leader."

As we left the restaurant, the wait staff stood at attention, and the maître d' saluted.

"At ease," Madeline commanded.

The maître d' raced ahead and held the driver's side door of the van open for Madeline. Once we were all belted in, she shot off with the whole wait staff on the curb waving.

"You have a decided effect on people," I said to Madeline.

"Once they know I mean business, they get in line. Enlisted people respect a decisive officer."

"Ain't she a dynamo?" Henry said.

Back at the Pacific Vista Nursing Home, Madeline punched the buzzer and the door immediately clicked. We entered to find the nurse who had been there earlier, now standing at attention.

"Welcome back," the nurse said.

"At ease," Madeline replied. "Resume your duties."

The nurse scampered away like a flea escaping a soapy wet dog.

"I saw a spot of mud on the floor," Madeline said. "I'm taking Henry along to whip the cleaning staff into shape. We'll meet the rest of you in the jerk's room." She lifted up Henry, tucked him under her arm, and strode off toward a man wielding a mop at the end of the blue hallway.

"Ain't she a beaut?" trailed back from the hallway.

The rest of us headed to my room. The curtain was parted, and Ralph lay in his bed.

"I hear Paul and Marion's footsteps but don't recognize the other person," Ralph said.

"I'll be damned," I replied. "Not only can you recognize our sound, but you can tell how many of us there are. How do you do that?"

"My hearing makes up for my eyes. Are you going to introduce me to your friend?"

"Meyer Ohana, meet Ralph Hirata. Ralph, Meyer and I knew each other when I lived in a retirement home in Kaneohe. Meyer, Ralph is my roommate and a World War II hero. You both have as good eyesight as I have overnight memory."

Meyer shuffled over, found Ralph's hand, and shook it.

"You must be the friend that Paul used to read to," Ralph said.

"That's me," Meyer said. "I have macular degeneration."

"He's been reading to me as well, since I can't see worth a tinker's damn. Paul, why don't you read both of us a story?"

"I can handle that." I grabbed my O. Henry book and brought it over to Ralph's side of the room. Marion moved chairs for Meyer and me to sit on and announced that she was going to go watch Madeline in action.

I opened the book. "Here's one titled 'Proof of the Pudding.' "

"I ate some of that for dessert tonight," Ralph said. "Two servings' worth."

"We had Chinese food with fortune cookies for dessert," I said. "My fortune says I flirt with danger, so let's dive in."

In this story the wives of editor Westbrook and writer Shackleford Dawe are friends. Dawe's stories keep getting rejected by Westbrook, who feels the endings aren't literary enough. Dawe objects, saying people don't fly into blank verse during emotional crises but use common language and that's how he ends his stories. They make a bet to prove who is right. Dawe says he'll leave a letter for his wife that he's run off. He and Westbrook will hide in the next room and listen if she responds with literary or common language. When Dawe and Westbrook get to the house, they find a letter from the two wives indicating they have both run off to join the chorus of an opera company. Dawe responds with a soliloquy to make Shakespeare proud, and Westbrook reacts with slang and cursing.

I put the book down.

Meyer sighed. "Good old O. Henry. Always a twist at the end."

"Yup," Ralph said. "Things don't turn out like you're expecting."

I paused, in thought. My fortune and the story. I had placed myself in danger, trying to help solve Linda Rodriguez's assault and murder. I hadn't been able to figure out anything useful yet. Had I been looking for the expected and missed the unexpected? I'd have to get back to my snooping and figure it out.

Madeline, Henry, and Marion returned. Madeline no longer carried Henry under her arm.

"Who's there?" Ralph asked. "I hear Marion and two other new sets of footsteps."

"Henry and Madeline Palmer," I said. "They are the rest of our dinner party. Henry and Madeline, meet Ralph Hirata."

They both came over and shook Ralph's hand. Fortunately, Madeline refrained from breaking any of Ralph's knuckles.

"Henry, you and Ralph have something in common," I said. "You're both very observant but in different ways. Henry sees things the rest of us miss, and Ralph can hear things other people can't. Henry, care to astound us with something you've seen?"

"Sure. That tube of face makeup I spotted earlier. You put it on your nightstand. It's not there now."

I gaped. *Uh-oh.* Sure enough, it had disappeared.

"Ralph, did anyone come into my side of the room while we were at dinner?" I asked.

He chuckled. "It was like a regular parade. I think everyone wanted to check to see if you had snuck back in or something. The cleaning supervisor, the security guy, and one set of footsteps I didn't recognize."

I definitely had some work to do.

"Time to hit the road," Madeline bellowed.

Meyer jumped up from the chair as if goosed.

Madeline clapped her hands. "Chop, chop."

Meyer, Henry, and Madeline said goodbye to Ralph, and I accompanied them out to the lobby.

Upon seeing Madeline, two nurses and a member of the cleaning crew shot to attention.

"Don't stand there, open the door," Madeline ordered.

One of the nurses dashed over and punched in the code. The door beeped open, and before you could say "tornado," Madeline shoved Meyer and Henry through the open door.

In the distance I heard, "Ain't she a beaut?"

I sniffed the aroma of pine cleaner and noticed the floor sparkled. The nursing home should hire Madeline to run the place.

I needed to find Benny. I looked down each of the three hallways but didn't spot him. "Is the security guy around?" I asked one of the nurses.

"Should be on the second floor."

I headed upstairs and found him speaking to a nurse. I went up and tapped him on the shoulder. "I need to speak with you."

He finished his conversation and motioned me to join him in the second floor break room.

"What's on your mind, Mr. Jacobson?"

I looked around to make sure no one was in hearing range. "I found something suspicious in my room earlier this evening. A tube of face makeup."

"Not something you use, I assume."

"Nope. It was under my bed. I guess no one noticed it earlier. I put it on my nightstand to show you later and went out to dinner with Marion and some friends. When we returned, the tube had disappeared."

"Any idea who took it?"

"My roommate, Ralph Hirata, who's blind, has excellent hearing. He said the cleaning supervisor, one unknown person, and you entered my room."

"Yeah. I came in to check on you but saw you were gone. I didn't notice anything on your nightstand."

"Who might have been on the first floor the last two hours?"

Benny thought for a moment. "Puna Koloa was going off duty, and Sal Polahi and Ken Yamamoto were starting their shift."

I thought back to my journal. "I've met all three."

"I'll do some more checking on them," Benny said.

So will I.

I returned to my room to find Marion reading my O. Henry book. Ralph lay in his bed so I stepped over to him.

"Hey, old buddy. You said I had some visitors while I was out to dinner."

"Yup."

"You mentioned the cleaning supervisor. Is that Hugh Talbert?"

"That's him."

"And the footsteps you didn't recognize. Let me know if you

hear them again."

"Will do. Why the interest, Paul?"

I thought for a moment. How much did I want to say to Ralph? "Something's missing from my room. I don't know if I misplaced it or someone took it."

"You should report it to security."

"I'll speak with the security guy if it doesn't turn up."

"I like your friend, Meyer. He's a real gentleman. Your other friends are . . . interesting."

"That's a mild way of saying it. Henry Palmer is a piece of work, and his new wife, Madeline, will probably be running for governor of the state of Hawaii one of these days."

"You know how to pick 'em, Paul."

"That I do."

CHAPTER 20

Marion looked up from the O. Henry book she had been reading on my side of the room. "What's this about Paul picking something?"

"Ralph was merely commenting on my ability to select interesting friends. But I'm also an expert at picking beautiful wives." I winked at Marion.

She gave me her winning smile that made my pulse rate increase twofold. "Don't forget you need to update your journal."

"Speaking of which, Ralph, you should write up your adventures from World War II."

"Writing and I don't get along so hot with my eyes having gone in the tank."

"You're a good talker. Do an audio recording. I bet your relatives would enjoy hearing some of your tales."

Ralph yawned. "I'll put that on my bucket list. It's time to kick you out of my side of the room, Paul. I'm ready for some shut-eye."

"We'll catch up in the morning." I pulled the curtain and turned off his light.

Returning to my side of the room, I asked Marion if she wanted to take a little stroll.

"I'm right in the middle of a story," she said. "Let me finish it first."

"Go ahead. I'll wander around the halls for a while, and then

Mike Befeler

we can go outside." I wanted the chance to do a little checking on some of the staff here anyway.

I wandered up to the nurses' station and asked for Ken Yamamoto. The on-duty nurse informed me Ken was helping a resident get into bed but would be back shortly. As promised, he showed up in five minutes.

The other nurse spoke to him, and he stepped over to where I waited. "Ah, Mr. Jacobson. The Jesse Owens fan."

I remembered what I had read in my journal. "That's right, you and Sal Polahi were debating the best athlete of all time. I put in my own dissenting vote."

"You wanted to speak with me, Mr. Jacobson?"

I quickly improvised. "That I did. Did you happen to go into my room while I was out at dinner? I found a silver dollar on the floor and thought you might have dropped it."

"Nope, wasn't me. I didn't go in."

"Did you see anyone else go into my room?"

"No."

"I guess it belongs to someone else. I'll keep asking around."

I next found Sal Polahi and asked him if he had been in my room.

He looked at me askance. "Why do you ask?"

I went through my silver dollar spiel again.

"Couldn't have been mine since I wasn't in your room."

Not having elicited anything useful from him, I decided to next track down Hugh Talbert. I traversed the halls and, not finding anyone who matched the description from my journal, took the stairs to the second floor. There I spotted a man with a gray mustache and beard and figured it must be my target. I approached him and called out, "Mr. Talbert?"

His eyes met mine. "Yes?"

"I'm Paul Jacobson from the first floor. We've spoken before."

"I remember."

152

I didn't, but it was a good thing I had written in my diary. "I understand you stopped by my room earlier this evening. I found a silver dollar on the floor and thought you might have dropped it."

"Not me. I haven't seen one of those in years."

I scratched my head. "I can't figure out who else might have lost it. Did you see it on the floor when you went in my room?"

"No, I'm not sure I would have noticed it. I was just checking to make sure your doorknob wasn't stuck. I didn't go far into your room. We've had complaints of doorknobs sticking, so I checked all the rooms earlier."

"Did you happen to see anyone else go in? I'd sure like to return it to the rightful owner." *Right.*

"Nope. Didn't see anyone besides Mr. Hirata in his bed, but he isn't able to move enough to get to your side of the room."

"I guess I'll keep looking."

I returned to my room and asked Marion, "You ready?"

"No. You took so long I started another story."

I slapped my forehead. "As they say, in life timing is everything."

"I only have another page to go. Be patient."

"At my age, I'll do that rather than being a hospital patient."

After receiving a well-deserved wife's glare, I waited until Marion had finished her story. She closed the book, put it on my nightstand, stood, and took my hand. "Now our moonlight promenade."

Marion signed me out, and we walked outside into the warm Hawaiian air. I heard bugs buzzing, the rattle of a car that needed a new muffler, and some background rock music. Ah, the music of the night. I took a deep breath and smelled the aroma of jasmine. Marion squeezed my hand.

"I struck out again on finding anyone suspicious," I said. "I haven't been able to track down or even get vibes on who caused the trouble around the nursing home."

"Don't get too nosy." Marion snuggled against me as we walked. "I don't want you involved in any more incidents."

"I'll be careful."

"And remember. A few more days and then we're going back to the mainland. It's time for you to retire as an undercover operative."

"Maybe you and I can do some under the covers investigation." I waggled my eyebrows.

"That's another reason for you to leave the nursing home. Nothing like that will happen when we're sleeping in different buildings."

"That's a good incentive. I'll wrap up my investigation one way or the other in the next couple of days."

"It was nice of you to read to Ralph and Meyer tonight."

I shrugged. "Hey, it's a small thing I can do to help my sight-impaired friends. And Ralph is helping me. He heard who entered my room while we were out eating. I wish I could level with him on why I'm in the nursing home."

"But Detective Chun wants it kept secret."

"Yeah, I haven't spouted off. Ralph makes up for his lack of eyesight with acute hearing. I think he could assist, but I'll keep my yap closed."

"I think it's time to turn the complete investigation over to the police. We can leave it up to Officer Makoku to track down the culprit."

"He's doing his best, but we're up against a wily cuss. I certainly don't have a clue who's been causing all the trouble. Maybe, I should check in with my consultant. I could call Jennifer and see if she has any recommendations."

"It's too late for that with the time difference between here and Colorado. It's the middle of the night there."

"Damn time zones. I always forget."

"Let's get you back. It's time for you to take your pills."

"On second thought, I think we should stroll for the rest of the night."

Marion swatted me. "You'll do anything to keep from taking pills."

"Darn right. My delicate throat can't handle those huge rocks."

In spite of my protesting, Marion steered us back to the nursing home. She pushed the button, the door clicked open, and the odor of disinfectant and laundry detergent invaded my nostrils. Marion signed me in.

"Oh, for the days of being able to move around without someone having to sign me in and out," I lamented.

"I know. Your freedom has been compromised."

Back in my room, Marion forced me to take my pills. Damn. Too bad she wasn't the one who forgot things. Next, she handed me my journal from her tote. She picked up the short story book to read while I wrote about the latest adventures in the life of Paul Jacobson. I only hoped there would be many more days to document.

CHAPTER 21

My eyes shot open. I lay in some kind of hospital bed. Had my old ticker gone on the fritz and was I recovering? I patted my chest. No tubes attached. I sat up. No, everything appeared to be in order, and all my limbs were still attached. "Where the hell am I?" I muttered.

"Is that you, Paul?" a voice said from behind a curtain.

"It's me. Who's speaking?"

"I'm your roommate, Ralph," the voice announced. "Pull the curtain, and you'll be able to see me."

I dutifully obliged and found an old guy lying in a bed similar to the one I'd escaped from.

"What is this joint?" I asked.

"You're in the Pacific Vista Nursing Home."

"Damn. Have I lost all my marbles and been sent to the dust bin?"

"You and your memory, Paul."

"I hate to admit it, but I don't know who the heck you are, Ralph."

He chuckled. "Marion warned me that you always wake up in this state of confusion."

Now I was really confused. "Is Marion a nurse?"

"No, she's your wife."

I whacked the side of my head, but that didn't shake lose any cogent memories to help the situation. "I had a wife once, but she died."

"You have a brand spanking new one," Ralph said. "You've been married five months. She's a peach."

"I guess that's better than a lemon, but I don't remember her one iota. What do they have you in here for?"

"I can't see and can't move. Other than that, I feel like I'm twenty years old."

I squinted at him. "I hate to say it, Ralph, but you look like a prune and not a twentysomething."

"Hey, I can't help it if I'm a little weathered."

"You're a lot weathered."

At that moment a young chick in her seventies strolled into the room and planted a juicy kiss on my cheek.

"Are you on the welcoming committee?" I asked.

"Paul's in a bit of a quandary, Marion," Ralph said.

I eyed the woman. Was she the Marion Ralph claimed I was hitched to? My heart thumped. Nice looking old broad. She smiled at me.

"Umm, are we . . . uh . . . married?" I asked.

"Very married."

"Hot damn. But what am I doing in this place?"

Marion handed me a notebook. "Why don't you sit down and read this?"

Not being one to ignore the request of a beautiful woman, I plopped my sorry behind down on a chair and read what turned out to be my diary. Holy macaroli. What a weird life I lived.

When I finished reading, I handed the journal back to Marion. "Thanks for the clarification . . . I guess."

A CNA came and helped Ralph into a wheelchair.

"You going to join me for breakfast, Paul?" he called out.

"I'm going to take him out," Marion said.

"Gee, I'm in demand."

"Get dressed," Marion commanded.

I obeyed, and once I was in presentable attire, true to her

word, Marion led me to the front of the building, signed me out, and steered me to a small coffee shop three blocks away.

After we ordered and our meals arrived, Marion said, "I want to speak with you in private. Ralph doesn't know about your mission in the nursing home."

"I'm trying to digest it myself along with the scrambled eggs."

Marion handed me a little electronic gadget. "Here's the cell phone you're supposed to keep with you."

I turned it over in my hand. "I have no clue how to use it."

"That's why I brought it for you. Here let me show you." She talked me through its operation.

"Okay," I said. "I think I can handle it. But why do I need it?"

"Detective Chun thought it would be important for you to be able to call him the moment you learn something useful."

I stashed it in my pocket. "I guess it beats smoke signals."

I paid the meal ransom, and we strolled back, enjoying the sunny morning. After Marion signed me back in, we returned to my room.

Loud footfalls thumped out in the hallway. A large woman with platinum blond hair burst into my room.

"Hello, jerk!" she shouted. "I've come to abduct Marion."

Marion waved. "Hi, Madeline. Ready for our shopping spree?"

I looked from Marion to Madeline, reviewing what I had read about Henry's new wife. "I bet you two will take Honolulu by storm."

Madeline rubbed her hands together. "Darn right. We'll shop until the salespeople drop."

"Where's Henry?" Marion asked.

Madeline waved a large hand, almost hitting me in the face. "He wimped out. Doesn't like shopping."

"I can't blame him," I said. "It's not one of my favorite activities."

Madeline poked me in the stomach, causing me to gasp. "You men. Don't appreciate the finer things in life. Let's get going." She grabbed Marion's arm and whisked her out of the room.

I watched as the two of them disappeared.

Whew. Typhoon Madeline had struck and moved on. I was sure she and Henry deserved each other.

With nothing better to do, I decided to snoop. I wandered up to the nurses' station in the front of the building and watched a nurse fill out a form on the counter. Probably reporting that a large wild woman had dragged Marion out the door. The front lobby area was crowded. People kept coming through the front door. I walked down each of the three color-coded hallways before climbing the stairs to the second level. After all the activity at the front of the first floor, not much was going on up here other than a woman with a walker who almost impaled me. This was a dangerous place.

I passed a snoozing woman in a wheelchair who did nothing more than dribble some spittle on my shoe. At the end of the light green hall, I came to a door, open to a nook off the main corridor. It was a recess approximately six feet long that contained some excess chairs stacked along one wall. It, in turn, led to another door that stood ajar. I didn't remember seeing this spot before, but who could tell with my slipshod memory? Opening the second door, I saw that it led into a deep storage closet. A shelf held toilet paper, paper towels, and cleaning supplies. Something sparkly rested on the floor right near the shelf. I stepped all the way into the closet and bent over to look. It was a quarter. My lucky day. I pocketed it, figuring I could use it and seven of its friends to buy a can of pop.

The door slammed shut, bathing me in darkness. *Uh-oh.* I turned back to the door and fumbled around for the handle. I heard some scraping sounds outside. Finally locating the handle, I turned it, but the door didn't budge. I pushed, but it didn't give. Damnation. I was locked in. Not my lucky day. I shouted and pounded on the door. Then I realized my predicament. With the two doors between me and the hallway, if whoever had locked me in had also shut the outer door, no one would hear me. I wondered how often someone came into this storage closet. If the cleaning crew had finished on the second floor for the morning, no one might come here until the next day.

There had to be a light switch here somewhere. I ran my hand around the door jamb and found a toggle. *Success.* I flipped it. Nothing. Wiring problem? Burned-out bulb? Sabotage? In any case, I only had darkness for company.

I stood back and rammed my shoulder into the door. It didn't give, but pain shot through my whole right arm. I couldn't force my way out. *Think.* How to get out of this place? I began to imagine I couldn't breathe. Was I suffocating? I groped around the floor. There should be some air coming in. I took a deep breath. Merely a mild panic attack. *Okay, use your noggin, Jacobson.* There had to be some simple way to alert someone. I snapped my fingers. I had that electronic doodad in my pocket. I fumbled around in the dark and managed to remove the cell phone. In my haste, it slipped out of my hand and crashed to the floor. Damn. I hoped I hadn't broken the cussed thing.

I dropped onto my hands and knees and patted the floor. It had to be here somewhere. It couldn't have gone very far. No luck. I tapped my hands along the floor until I reached the door and then worked my way deeper into the closet. Eventually, my hand struck something right near the shelf. *Jackpot.* I sat on the floor and carefully opened the phone. Lo and behold, a little blue screen and white backlit numbers shone. It provided enough illumination to see around the room. Now, what had Marion taught me earlier? Good thing I had a photographic memory during the day. I followed her instructions and punched the keys. The phone began to ring.

"Detective Chun," came a voice.

I put the phone to my cheek. "Detective, this is your favorite undercover operative, Paul Jacobson."

"I can't hear you," the voice said.

I adjusted the phone, and repeated my name.

"What can I do for you, Mr. Jacobson?"

"You can send out the posse. Someone locked me in a closet."

There was a pause on the line. "Locked in a closet?"

"Yes, I'm ready to come out of the closet, so to speak. Can you have someone come rescue me? I'm stuck on the second floor of the nursing home. I've shouted and banged on the door, but no one can hear me."

"Was this an accident?"

"No. Someone deliberately locked me in. I'm at the end of the light green hallway on the second floor."

"Sit tight, I'm on my way."

"I don't have any choice but to sit tight."

I closed the phone, returned it to my pocket, and remained on the floor slumped against the wall. I thought momentarily of breaking into a sad ditty such as "Swing Low, Sweet Chariot," but even I couldn't stand the sound of my own voice.

While I waited, I reviewed my predicament. My snooping had come to the attention of someone with less than honorable intentions. Whoever that person was, I had put myself in a position where he had snuck up on me and locked me in this closet. I was fortunate he hadn't bashed me over the head.

A realization struck me as if I'd been slapped in the face. Most of the assaults on yours truly had happened at night. This one occurred during the morning. Detective Chun could check to see who from the night staff happened to be hanging around this morning. Probably not very many of them still here. That might indicate who the culprit was. We'd nail the sucker.

On that happy note, I bided my time until I heard a scraping noise and the door popped open.

"I'm saved," I shouted. "Detective Chun, I presume."

"At your service, Mr. Jacobson."

I stood and joined him in the outer storage area.

"Someone placed a chair against the doorknob to lock you in," he said. "Did you see who did this?"

"No, but you should be able to catch the SOB. I figure the person after me works at night. You only have to find who from the night shift is still here."

"That's the problem, Mr. Jacobson. I already asked that question. It turns out this morning the nursing home held a monthly all-hands meeting that adjourned right before you called me. Staff members from all shifts were in the facility at the time you were locked in."

CHAPTER 22

Detective Chun arranged for someone to come and check for fingerprints on the doorknobs and the chair used to lock me in the closet. He wasn't hopeful they'd find anything useful, but indicated they needed to make sure. He admonished me to be careful and accompanied me back to my room.

Ralph heard me enter and called out, "There you are. What have you been up to, Paul?"

"Playing a game of hide-and-seek."

He squinted in my direction but didn't question my statement. "Since you ran out on me for breakfast, are you going to join me for lunch?"

"Wouldn't miss it. When do you want to go?"

"I'll call to have someone get me into my wheelchair."

Ralph pushed his call button, and in a few minutes a female CNA appeared to help him into his conveyance. I offered to wheel him, and the CNA disappeared for other duties.

In the hallway, a woman in an automated wheelchair blocked our path. She spun it around to face us.

"Hey, Ralphie. Look what I got. A brand-new electric wheelchair. This beauty is a humdinger."

"Paul, do you remember Alice Teng?" Ralph asked.

I peered at the small woman doing wheelies in her chair. "I recall the name from my journal."

"I don't need anyone to push me anymore," Alice said. "I can whup your fanny in a race by myself."

"I don't know," Ralph replied. "I have a pretty good motor with Paul pushing me. You up to the challenge?"

"Eat my dust." Alice spun one last time, aimed her wheelchair down the hall, and took off for the dining area.

With the gauntlet thrown down, I responded by pushing Ralph's wheelchair at full tilt. Alice built up some speed, but I gained traction and caught up halfway down the hallway. I pulled ahead as a woman in a walker thumped out of a room. We were on a collision course. I veered in front of Alice to avoid the woman but overcorrected and bonked into the wall. We rebounded into Alice's path. She put on her brakes but not in time. She bashed into my leg. I dropped like a wounded duck and collided with the woman using the walker. She managed to keep her balance, but I ended up on my butt, completely enshrouded by a tipped walker, an electric wheelchair, and Ralph's non-automated model.

At that moment Marion and Madeline came through the entryway. Marion held shopping bags in both hands.

"Paul, what are you doing?" Marion called out.

"Can't you tell? We're having a wheelchair race."

Madeline strode toward us, reached over, and lifted me up as if picking up a rag doll. "What kind of trouble are you causing, jerk?"

I landed on my feet, leaned over, and rubbed my leg, making sure I wasn't bleeding. "Only the usual."

"Dang blamed amateur drivers." Alice shook her fist at me. "You should have your license revoked."

"Hey, no worries. I gave up my driver's license years ago."

Madeline righted the walker, and the woman holding it continued on her way toward the dining room as if accidents like this were an everyday occurrence.

Alice maneuvered around us and zipped forward, raising her fist in the air. "Whupped 'em again."

"You two ladies want to join us for lunch?" I asked.

"Sure," Madeline said. "I'm starving."

"I'll drop the bags in your room, Paul." Marion headed past us.

I pushed Ralph's wheelchair the rest of the way, and we seated ourselves at a table for four.

"Madeline, Ralph was with the Four Hundred Forty-Second in World War II. Ralph, Madeline was a WAVE."

Madeline grasped Ralph's hand. "Good to see you again. I had a friend married to a man in the Four Forty Second. She crewed for me on a Transpac yacht race. Name of Helen Okawara."

Ralph sat up straight in his wheelchair. "The Helen Okawara who lived in Aiea?"

"That's the one."

Ralph grinned. "I knew her. Married to Buddy Okawara."

"Yeah," Madeline said. "I met him. He told lots of stories of the campaign in Italy and how he survived."

They exchanged stories like long-lost friends. In the meantime Marion returned from stashing her shopping treasures.

"Did you deplete our savings account?" I asked.

She patted my hand. "There should be enough left to get us back to the mainland. I even brought you a present—a new Hawaiian shirt."

"Good. You can't have too many of those."

We ate spaghetti and meatballs, with Madeline having a heaping second serving. After we finished, Alice Teng scooted over to our table. "Any of you wimps ready to race back? Double or nothing."

"I've retired from the circuit," I said.

"I'll push Ralph," Madeline volunteered.

Alice eyed Madeline. "You think you can keep up with me, girlie?"

"We'll leave you so far back, you'll only have oil on your forehead."

"Oh, yeah. Who's going to do that? You and who else, girlie?"

The combatants lined up.

Alice spun around in a wheelie. "Let's see what you're made of." She aimed her chair down the hallway. "First one to the green light. Ready, set, go!" She took off.

Madeline leaned over and pushed so hard that Ralph's front wheels shot up in the air. Ralph gasped.

It was no contest. Madeline passed Alice in two steps and won by half a hallway. When we all gathered in front of the shower room, Alice held out a hand. "You beat me fair and square, Ralphie. You have some engine there."

Ralph groaned. "I think I have whiplash."

Madeline dusted her hands together. "Let me know if you ever want a rematch."

"No thanks, girlie. I'll stick with the guys. You're too much for me."

Later that afternoon beeping sounds emerged from my pocket. I reached in, removed the electronic gadget, and looked at it.

"You need to open it and put it to your ear," Marion said.

"Right." I did as instructed. "Hello?"

Detective Chun's voice announced a lack of success in locating any useful fingerprints or any clues indicating who had locked me in the closet that morning. With another reminder to be careful, he signed off.

Marion stuck around for dinner, and I changed into my new gold Hawaiian shirt to show up all the other old farts. I wheeled Ralph to the dining area with no challenges from Alice Teng, and we arrived without any traffic accidents.

Ralph regaled us with his World War II exploits, and I related my triumph over supply requisitions.

I dreamt I lay in a dark alley. I heard a cat yowl. I sniffed and smelled rotten garbage. The walls pressed in on me. I squirmed. I heard footsteps. My eyes shot open. I was in bed in a strange place. I heard real footsteps. A dark shape moved through the doorway toward my bed. Something wasn't right. "Help!" I shouted.

The figure in the doorway turned and disappeared.

"What's going on?" came a voice from behind a curtain.

I squirmed out of bed, went over to the curtain, and opened it. A withered old guy lay in bed, his unfocused eyes blinking.

"Paul, you shouted for help."

I looked at the guy. I didn't know who the hell he was. "Someone was sneaking toward my bed. Where am I?"

He introduced himself as Ralph Hirata and explained where I was.

"Why would I be in a nursing home?"

His unfocused gaze pointed near me. "You have memory problems."

"You can say that again."

"You have memory problems."

"Okay. So I have a roommate who's a joker."

Ralph tapped the railing on his bed. "You may want to call your wife, Marion."

"I don't think I'll call my wife, Marion, Joan, or any other name. Best I can remember I'm a widower."

After he explained my marriage situation, I had a nurse place a call, and in half an hour an attractive silver-haired woman arrived and planted a kiss on my cheek. She gave me something to read, and everything became as clear as pea soup.

Upon learning of my undercover assignment, I whispered to

Marion, "A man was sneaking into my room around five-thirty."

"I better find Benny Makoku to let him know." Marion left the room and returned in a few minutes accompanied by a man with a ponytail. He signaled for me to join him outside my room, and we walked to an alcove to speak in private.

"What happened, Mr. Jacobson?"

I looked around to make sure no one could hear me. "I awoke to see a man sneaking into my room."

"Did you get a look at him?"

"No. It was too dark. I shouted and scared him away."

"Any sense of his physical stature or age?"

I shook my head. "No. Too dark, and I was disoriented from being abruptly awakened."

"I'll do some checking."

He took off, and I sat there, gathering my thoughts.

From what I read in my journal, too many unexplained things had happened to me. I was supposed to be helping to find someone who had assaulted and later killed a woman here in the nursing home. Now that person had turned his attention to me. Not a position I coveted. This threat needed to be resolved before someone turned me into minced dog food. We had to find the person responsible for all these problems.

CHAPTER 23

News of the day got worse. Another woman in the Pacific Vista Nursing Home had been assaulted overnight. When overhearing two female nurses talking about the attack, a shiver ran down my spine. The perp had done this deed before sneaking into my room. Holy Shinola. This place gave me the creeps.

Benny Makoku took me aside and gave me the specifics. "Someone sexually assaulted Mrs. Annabel Dempsey in the middle of the night. She thought it was just a dream, but physical evidence of an attack was found when she complained of pains in her abdomen this morning. She also says a pearl necklace is missing. Same MO as the other assault."

"And I don't feel like I've been able to help jack squat," I said. "I'm supposed to be tracking down information so you can catch and arrest the SOB. I've been as useless as wheels on a submarine."

"We'll catch him, Mr. Jacobson. We'll catch him."

On that happy note, he departed, leaving me with my thoughts.

Later that afternoon I decided to pay a visit to Mrs. Dempsey. Thanks to Ralph's superb memory and knowledge of residents' locations, I found my way to her room along the blue hallway of the first floor where she was resting peacefully in her bed.

"Mrs. Dempsey, I'm Paul Jacobson. We haven't met before. I live in the beige hall here on the first floor. You may know my roommate, Ralph Hirata."

"Everyone knows Ralphie." She squinted at me. "But I don't believe I've seen you before."

That was encouraging. At least she didn't think I had attacked her. "I haven't been here very long. How are you feeling?"

"I went to the hospital for a checkup this morning. I'm fine now. Thanks for asking."

She didn't look worse for wear, so I decided to press on. "Did you get a good look at the man who came into your room last night?"

"The police asked me the same question. I thought I was having a dream, but now I realize there was really someone here. It was dark. I think he was a haole guy, maybe in his sixties."

"Any distinguishing characteristics?" I sounded oh so investigative.

"A beard and mustache."

"And his voice?"

"He didn't say anything. I was in that half-asleep, half-dream state and wasn't really aware of what was going on, but this morning I didn't feel so hot."

"What was he wearing?"

"Hmm." She put her hand to her cheek. "The only thing I remember is material that felt like a sweatshirt."

I looked around her private room, trying to figure out something useful to ask. The perp apparently didn't want to take a chance on assaulting anyone in a semiprivate room where a roommate might overhear. Except when he went after me. He had come into my room once to try to smother me and again this morning, but I was a special case. There had to be some way to identify this guy.

"Was he fat or skinny?"

She shrugged. "Average build."

I ran out of questions. D-minus on my investigation exam. "I'll let you get some rest. Thanks for speaking with me."

On that note, I skedaddled. I spent some time pacing through the halls, trying to think of something useful. *Nada.* I tried to picture someone skulking along the hallway, checking to make sure no one else was in sight, then ducking into Mrs. Dempsey's room. Afterwards, he must have peeked out and, once assured of no observers, returned to his responsibilities. No one had seen him entering or leaving her room.

Back in my hallway, a short woman with spiky gray hair accosted me. She poked a finger in my chest. "You're that Jacobson guy. You got any soap for me?"

The word *soap* clicked. "I have short-term memory loss. Are you by any chance Louise Wilkins?"

She patted her chest. "That's me."

"I don't have any soap on me. I'll try to bring you some in the future."

"If you do that, I'll be mighty appreciative."

She padded away.

When I returned to my room, Marion was waiting for me.

"We have an appointment," she said.

"Oh?"

"I'll tell you about it on our way there."

She escorted me to the front desk and requested a taxi be called. After she signed me out, the attending nurse buzzed the door open for us. Outside, we waited by the curb.

I grabbed her hand. "Why the secrecy?"

"I didn't want to talk in front of Ralph or any of the staff. We're going to police headquarters to meet with Detective Chun."

"He and I just can't see enough of each other," I said.

A pleasant cabby picked us up.

"Where to?" he asked.

"The police department on Beretania," Marion said.

He smiled. "My brudda works there."

"We're just going for a visit," I said.

After a short trip he deposited us at our destination. I paid the tariff, adding a nice tip, acknowledged by a big smile and a wave of the hand as the cabbie drove away. I was happy to finance his next malasada break.

Inside, we were escorted to a meeting room, and in five minutes Detective Chun appeared, carrying a manila folder stuffed full of paper.

"Thank you for joining me, Mr. and Mrs. Jacobson."

"And here you pulled me away from all the excitement of a bingo game," I replied. "This might have been my winning day."

Marion swatted me. "You weren't planning to play bingo."

"I know. But I have to make the good detective feel a little guilty. What's up with having us come here?"

Chun tapped the manila folder. "I want to review with you what we've learned and hear if you've come across anything else that will assist the investigation."

Given my less than stellar work so far, I doubted I'd have anything to add. I hunched over the table to listen to Chun's spiel.

"As we've discussed before, we initially had three persons of interest: Dr. Burber, Fred Langley, and Hugh Talbert."

"From what I read in my journal, I spoke with each of the three, and not one of them gave any indication of being the guilty party."

Chun pursed his lips. "Our conclusion as well. None of the three was in the Pacific Vista Nursing Home last night. Dr. Burber wasn't scheduled to make any evening calls. No one reported seeing him, and we double-checked the sign-in log."

"That eliminates him," I said, helpfully.

"Fred Langley didn't visit his mother yesterday either, and Hugh Talbert took the night off. We're back to square one on finding a viable suspect."

"Besides, Fred's only half haole," I said. "No other haole guys in their sixties?"

"No, that's the problem," Chun said. "We suspect the perp is a staff member, but everyone else is younger, and not many of them are haole."

"Anyone who might have a criminal record?" Marion asked.

Chun scowled. "We've done another detailed background check on all the males who work at Pacific Vista, but nothing jumps out. We have a list of the people on last night's shift. I want you to go over the names, Mr. Jacobson."

"Fortunately, I've been keeping an accurate journal and read it this morning. Let's take a look."

He slipped a sheet of paper toward me. I picked it up and scanned down the twenty names. I recognized Dan Aukina from the cleaning crew; Puna Koloa, ex-wheelchair racer; and CNAs Ken Yamamoto and Sal Polahi.

"Only four names ring a bell," I said.

"Anything to make you suspicious of one of them?"

I bit my lip and concentrated. The events from my journal swirled in my head. I had only spoken with Dan twice. Nothing suspicious about him, except my erroneous observation when I thought he had stolen a pen. Puna would be hard to disguise as someone with an average build, so that eliminated him. That left Ken and Sal. Anything there to implicate one of them as the attacker? Like a puzzle piece falling into place, it clicked. I slapped my forehead. It was so obvious. How had I missed it?

"We've been on the wrong path." I practically bounced up and down in my chair as if on a fanny trampoline. "The perp is a younger person appearing to be older. You need to check out one guy in particular. Ken Yamamoto told me he's an amateur actor. I bet he has the ability to make himself look older."

Chun scribbled a note. "Anything else?"

I was on a roll. "All the women described the attacker as being haole. Ken couldn't pass for being white unless he also changed his skin color." A second puzzle piece clicked into place. "Someone left a tube of face makeup in my room. In addition to changing his face to look older, he could have applied the makeup to make his skin lighter."

Chun shot out of his chair. "Wait here. I need to make a phone call." He stepped out of the room.

In a moment, a pleasant young woman entered. "Detective Chun asked me to get you some refreshments. May I offer you some coffee?"

"Sure," I said. "And also one of those non-fat police malasadas."

She grinned, displaying sparkling white teeth. "I'll see what I can find."

She reappeared with a tray holding two cups of coffee and malasadas. Marion and I guzzled and munched happily. In fifteen minutes Detective Chun and Benny Makoku raced into the room.

"Mr. Jacobson has come up with a lead for us," Chun said.

Benny smiled at me. "Way to go. Who is it?"

"One of the CNAs on night shift. Ken Yamamoto."

Benny's eyes widened. "That young kid?"

"Yeah," Chun replied. "He may have changed his appearance to look like an older haole guy. I want you to keep a close eye on him tonight."

"Will do," Benny said.

"I'm worried that he will still be working in the nursing home," Marion said. "Can't you arrest him?"

Chun shook his head. "We don't have any definitive evidence

yet. Mr. Jacobson has put forward an interesting theory, but it's all circumstantial at this point. We need to find a more definitive link between Yamamoto and the crimes."

"Why not bring him in for questioning?" Marion asked.

"Too soon," Chun replied. "I don't want to alert him that we suspect him. I'll assign a team to put him under surveillance when he's outside the nursing home. Officer Makoku will be watching him carefully on the night shift. And, Mr. Jacobson, I'd like you to strike up a casual conversation with Yamamoto this evening as well. See if he matches in any way the intruder you saw this morning."

I saluted. "I'm on it like gravy on mashed potatoes."

Chun looked at me askance. "Don't do anything too obvious. Only observe him. I don't want you put at any risk."

"That's my concern," Marion said. "With an intruder having been in Paul's room several times, I don't want him threatened again."

Marion was right. In spite of Benny Makoku being there, the perp had snuck into my room again this morning. Benny couldn't be everywhere. But if he was keeping an eye on Ken Yamamoto, and Ken tried to do anything to me, Benny would catch him. I wondered if Benny had the endurance to last a whole shift without taking a restroom break.

"I'll be careful," I said. "We'd agreed to give this a try for a few more days. Let's see if we can nail him tonight."

CHAPTER 24

We took a cab back to the nursing home, and along the way Marion took out her cell phone, placed a call, and handed it to me. "You need to talk to Jennifer."

Denny answered.

"How are things in the wilds of Colorado?" I asked.

"Wild enough. Jennifer and I went skiing at Vail today and barely escaped being stranded in a blizzard on the way home. We have a foot of snow on the ground now."

I looked out the window. "Not much of that here. Speaking of Jennifer, is my slope-swooshing granddaughter around?"

"Here she is."

I heard a little background crackling sound and then, "Hi, Grandpa."

"Hello to you, too."

"Have you solved the crimes at the nursing home?"

I cringed as a bicycle cut in front of a car coming the other direction and missed being crunched by inches. This reminded me of Alice Teng and her electric wheelchair. "Not yet, but we finally have a solid lead."

"I bet it's someone on the staff."

I sputtered. "How did you know that?"

"It's obvious, Grandpa. With all that's happened, it doesn't seem reasonable that a visitor has been causing the problems. And I can't imagine any of the residents as the guilty party. After all, it is a nursing home."

"I don't know," I replied. "We have some pretty wild characters living in Pacific Vista."

"My vote goes to someone working there, Grandpa."

"The Honolulu Police Department should hire you as a consultant."

"I'll just help you, Grandpa. Tell me who you think is the culprit."

I turned my head toward Marion, who watched me intently as if her eyeballs might pick up the conversation. "One of the certified nurse assistants who is an actor. We think he may have disguised himself."

"Hmmm. That could be. But be careful not to make too many assumptions."

"Spoken like a true investigator," I said. "That's why Benny Makoku and I are going to check him out tonight."

"Be careful, Grandpa. He might be dangerous."

"I'll be on my toes."

"I have a geezer joke for you, Grandpa."

"Are you sure you won't get in trouble?"

"Nah. My parents are watching *Dancing with the Stars*."

"I've heard of dancing under the stars. What the heck is that?"

I heard a loud exhale of air. "People dance around and get judged for their dancing skills, and viewers vote on the one they think is best. I'd rather watch a movie."

"I've never been one for dancing either. No one ever called me twinkle toes. Let's hear your joke."

"Okay. It's a series. What do you call an old man who makes fun of people?"

"I give."

"A geezer teaser."

I groaned.

"What do you call an old man gasping for breath?"

I smiled. "I know that one. A geezer wheezer."

"Good, Grandpa. And what do you call an old man with a cold?"

"Hmmm. That must be a geezer sneezer. I'll add one. What do you call a nice old man?"

Jennifer giggled. "Someone like you. A geezer pleaser. Uh-oh. Here comes Mom. Must be a commercial break. No more geezer jokes. Let me know what happens with the investigation."

"Will do."

After handing the phone back to Marion, I watched the traffic around us until we reached the nursing home, thankful not to spot any more Kamikaze bicycles. But I did see a pedestrian scamper to safety as a truck shot past. As Jennifer indicated, I'd have to be careful when I poked around tonight.

That evening after Ralph and I finished dinner, I wheeled my buddy back to our room, and a woman CNA stopped by to help him into bed.

"Would you mind retrieving my memorabilia box from the closet?" Ralph asked.

"No problemo." I brought the shoebox down and gave it to him.

He sorted through it for a moment, and his head jerked up. "My Bronze Star is missing!"

"Let me take a look." I dumped the contents out on his bed. "You're right. There're lots of papers and other medals here but not the Bronze Star."

"I wonder . . . Paul, you dropped the box when you put it away for me before. Please check to see if my Bronze Star fell on the closet floor."

"Sure." I went into the closet, settled onto my hands and knees, and patted all over. "Can't find it."

"I hope someone didn't steal it," Ralph said.

I immediately thought of the perp who had been sexually assaulting women and stealing jewelry. Could he be branching out into old war medals?

"Is the Bronze Star valuable?" I asked.

"I can't imagine it being worth a whole lot to anyone but the recipient."

"Tell you what. I'll have the security guy stop by."

I picked up the phone and called the nurses' station.

"Could you have the night security man come to my room? My roommate, Ralph Hirata, thinks something of his might have been taken." Then an idea occurred to me for beginning my evening campaign. "Also, is Ken Yamamoto around?"

"He's with another resident," the voice on the phone replied.

"I need to take a shower. Please have Ken come help me when he's available."

"I'll let him know."

After I hung up the phone, Ralph called out from his side of the room, "Why do you need assistance to take a shower, Paul? You move around fine."

"Yeah, but the last time I tried to do it on my own, they had a hissy fit. I figure I won't fight city hall."

Benny Makoku stuck his head in the room. "You asked for me, Mr. Jacobson?"

"Yeah, Ralph here is missing an army medal he received during World War II. It was in a box in his closet, and now it's missing."

"Describe it," Benny said.

"It's a Bronze Star," Ralph replied.

"Wow. I've seen a couple of those. Let me take a look." Benny rifled through the closet but also came up empty-handed. "I'll write up a report and ask the staff to look for it." He strode out of the room.

"That's a pisser to have your Bronze Star go missing,"

"Yeah. I can't figure out why someone would take it. *C'est la vie.*"

"You're being awfully cavalier," I said.

He shrugged. "Nothing I can do about it."

"While I'm waiting for my shower do you want to hear a story?" I asked Ralph.

"Sure."

I retrieved my O. Henry book and selected a story called, "After Twenty Years." A policeman on patrol comes across a man in a doorway at ten p.m. The man named Bob says he went west to seek his fortune and agreed to meet his friend Jimmy in exactly ten years on this date at ten p.m. right here. The police officer leaves. Another man appears. Bob at first thinks it's Jimmy, but realizes his companion is too tall. The man arrests Silky Bob, saying he was warned that the wanted man would be here from Chicago. The man hands Bob a message from the policeman, that says: *Bob, I came on time. When I saw you, I realized you were a wanted fugitive from Chicago. I couldn't arrest you, but I had a plainclothesman do it.* The note was signed Jimmy.

Ralph chuckled. "Good story. With O. Henry, things aren't always what they appear to be."

"Ain't that the truth? Kind of like around here. A war veteran who can't see but has great hearing, a wheelchair-racing old broad, you name it."

"I'm really tired tonight, Paul. Would you turn off my light and pull the curtain?"

I did as requested and adjourned to my side of the room to read. I heard Ralph snoring. He certainly had no problem falling asleep. Partway into my second story, a young man appeared in the doorway. "Mr. Jacobson? You wanted help with your shower?"

"Are you Ken Yamamoto?"

"Yes. You don't remember me?"

I tapped the side of my head. "My short-term memory isn't so hot. I'm ready."

I followed him down the hall. No time like the present to get started. "Aren't you the guy who's interested in acting?"

Ken came to a halt and stared at me. "I am. I thought you had problems with your memory."

Oops. "I . . . uh . . . don't remember stuff so hot, but Ralph mentioned a CNA who acted. I thought that might be you."

He crinkled his nose. "I act in an amateur theater group."

"You must get to play a lot of different roles."

He shrugged. "I've been heroes, villains, and supporting characters."

"Ever get to play an older man?"

"One time I put on makeup and a wig to look like an old man. I slumped over and used a cane."

"Bet you couldn't look as old as me," I said.

"I don't know. With the right props and makeup, I probably could."

"What kind of goo do you use to change someone's appearance?"

"There are all kinds of theater cosmetics. Why the questions?"

Uh-oh. "Uh, I was wondering if you could make someone like me look younger."

"That's harder."

We reached the shower. He adjusted the water for me and helped me into the stall. While I scrubbed, I thought of my next line of attack. I had to be careful not to make him suspicious. But as an old fart I could ask dumb questions.

After I dried off, I asked, "Do you have any of that acting face putty stuff around?"

"I keep a kit in my locker here at the nursing home. When I'm in a play, I work split shifts and don't have time to head home in between."

"I didn't know the staff had lockers."

"Sure. Off the break room, there's another room with lockers and men and women's restrooms where we can change."

He escorted me back to my room and left me with my thoughts. I changed from my bathrobe and slippers into Bermuda shorts, a T-shirt, and flip-flops for one more reconnaissance trip.

I went to the nurses' station in the lobby and waited until no one was watching me. I ducked into the empty break room and found the door to the adjoining locker area. Before you could say peeping Paul, I was inside. Sure enough, lockers lined one wall, and names on masking tape indicated the respective owners. I located Ken's. Fortunately, none of the lockers had locks. I quickly opened the locker and peeked inside. Hiking shorts and a T-shirt hung on hooks. A box rested on the bottom of the locker. With a quick scan around to make sure no one could see me, I opened it to find a whole collection of goodies: cheek rouge, a rouge brush, swab applicators, cream foundation, different pigments of cream makeup, stage blood, a lip pencil, an eyebrow pencil, liquid latex, nose and scar wax, hair coloring, mustaches, beards, a powder puff, a sponge, spirit gum adhesive, spirit gum remover. and makeup in cakes and tubes.

Bingo.

I wondered if one of these tubes had been the one Henry had spotted on the floor of my room.

I heard footsteps. *Uh-oh.* A drop of sweat formed on my forehead. I fumbled with the lid of the box but managed to close it. I quickly shut the locker. I turned around to see Ken Yamamoto enter the locker room.

"What are you doing here, Mr. Jacobson?"

Chapter 25

My heart raced as I stared at Ken Yamamoto. "I don't know what I'm doing here. I get disoriented sometimes."

He eyed me warily. "Let me help you back to where you belong." He took my arm to guide me out through the break room, into the hall, and to the door of my room.

"Can I leave you on your own?" he asked.

"Yeah. I'm fine now."

After he left, I stomped into my room. Damn. That was close. He almost caught me looking in his locker. Did Ken suspect me of snooping? Had I violated what Detective Chun asked—to not be too obvious? What a lame undercover operative I turned out to be. I didn't dare do any more investigating after that. I punched my bed.

"I hear some frustration being vented over there," Ralph said from his side of the room.

"I thought you were asleep."

"I woke up when you burst into the room."

I parted the curtain and moseyed over to Ralph's bed. "Darn right. I'm trying to figure out something that isn't making any sense yet."

"Paul, I know you're up to something. You asked me not to mention it again, but I have to. You hold these hush-hush meetings with people and disappear for extended periods. I may not be able to see what's going on, but I sure hear some things that make me wonder about you. Besides, you're too healthy to be living here."

I eyed him warily. "But my memory is crapola."

"Sure, you don't remember things when you wake up in the morning. But you're intelligent and recall things fine during the day. You have your eyesight, hearing, and mobility. Marion can take care of reminding you. Why shouldn't you be living with her rather than having her come visit you here? Besides, you're keeping a journal. Between Marion and your journal, your memory works fine. There's no reason for you to be in a nursing home."

"Maybe I just like your company, Ralph."

"I appreciate that and am glad we met. But for whatever reason you're here, it won't last long. When will you level with me?"

I bit my lip. I had promised Detective Chun not to discuss my real mission, but Ralph was on to me. He'd keep after it until I told him what was happening. What harm could it do? Maybe Ralph might even aid the investigation.

I pulled up a chair, sat, and let out a deep sigh. "All right, Ralph. I'm not supposed to tell anyone, so you have to promise to keep this to yourself."

"It will stay between the two of us. On my honor as a member of the Four Forty-Second."

That pledge convinced me. I leaned close and whispered, "I'm here undercover to help the police with an investigation."

"The attacks on the women. That's why you asked for Mrs. Rodriquez's room number a while back."

"Nothing gets by you, Ralph."

"I suspected there was some logical explanation for how snoopy you are. It all makes sense now."

"But I'm not a trained investigator. I met Detective Chun in December when Marion and I vacationed in Honolulu with my son, daughter-in-law, and granddaughter. I inadvertently helped the police solve a case then. Chun thought I might be able to help here, given I'm older than dirt and can blend in with the rest of you old farts in this nursing home."

"Blend but not fit in exactly. That's why I knew something wasn't kosher." Ralph cupped his hands and whispered, "What have you learned so far?"

I thought back to my journal notes. "Initially the police had three persons of interest. The first was Dr. Burber."

"And you asked him to examine your back even though you really don't have a back problem."

"Man, nothing gets by you. Because of your exercise class, my back felt a little stiff that day, so it gave me an excuse. It's been fine since."

Ralph gave me his rheumy, unfocused stare. "Go on."

"The other persons-of-interest included Aiko Langley's son, Fred, and the cleaning staff night supervisor Hugh Talbert."

"Why did the police suspect Dr. Burber and these other two?"

I looked around to make sure no one in the hallway overheard us. "The attacker was identified as haole in his sixties. Those three were the only people here the nights of the attacks who fit the description."

"Are you getting close to discovering which one it is?"

I clenched my teeth. "That's the damn problem. Each of them has an alibi, and my futile attempts to interview them led to no useful information. But we have one new suspect—one of the CNAs, Ken Yamamoto."

"Not exactly a haole guy in his sixties."

"True. But I learned something interesting. Ken's an actor." I leaned even closer. "And he has an actor's makeup kit in his employee locker here at Pacific Vista. It contained all kinds of face goo and coloring."

"You've been rifling through people's belongings?"

I gulped. "In the interest of catching a killer. Ken may have disguised himself as an older man and changed his skin color."

"Hmmm. It's possible that he changed his appearance, but I don't buy he's a sexual predator and murderer. I've gotten to know Ken a little. He's very passionate about his acting. No, I don't believe he's your man."

"Tonight I made a lame attempt to discuss stage makeup with him but wasn't able to elicit anything useful."

"And I don't think you will."

CHAPTER 26

I pulled out my cell phone and called Detective Chun. He didn't answer so I left a message that I found an actor's makeup kit in Ken Yamamoto's locker. I shut the phone with no new ideas on what to do next.

I decided to go find Benny Makoku to relay the same information. I found him in the break room drinking a cup of coffee. I sat down beside him.

"I found an actor's makeup kit in Ken Yamamoto's locker."

"Doing a little illegal snooping?"

I shrugged. "Hey, there was no lock on the door. I happened to open it and found a box. One thing led to another and the box popped open."

A glint shone in Benny's eyes. "Amazing what will happen sometimes."

I took a deep breath. "This afternoon I mentioned finding a tube of makeup in my room some days ago."

Benny arched an eyebrow. "Yeah?"

"Since I can't remember specifically, I can't say for sure, but the one on the floor in my room could be like some of the tubes in Ken's makeup kit."

"Too bad you don't have that tube from your room."

"It disappeared. Ken may have realized he had lost it and came back to retrieve it."

Benny gave me his policeman's stare. "Interesting, but it may only be another piece of circumstantial evidence. We don't have enough to prove Ken's guilt."

I groaned. "Yeah, that's the problem."

"We don't even know for sure if all the crimes have been committed by the same person."

"I'd bet my Social Security check that there's only one perp doing all of this."

"You're probably right."

"I left a message for Detective Chun," I said. "You can fill him in on the details when you next speak with him."

"I'll watch Ken but also look for any indication of who else might be involved," Benny said.

"That's a good idea. No sense jumping to conclusions, not that I can jump much anyway."

With that, I returned to my room.

When Marion stopped by with my journal for my nightly update, I said, "I have a confession to make."

She eyed me warily. "What have you been up to, Paul? You aren't romancing one of the nursing home ladies, are you?"

"Nothing like that. Detective Chun told me not to divulge my mission here. I mentioned it to Ralph tonight."

"But it's not going any farther," Ralph said from his bed.

Marion actually smiled. "To tell the truth, I'm glad you know, Ralph. I'm worried about Paul. It's good to know someone else is aware of what he's doing."

"That's right," Ralph said. "I'll keep my eye on him."

"With your eyesight, that won't do me a lick of good," I said.

"I'll keep an ear on him instead."

"That's more like it," I replied.

Marion fidgeted. "I still think you should wrap up here, Paul. It's a dangerous place."

"We World War II survivors will team up," Ralph said. "Not to worry, Marion. I've got his back."

Marion took a notepad out of her purse, jotted on it, and

placed the note on my nightstand. "Here's the phone number and address of where I'm staying. If you wake up and feel threatened in any way, call or have someone bring you to the condo."

I saluted. "Will do."

"I'll also leave instructions with the nursing staff that someone can accompany you to the condo if you request it."

"And I'll remind him where to find the note," Ralph said. "I'll be Paul's memory, and he can be my eyes."

"As you said, Ralph, we can be quite a team."

"I'm not buying this." Marion crossed her arms and gave me a wifely evil eye. "It's become too dangerous. You need to quit this travesty as soon as possible."

"But I've made a commitment to Detective Chun," I said.

"You have a commitment to our marriage as well. Maybe it's just as well we're sleeping in different places."

Uh-oh. I had stepped in it again.

Marion threw my journal at me. "Write in this, although I don't know what good it will do you. Maybe I should go back to the mainland without you."

I gulped. I didn't know how to get out of the doghouse. I heard a shuffling sound, and a woman entered the room. She wagged an index finger at me. "Why aren't you in bed, Junior?"

I figured this had to be Evelyn Newberry. "I'm not quite ready. I haven't finished my homework yet."

"Junior, you get it done and then lights out," Evelyn said. "And, Sonny, have you completed your homework?"

"I'll be done soon," Ralph said.

Evelyn turned to Marion and her eyes lit up. "Sis, it's good to see you here again. Another family reunion."

In spite of how pissed off she was, Marion jumped in. "I'll take care of Junior and Sonny. I'll make sure they finish their homework and get to sleep."

"Much obliged. These boys are a handful. Don't let them sass you, Sis." Evelyn turned and padded out of the room.

On that note, I documented the day's events.

The next morning I awoke in my usual jumble, and the kind man sharing a room with me identified himself and explained where I was.

"How in the hell did I end up in a nursing home?" I asked.

"Can you see anyone who might overhear us?" Ralph asked.

I walked over to his bed. "No, we have the place to ourselves."

"You're here helping the police."

That stopped me cold in my tracks. "You've got to be kidding."

He explained the situation and even told me of my brand-new wife named Marion. "And she should have been here by now to give you your journal to read." He proceeded to describe how my diary was my memory crutch. "You and Marion had a little tiff last night. She's not happy that you're remaining in the nursing home. You better give her a call. The number's on your nightstand."

I located a piece of paper that contained a phone number and address. "Now I need a phone."

"You have a cell phone," Ralph said. "Look around for it."

"You're a wealth of information." I located a tiny electronic gadget in the pocket of my Bermuda shorts. "Do you know how to work one of these?"

"Bring it over," Ralph said.

I gave it to him. He ran his hand over it and pushed some buttons. "Although I can't see, I can get it set to make a call. You punch in the phone number and hit this button." He fingered a button and handed the phone back to me.

"Jeez. The blind leading the memory-challenged." Following the directions, I placed the call. It rang and cut over to a recorded voice saying to leave a message for Marion.

"This is your abandoned husband," I said. "Where are you?" Then I hung up and tossed the gadget on my bed.

"Now what?" I asked.

"If Marion isn't here in five minutes, you better go to her condo," Ralph said. "You can't walk out of this place on your own, but Marion left instructions at the nurses' station at the front of the building to have someone escort you. She indicated it's only a short walk away."

I dressed, and after the five minutes had passed with no Marion, I picked up the note and headed to the front counter.

"I need to take a short walk to my wife's condo," I announced to a cheerful nurse who sat behind the counter.

"Oh, yes, Mr. Jacobson. Your wife left instructions to have someone accompany you. I think our night security officer is just now getting off duty. He can go with you."

She placed a call and in a few minutes a guy with a ponytail appeared. "You need an escort, Mr. Jacobson?"

"That I do."

He pushed some buttons by the door, a buzzer sounded, and he held the door open for me.

Once we were outside, he said, "To give you an update, I spoke with Detective Chun after our chat last night."

I came to a screeching stop. "You know me, but I don't know you or remember the conversation."

He smiled. "Your short-term memory problem. I understand. I'm Benny Makoku. I'm a police officer undercover as the night security man at the nursing home. We're working together."

"I'll be damned. This is news to me."

"I can't imagine what it must be like to wake up each morning not remembering the day before."

I handed him the slip of paper. "Here's where I'm headed. If you need to go home, point me in the right direction, and I can continue on my own."

"I'll come with you. Besides, I have a key to the condo, which you'll need to get in if your wife isn't there."

"Good point. Maybe you can educate me on what's going on since I'm in a fuddle this morning."

He filled me in on the attacks and murder. "We suspect Ken Yamamoto, one of the CNAs at the nursing home. We're close to arresting him."

My head swirled with this foreign information. I decided to take it one step at a time. What other option did I have?

When we reached the condo, I rang the bell. No answer. I knocked loudly. Still no answer. "I guess we'll need to resort to your key."

Benny unlocked the door and led me inside. No one there. A chair lay on its side. There was an eerie silence, punctuated by my breathing.

"This doesn't look good," Benny said.

I entered the bedroom. Blankets from the bed covered the floor. I noticed a spiral notebook on the dresser. I picked it up and discovered this was the journal Ralph had mentioned. I tucked it under my arm.

Next thing I noticed—a piece of paper on the pillow of the bed. I picked it up and read, "Paul Jacobson: Stay out of what doesn't concern you if you want to see your wife alive."

CHAPTER 27

Duly threatened by the note left on Marion's pillow, I wiped away sweat rolling down my forehead. I looked around the room wildly. "Benny, you better come see this," my voice croaked.

He loped into the room, and I handed him the note. His eyes widened. "Come into the living room with me, Mr. Jacobson."

I followed him, and he waved me to sit on the couch. "Stay right there."

I sank into the soft, well-used sofa. He took out his cell phone to place a call. I overheard him addressing Detective Chun and requesting a crime scene investigator and backup officers to search for Marion. I hoped they enlisted everyone, including the Royal Canadian Mounted Police.

What had I gotten into? I little while ago I awoke not even knowing I was remarried, and now my wife had been kidnapped. What kind of husband would let this happen? I needed to do something to help find her. *Think*. What could I accomplish? Certainly not anything while sitting on my butt. I pulled myself off the couch.

Benny gently pushed me back onto the couch. "Please stay right there, Mr. Jacobson. I don't want the crime scene further compromised."

I realized he was right. At the moment I needed to stay out of the way of the investigation. With nothing better to do, I opened my journal and read. It became obvious that my snooping had caused this latest fiasco. Whoever had been attacking women at Pacific Vista had abducted Marion. A pang of fear seized my chest. What had happened to Marion? And none of this would have occurred if I hadn't been nosing around.

Even with my speedy reading, it took me over half an hour to get through the document. The names and events swirled in my defective brain. I tried to imagine who the culprit might be. With my memory, I drew a complete blank. My chest sank as if full of lead. Last night Marion and I had argued. She wanted me out of the nursing home caper, but I had insisted on continuing. And because of my stubbornness, something bad had happened to her. What a jerk I'd been.

By this time, the condo was swarming with people. I sat tight, not wanting to interfere with the police work. I watched a woman carrying a black bag disappear into the bedroom. In a few minutes I saw flashes coming from a camera. Someone else was dusting the knob of the door into the condo. Some of the powder drifted through the air. I sneezed, depositing some of my DNA on the couch.

Eventually, a man in a crumpled suit arrived and addressed me. "Mr. Jacobson, I want to hear exactly what happened this morning."

"You must be Detective Chun," I said through teary eyes.

"The same."

I took a deep breath and recounted everything that transpired since waking up. "Then I sat on this couch reading my diary. That's it."

He tapped his notepad. "Any idea how someone knew where to find your wife?"

I tried to figure out this puzzle. Nothing at first occurred to me. The police wouldn't have divulged her location. Maybe someone had followed Marion or me. That might get them to the building, but I doubted someone followed unnoticed to her individual condo. Then like being hit on the head with bird poop, it struck me.

"Damn. Marion left me a note last night with her phone number and address so I'd know where to go if I needed to get away from the nursing home. I found it on my nightstand this morning. If someone snuck into my room during the night, he could have found that information and acted on it. Benny has the note."

Chun strode over to where Benny stood. They spoke in hushed tones for a moment. Benny nodded, pulled the note from his pocket, held it gingerly, and dropped it in a paper bag that Chun held open.

The detective came back to me. "We'll check it for finger-prints, but with you and Benny having handled it, I'm not expecting anything useful."

"Since I can't do anything to help here, may I be excused to go back to the nursing home?" I asked.

"Yeah. That will be fine. Can you find your way?"

I tapped my temple. "Locked and loaded. I remember the route from coming here with Benny earlier. I'll be fine."

I headed back, hoping that Detective Chun and his crew could locate Marion. My steps were as heavy as if I wore cast-iron boots. What a turn of events.

A block away I paused to look first at the sky with white clouds sailing toward the ocean and next at the side of Punch-bowl. Grass, shrubs, and trees lined the hillside above the roofs of nearby houses. It would be nice to take a hike and get away from this mess. I resumed my trek, realizing I shouldn't distress the police with another disappearance.

Back at the geezer and geezerette farm, I rang the bell and someone inside buzzed me in. After signing myself in to the consternation of the attending nurse, a short woman with dark black hair, I shuffled to my room like a kicked dog.

"You're back, Paul," Ralph said.

"There you go again. I didn't say a word, but you knew it was me."

"Of course. Although you're walking like you're not very happy."

"You can tell all that from my feet?"

"Absolutely. You usually have more bounce to your step."

"All the bounce has been wrung out of me. This hasn't been a good day. Someone abducted Marion."

"Oh, no! Tell me what happened."

I slumped into a chair near Ralph's bed and gave him the gory details. "The worst part is that I'm responsible for the bad guy going after Marion."

"You don't need to shoulder the blame, Paul. You've been trying to help. The police asked you to do this."

"Yeah, but I can't get pissed at them. The cops have their job to do. I'm the one who decided to work undercover. If I had listened to Marion and quit last night, this wouldn't have happened to her."

I had no chance to wallow in self-pity, because there was a commotion outside my room and a large woman burst in. She wore a bright blue muumuu the size of a tent and had platinum hair.

She stomped up to where I sat and placed her huge hands on her solid hips. I expected fire to shoot out of her mouth. "What's going on, jerk?"

Although she blocked most of my view, two men followed in her wake into the room.

"Hello, Madeline," Ralph said.

She turned to him. "You're the jerk's roommate, Ralph."

I put the pieces together from my journal reading. "I take it our room has been invaded by Madeline Hightower Palmer, Henry, and Meyer."

"That's right," Madeline announced. "We've come all the

way from Kaneohe to pay a social visit."

"It won't be that social," I said. "Marion has been kidnapped. I think someone on the staff here did it."

"What! I'll get to the bottom of this. Meyer, you stay here." Madeline picked up Henry, tucked him under her large arm like a football, and charged out of the room as if headed for the goal line. I heard loud footfalls, shouting voices, and mumbled undertones in the background. I pulled up another chair for Meyer.

"You get drafted for this visit?" I asked Meyer.

He made a sour face. "I had just finished breakfast when Madeline appeared at the care home and literally dragged me out to her car. Henry was there. I thought I was the one kidnapped. That woman sure drives fast. Even with morning traffic, we made it from Kaneohe, through the Pali tunnel, and into Honolulu in twenty minutes. She blasts her horn and people move out of the way as if she were driving an emergency vehicle."

I heard some more shouting. "I better go see what trouble Madeline is causing with the staff. I'll leave you two sight-impaired gentlemen to compare notes."

Outside my room, I found the hallway empty, but heard Madeline's commanding voice from the front of the building. When I reached the nurses' station, I saw her standing in front of three neatly-formed rows of nursing staff, everyone standing at attention. She paced in front of them like a sergeant training the troops.

Madeline thrust her arm toward the group as if hitting a tennis backhand, causing people in the first row to flinch. "I want answers, and I want them now. Who knows what happened to Marion Jacobson?"

One short, quivering woman stammered, "This . . . this is shocking. I . . . I didn't know she was kidnapped."

"Now you do." Madeline slapped the back of her right hand into the palm of her left hand. "Well?"

"I came on duty two hours ago. I know nothing."

Madeline pointed to a skinny man, next in line. "You."

He winced. "Same. I'm on first shift as well. This is news to me."

"Next." Madeline glared at a stocky woman.

"I've been here all night and haven't left the building. I'm working overtime as it is." She burst into tears.

Madeline poked a finger at a very large man. "Name and rank."

"I'm Puna Koloa." He brought his large body to attention. "Certified nursing assistant."

"Did you see anything?"

He shook his head. "Nope. I also just came on duty for the day shift."

Henry waved to me to follow him. He headed down the blue hallway. Once we were out of sight of the troop inspection, he said, "Madeline wants us to look for clues, jerk."

"Be happy to, but don't know what we'll find here. The police are checking the condo where Marion was abducted."

"That's the point," Henry said. "They may not think to look around here. Let's see what we can find."

We scoured the hallway and headed back past Madeline, now interrogating the second row of staff. "Move!" she shouted at us.

I immediately doubled my pace to escape into the next hallway.

Who needed waterboarding when you had Madeline?

After traipsing through the three downstairs hallways with no clues, we headed upstairs. There, completing one hallway unsuccessfully, we next came to the end of the light green one. A door stood open. We went through into a storage room. I turned on the light.

"This might be the place where someone locked me in yesterday." I pointed to the inside door. "I described a storage area with second interior room in my journal."

Henry walked around the room, inspecting the walls. He only lacked a magnifying glass and a deerstalker. He came to an abrupt stop. "Here's something." He pointed to a tiny smudge on the inside door.

I peered at it. "Kind of grayish pink."

"Same color as that tube of makeup that was under your bed on our last visit," Henry said.

CHAPTER 28

Henry and I returned to my room to find Meyer and Ralph deep in conversation.

"What's going on?" I asked.

"We were swapping Paul Jacobson stories," Meyer said. "You've been a good friend to both of us."

"As well as providing much needed entertainment," Ralph added.

"I'm glad I can contribute to an improved quality of life. Now, if you'll excuse me, I need to reach Detective Chun." I picked up my cell phone thingy and used it to call Detective Chun, thankful that Ralph had shown me how to use it earlier. I was such a klutz with electronic gadgets that a blind guy had to train me.

Chun answered on the third ring.

"Detective, this is Paul Jacobson. I'm back at Pacific Vista. We've found a clue you will want to check out."

"I'll be there as soon as I can. I have an idea where Marion might be."

My heart fluttered. "That's top priority. Go find her."

"I'll let you know as soon as we have further information." The connection went dead.

I stared at the phone. I assumed he had consciously cut off on his end rather than that a boulder had fallen on him.

"I'm starving," Henry groused. "Where can you get something to eat around here?"

Food had been the last thing on my mind. I checked my watch. "It's time for lunch, if Madeline let the kitchen staff prepare the food."

As if on cue, thumping sounds came down the hallway, and Madeline burst into the room like a gale force wind blowing open shutters. She glared at me and then smiled at Henry. "How's my honeybunch?"

Henry gave a goofy grin. "Just fine, sweet cakes."

I rolled my eyes. "Okay, let's pass on the endearments. Honeybunch is hungry."

"Let's go test the chow in this joint," Madeline said.

"Did you let the staff get back to their duties?" I asked.

Madeline raised a fist. "Yes. I whipped them into shape. They didn't know diddly about Marion's abduction, but they'll report anything they find."

"I'm ready to eat, too," Ralph said. "I need help getting into my wheelchair."

"No problem." Madeline took two giant strides over to Ralph's bed, lifted him up as if grabbing a Chihuahua, and deposited him in his wheelchair. She pushed him toward the door. "Let's go, troops."

Ralph stared vacantly, a dazed look on his face.

"Ain't she a beaut?" Henry said.

We all sat at one table, and a woman wearing a white smock scampered over immediately to serve us. She stood at attention by Madeline's side. "Is there anything else?" the woman asked.

Madeline waved her hand. "You're dismissed."

The woman disappeared at full trot into the kitchen.

I hardly ate, worried as I was over Marion's disappearance.

After Madeline and Henry cleaned up every scrap and crumb of food, Madeline poked a finger in my chest. "What are the police doing to find Marion?"

"Detective Chun said he had a lead," I replied.

"Well, let's not sit here." Madeline slammed her fist on the table, overturning the salt and pepper shakers. "We'll go help."

"I'll stay here with Ralph," Meyer said.

"We're off." Madeline jumped to her feet, knocking her chair over, tucked Henry under her arm, and grabbed my hand to drag me toward the door.

The CNA on duty saw us coming and buzzed the door open without even asking anyone to sign me out. Madeline sure knew how to get results.

Out on the sidewalk, Madeline demanded, "Which way?"

I pointed with my unencumbered hand. "That-a-way."

Before you could say "giddyup," we were galloping along the sidewalk toward the condo. Once we arrived at the building, we made our grand entrance and found Detective Chun in the hallway. Madeline released my hand and set Henry down with a thump. I rubbed my hand. Nothing broken, but it was numb from wrist to fingertips.

"Where's Marion?" Madeline shouted.

Detective Chun took a step back as if trying to avoid being assaulted. "We think she's in this vacant apartment." He pointed to a door. "The lock has been jammed. I'm waiting for a locksmith to arrive."

"We don't need any stinkin' locksmith," Madeline said. She raised a gigantic leg and slammed her foot into the door. Splinters flew, and the door shot open. She pushed Chun into the room. The rest of us followed.

No furniture in the living room. Brown-stained carpet covered the floor, and the off-white walls displayed smudges that looked like kids had been finger-painting. Chun staggered through the empty room with Madeline prodding him forward. Henry and I followed.

"Go, go, go," Madeline shouted. "Check all the rooms."

In one of the vacant bedrooms, I heard a muffled sound coming from the closet.

"In here!" I shouted.

Madeline steered Chun into the room. He escaped from her grasp and turned to face her. "Let me take it from here," he said.

Madeline saluted. "Go for it, Detective."

Chun took a handkerchief out of his pocket and turned the closet door handle. The woman who must have been Marion lay on the floor with her hands and feet bound with duct tape and a strip over her mouth. He took out a Swiss Army knife and sliced the tape from her arms and legs and helped her to her feet.

She staggered out of the closet. With her arms free, she reached up and tore the duct tape from her mouth. "Ouch."

I got what seemed like my first look at my wife. In spite of her ordeal, she appeared darn good to me. I stepped over and gave her a hug.

She began crying. "Oh, Paul. I was so frightened."

I released her and clenched my fists. "Did he hurt you?"

"No. He only bound me."

I held her again in a fierce embrace. "This is all my fault. I'm so sorry."

In the meantime, Detective Chun was on his phone. In moments a crime scene investigator arrived to collect evidence, and an EMT strode in to check Marion.

Madeline looked at her watch. "Holy Moly! I need to get back to Kaneohe. I have a yacht race this afternoon." She grabbed Henry and tucked him under her arm. "Glad Marion is safe. See you soon, jerk." With that she and Henry sailed into the afternoon sun.

Marion declined any further medical attention, and we adjourned to Marion's apartment where we could sit on furniture.

Chun pulled up a chair to face Marion.

"Tell me exactly what happened," he said.

"I was sleeping when suddenly a hand slapped tape over my mouth. Then he bound my hands and feet and wrapped me in a blanket covering my face and body. He carried me over his shoulder until I ended up where you found me."

"Did you see your assailant?" Chun asked.

Marion shook her head. "It was too dark in my apartment, and with the blanket over my face I couldn't see anything."

"Any impression of the abductor?"

"It was a man. He was strong and had no trouble carrying me. I couldn't tell his height or age. He said nothing."

"Do you have any idea what time the man appeared in your condo?" the detective asked.

Marion bit her lip. "I woke up at three-fifteen to use the bathroom but went right back to sleep. It was pitch black when he appeared."

"Most likely between three-thirty and five-thirty," Chun said. "I'm going to check to see if our person-of-interest Ken Yamamoto was off duty during that time." He stood and went into the bedroom.

"Are you sure you don't need any medical attention?" I asked Marion.

She patted my hand. "I'm fine now that you're here, Paul."

My heart did a little pit-pat. I squeezed her hand. "I feel so awful about what happened to you."

Chun returned, a frown on his face. "I checked with Officer Makoku. He says he saw Ken Yamamoto several times during that time period. He already spoke with other staff members, and enough people spotted Yamamoto during the early morning hours that it seems highly unlikely he could have left Pacific Vista long enough to abduct Marion."

My stomach tightened. "So we still don't have a good suspect."

"We can't definitively rule out Yamamoto," Chun said. "I'll also work with the nursing home staff to check to see who was on duty the nights of the other attacks but not on duty last night. That may turn up some useful leads."

"When will I have my condo back to myself?" Marion asked.

"We may work here the rest of the day," Chun said. "I'm going to arrange a new apartment for you, Mrs. Jacobson."

He pulled out his cell phone and jabbered away for ten minutes. After he got off the phone, he told us to sit tight and disappeared while Marion and I snuggled together on the couch. It felt really good to be with her.

Chun returned in half an hour holding a key in his hand. "Follow me."

We went up to the next floor, where Chun ushered us into another condo. This one was larger and had a direct view toward the ocean.

"Nice digs," I said.

"We made arrangements for you to use it for a week," Chun said. "Mr. and Mrs. Jacobson, you can stay for that whole week or leave for the mainland sooner if you want. Mrs. Jacobson, we'll have your clothes moved from the other apartment later this afternoon. Is this apartment acceptable?"

Marion looked around. "This place will be fine."

"One other thing," Chun said. "We'll bring Mr. Jacobson's belongings from the nursing home as well. I'm pulling him out of there immediately."

Heat rose in my neck. "Wait a damn minute! I want to do everything possible to track down this guy." It was one thing for someone to throw a rock at me and try to smother me. It was something else when the jerk went after my wife.

"I know you do, Mr. Jacobson," Chun said. "But I don't

want to put either of you at any more risk, particularly after the attack on you, Mrs. Jacobson." He waved toward Marion.

Marion's eyes flared. "I want you to catch that SOB. Paul, you need to keep helping the police."

I clasped Marion's hand tightly. "I'm going to do everything in my power to assist, but I don't want anything else to happen to you."

"If I'm in a new condo, I'll be safe," Marion said. "Go catch the bastard."

I squeezed Marion's hand again, and she squeezed back. "You want me to stick with my assignment?"

I looked in Marion's eyes, and she nodded.

"I have one suggestion, though," I added. "Detective Chun, you should have a police officer check here periodically."

"I can arrange that," Chun said. "Are you sure you want to stay involved, Mr. Jacobson?"

I met his steely gaze. "Benny Makoku and I are going to nail this guy. Tonight might be the night."

CHAPTER 29

I stayed with Marion until late afternoon, when a female police officer arrived with Marion's belongings. The officer set the suitcase down on the living room carpet and a box of Marion's food supplies on the kitchen counter. "Is there anything I can do to further assist you?" she asked.

"No, thanks," Marion said. "I can take it from here."

After the officer left the apartment, Marion arranged her clothes and doodads and stashed the food in the refrigerator and cupboards. With her task completed, she stood with her right index finger on her cheek, regarding her new domain. "There, that should work for the next few days . . . until you catch the SOB."

"I'll be working it tonight to see if I can help Detective Chun and Benny Makoku find the perp."

Marion said she wanted to take a nap. I told her I wanted to take a walk to clear my head on my way back to the nursing home.

"They won't appreciate your signing yourself in," Marion said.

"No sweat. I read in my journal that I've done it before."

She gave me a kiss on the old puss. I put my arms around her and held her tight. Ah, young love.

"I'm so glad you're safe," I said. "I was worried sick earlier."

She patted me on the back. "Go take your walk, but stay out of trouble. I'll stop by tonight with your journal."

I departed and wandered around the neighborhood. Off to the side loomed a banyan tree full of squawking myna birds. I made sure not to actually walk under that tree. Late afternoon shadows fell. I smelled the aroma of someone grilling hamburgers.

I tried to piece together what had happened. The assaults on women in the nursing home. The attacks on Marion and me. The police had eliminated three men in their sixties as suspects. Next, the focal point became Ken Yamamoto. Currently, he didn't appear to be the one who had abducted Marion. Most likely someone else on the staff—someone who hadn't been on duty last night. Detective Chun would work that angle. I needed to find some way to smoke out the perp. The problem—I had no one in mind who could have done all of this.

I passed a noodle shop, and my stomach growled. I decided to fill my belly right now and skip dinner at Pacific Vista.

After a good time slurping and chewing, I continued my jaunt until the sun set. I figured I shouldn't be wandering around after dark.

Oops. I slapped my forehead. I had failed to show Detective Chun the clue Henry found near the closet on the second floor of the nursing home. I pulled out my cell phone and called Chun.

"Yes, Mr. Jacobson?"

"In all the commotion I forgot I had something for you to see at the nursing home. Henry Palmer found a smudge that looks like actor's makeup near the room where I was locked in the day before yesterday. Can you meet me at the nursing home?"

"I'll be there in fifteen minutes and bring a swab kit."

I headed right there, pushed the button next to the nursing home door, and was buzzed into the building. The attending nurse looked at me askance. "What were you doing wandering around on your own, Mr. Jacobson?"

"Taking my constitutional."

She shook her head. "In the future, go with someone."

"Yes, ma'am."

I waited in the lobby area. I found a two-year-old magazine with an article on cosmetics. I read how cosmetic companies designed modern makeup to treat the skin with care. I wondered if that applied to an actor's makeup as well. When Detective Chun arrived, he signed in like a good visitor, and I waved to him to follow me.

We went to the second floor, along the light green hallway and through the outer door of the storage area. I pointed. "I probably wouldn't have seen this myself, but earlier today Henry Palmer and I looked around Pacific Vista for clues, and he spotted it. Henry is very observant."

Chun bent over and inspected the smudge carefully. He took out a swab and dabbed the spot. "I'll have the lab check it out. Anything else I should be aware of, Mr. Jacobson?"

"No, I think you've drained me dry for the day, but I have one question for you. Have you found who wasn't on duty last night?"

"I'm awaiting a call from the night shift supervisor. I'm told she'll be here in an hour."

I rubbed my hands together. "Good. Maybe that will give us a solid lead."

We headed downstairs, and Chun departed. I ambled back to my room, where Ralph greeted me. "You missed dinner, Paul. We had mystery meat."

I snapped my fingers. "Darn, unlucky me."

Ralph chuckled. "I should have saved you some."

"Not necessary. I stopped for some real food."

"You had a visitor a few minutes ago," Ralph said.

"Yeah, I just met with Detective Chun."

"No, this was someone who came in the room."

"Anyone I know?"

"Very mysterious. When he entered your side of the room, I called out, but he didn't respond. His footsteps sounded the same as the man who snuck in two days ago in the early hours."

Now Ralph had my complete attention. "The intruder?"

"Same footfalls."

I gaped at Ralph. "And you'd recognize them again?"

"Sure."

"You and I discussed Ken Yamamoto. I want to verify one way or the other if he was this intruder. Let's have him come to the room, and you can either verify or rule him out."

Ralph waved his arm feebly. "If we need an excuse, I can ring to have him come help me to the bathroom."

I stood. "Let me go to the front desk to make the request. If you ring, someone else might respond."

"Okay."

I scooted out the door and practically raced to the nurses' station. Ken wasn't there, only a woman nurse. I tapped the counter to attract here attention. "Is Ken Yamamoto on duty?"

"Yeah, he arrived fifteen minutes ago to begin his shift."

"My roommate, Ralph Hirata, needs Ken to help him."

"He's adjusting Mrs. Teng's wheelchair. Somehow the wheel got dented today, and he said he'd fix it for her."

"When he's done, ask him to stop by."

I heard the front door buzz and the nurse pushed the button behind the counter to open the door. In came a guy with a comb-over wearing a shirt that read, "Mother is number one." From my journal account I could tell he was Fred Langley. He nodded to me and stopped to sign in.

I headed back toward my room and spotted an earring guy mopping the floor. He wore a gray sweatshirt and had a tattoo of a surfboard on his hand. "I bet you're Dan Aukina," I said.

"Yes. You have a good memory."

"Actually I don't, but I read well."

He looked at me quizzically. "Huh?"

I gave a dismissive wave of my hand. "It's a long story. Is your boss, Hugh Talbert, here tonight?"

Dan's eyes lit up. "Yeah. You have another thank you for us?"

I winked at him. "You bet."

I loped back to the room and sat down with Ralph again. "Ken Yamamoto is helping Mrs. Teng with her damaged wheelchair."

Ralph chuckled. "I heard about that. You missed all the excitement when you disappeared today. Going to dinner, Alice Teng was racing another resident who also has an electric wheelchair. Their wheels locked together. Alice's wheelchair bashed into the hall wall."

"Speeding doesn't pay."

"Alice may have to find another form of entertainment," Ralph said.

We waited until Ken strolled into the room. I sat there motionless, listening to his footfalls as he proceeded to Ralph's bed. I didn't notice anything unusual, not that I'd remember anything anyway.

"Mrs. Teng's wheelchair back in commission?" Ralph asked.

"Yeah," Ken replied. "She dented the wheel pretty bad. I needed to use pliers and a hammer to get it back in shape. It's amazing the trouble that woman gets into."

"I need help getting to the bathroom," Ralph said. "Someone younger and stronger than Paul."

Ken eased Ralph out of bed and half carried him to the bathroom. I waited. They returned, and Ken helped Ralph back into bed. Once he was situated, Ralph said, "Thanks."

"Any time."

Ken left the room.

"Well?" I asked.

"Not the same sound. He's not the one who came into your room."

CHAPTER 30

I was back to square one in finding a suspect for the crimes committed at the Pacific Vista Nursing Home. After being here for over a week, all I had to show for it was a rock thrown at me, a pillow thrust over my face, time spent in a locked storage room, and Marion ending up duct-taped in a closet. My assistance to the police had been next to useless. Here I thought I had helped at one time by linking Ken Yamamoto, his acting, and the makeup tube found under my bed. But he had an alibi for when Marion was abducted, and my eagle-eared friend, Ralph, had dispelled any idea that Ken had been the intruder in my room. With my results so far, I couldn't even claim amateur status as a sleuth.

My only other alternative was to parade everyone who worked here through our room to find out if Ralph recognized the sound of the intruder's footsteps. That would make me popular. I might have to resort to that if nothing else occurred to me, but right now I felt like a deflated balloon and wasn't up to the effort.

With nothing useful having been accomplished, I decided to entertain Ralph by reading him a story. He had been a good friend to me and deserved more than to be lying in bed by himself with nothing to do. "You ready for the next installment in the O. Henry saga?" I asked.

"That would be great, if you're up to it, Paul."

That was all I was up to at this point. I grabbed my book,

ensconced myself in a chair next to Ralph's bed, and scanned through the index of the short story collection. At first nothing jumped out, until a title caught my eye. Why not? "Here's one called the 'Love-Philtre of Ikey Schoenstein.' "

"With a title like that, it has to be good."

I licked my finger, found the first page of the story, and began reading the account of Ikey Schoenstein, a pharmacist, who admires Rosy Riddle from afar, but is too shy to make his intentions known.

I paused and put the book down. "I don't know if I can keep reading this story, Ralph. There's something here that bugs me."

"What's the matter?"

"This story is about a guy who sells pills. I hate taking damn pills. Someone's always trying to cram them down my throat."

Ralph chuckled. "You're one of a kind, Paul. You're going to let a little prejudice get in the way of a good story?"

"I guess I can grin and bear it." I picked up the book and continued.

Into Ikey's pharmacy comes Chunk McGowan, who divulges that he wants to run off and marry Rosy, but she had ended up with cold feet at the last minute several times before. Chunk asks Ikey if he has a potion that will make Rosy think positively of him so she won't change her mind again. Ikey puts together some sleeping powder, figuring that if Rosy falls asleep, it will put the kibosh on elopement plans. To be doubly sure, Ikey warns Rosy's father of Chunk's plans. Rosy's dad says he'll watch Chunk like a hawk and not let him steal Rosy. The next day Chunk comes in the pharmacy to say he's happily married to Rosy. Chunk says he didn't want to use the potion because he wanted Rosy to come away with him on her own volition and not under the influence of the potion. Instead, Chunk gave the potion to Rosy's father, figuring it would make him friendlier.

"Good story," Ralph said.

"Ikey got what he deserved," I replied. "Anyone who dispenses pills shouldn't end up with the girl."

Then in the way my miswired brain worked, the idea of sleeping powder and the wrong person getting it melded together. I experienced an aha moment.

"If you'll excuse me, Ralph, I have something to look into."

I dropped the book on the nightstand and charged out of the room faster than you could say "investigator on the prowl." I skidded to a stop in front of the nurses' station. No one in sight but a nice young female CNA who smiled at me.

"I need to see Ken Yamamoto," I gasped breathlessly.

"Here he comes." She pointed up the purple hallway.

I dashed in that direction to intercept him and grabbed him by the arm sleeve. "Ken, I have a favor to ask."

He eyed me warily. "What, Mr. Jacobson?"

"You mentioned your actor's makeup. Would you show me something to make me look younger?"

He chuckled. "You're on that kick again to appear younger. I could probably take off twenty years but not more than that."

"That's good enough. Do you have a few minutes to give me a demonstration?"

He looked at his watch. "Sure. I have to check on Mrs. Dempsey in thirty minutes, but I'm good until then. Follow me."

He led me through the empty break room into the equally empty staff locker room.

"Let me get out my kit." He reached in his locker and removed the box, which he took into the break room and set on a table. He opened it and began describing its contents. "I have different skin colors and different treatments I can put together."

"And I assume you can add facial hair."

"Yeah. That's easy. A little glue and a false mustache or beard."

"When you put actor's makeup on your face, does it rub off easily?" I asked.

"Depends. Some brands are more durable and resist contact and moisture. That kind's needed when it gets hot or during emotional scenes with tears. You don't want the makeup to run."

"Could you make my skin darker?"

He picked up a tube and tapped it. "Here's one that would make you look almost Hawaiian."

"What about making someone with dark skin look lighter?"

"Sure. I could become a haole with one concoction I have. Now, where is it?" He rummaged through the box.

He wrinkled his brow. "That's strange. I had two tubes. They're both gone."

CHAPTER 31

I watched Ken carefully, but he seemed genuinely surprised to be missing tubes of makeup from his kit. But, I reminded myself, he was an actor. I watched his eyes. Damn. He appeared disturbed by the disappearance. I couldn't decide for sure.

"Who else knows that you keep makeup in your locker?" I asked.

He scratched his head. "Everyone. I'm always sharing my acting stories. It's no secret that I have my actor's kit here."

Now I only needed to find who had taken Ken's makeup.

"Thanks for the lesson," I said.

"You're welcome . . . I guess."

I scooted off, leaving him staring into his kit.

Now what? My efforts had been two steps forward, one step backward. I didn't know if I was getting closer or going around in circles.

I wished I could frisk everyone to find the missing tubes of makeup. I thought back over the events. A tube of makeup had been accidently left in my room. The perp had noticed it missing and had later retrieved it. A smudge had been left near where I had been locked in. The bad guy had the makeup. He was apt to strike again.

I returned to my room to regroup and found Evelyn Newberry there lecturing Ralph. She wagged a finger at him. "Now, Sonny, I want you to be sure to go out tomorrow and get your fresh air. You're looking a little peaked."

"I haven't been out of this joint in six months," Ralph said.

"There. Just goes to show you. Go play catch with the kids in the neighborhood. It will do you a world of good." She turned, having heard me enter. "Here's Junior." She focused her attention on me. "I want you to make sure your brother gets some exercise tomorrow. It's important. Do you hear me?"

"I'll wheel him all over the place, if that helps."

She stamped her foot. "No. He needs to go outside."

"You up for a jailbreak, Ralph?" I asked.

"Why not? It would add a little excitement."

"Evelyn, I know you like to go outside," I said.

"It's Mom to you, Junior." A glint showed in her eyes. "I'd be up for a little exploration in the morning. I might join you boys."

"We'll make it a family picnic." I was getting into the swing of her fantasy world. "I'll make three sandwiches."

"Oh, you're making me hungry just thinking about it, Junior." She closed her eyes. "I'm seeing bright red."

"Huh?"

She gave a dismissive wave of her hand. "You know. Three is red."

"It's her synesthesia," Ralph reminded me.

"That's right. And if I pack two sandwiches?"

Evelyn licked her lips. "Ah, bright orange."

"What a world with your numbers and colors."

"I used to tell you boys stories with all the colors." Evelyn sighed and looked into the distance, her eyes unfocused. Then she brought her gaze back to me. "But it's late. Time to go to bed."

"But I'm not sleepy," I said.

Evelyn put her hands on her hips. "Now, are you going to mind me or am I going to have to get out your father's belt?"

An image of my dad whipping me at the age of ten flashed

into my mind. I had stolen a lollipop from the corner store. That ended my involvement with crime. That is, until I started helping with police investigations in my old age. "No thank you." I hopped into bed fully dressed. I didn't want to risk the wrath of a mentally confused woman.

"That's better. Nighty-night." She headed toward the door, flipped off the light switch, turned toward me, and blew a kiss. Then she was gone.

"Phew," I said, wiping my forehead as I got out of bed. "I thought I might be in for a whipping tonight."

"And I bet she could do it, too," Ralph replied.

This place continued to grow on me. Kind of like dandelions popping out of a lush green lawn.

I walked over and flipped on the light.

Moments later a man stepped into the room. "I wanted to stop by to see how your back is doing, Mr. Jacobson."

Back? Then it clicked. "You must be Dr. Burber."

He smiled. "That's right. I like to follow up after I've seen someone here."

I arched my back and stretched my arms. "Everything's copacetic. Thanks for asking."

"Good. Let me know if you have any reoccurrence." He turned and headed out of the room.

"This place is as busy as Coney Island," I said.

"You're a popular guy," Ralph said.

I needed to focus my defective brain. I paced around the room.

"Something bothering you, Paul?"

"Yeah. I'm trying to figure out who is causing all the problems around here. I visited with Ken Yamamoto again a little while ago. He's missing some face makeup that would turn someone's dark skin lighter. For a while I thought he had disguised himself and committed the sexual assaults and murder. Now it appears that someone else stole his makeup. We have someone wandering around here who might commit another crime. It fries me that we haven't been able to nail the bastard."

"Why don't you settle in for a good night's sleep and let it go until tomorrow." He winked one of his sightless eyes. "You know, until our picnic."

"I'm not ready for shut-eye yet, Ralph. I'm too keyed up after what's happened today. I think I'll walk around for a while."

"I'll leave it to you, Paul. I'm hitting the hay. If you're going past the nurses' station will you ask Ken Yamamoto to come help me to the bathroom again?"

"Will do." I headed out the door to become a hall walker. That was better than being a streetwalker.

At the nurses' station I waved to the same female CNA who had been on duty earlier. "Ralph Hirata needs Ken Yamamoto to come help him," I said.

She smiled at me. "Ken's tied up, but Sal Polahi could help. I'll notify him."

"Sounds good," I said. Next I walked along the blue hallway. I came to a stop halfway along the hall.

If I were the perpetrator, what would I do? If I had this thing for attacking old women, I'd wait until no one was looking. Then I'd put on my disguise and sneak into a room, do my deed, sneak out, and remove my disguise to return to my normal appearance.

This guy was sneaky. He had avoided detection by anyone else on the staff as well as Benny Makoku or my lame efforts.

Out of the corner of my eye, a motion caught my attention.

CHAPTER 32

Someone disappeared into a room partway down the hall. Being in full stealth mode, I tiptoed to the room and saw a name on the door, Annabel Dempsey. *Uh-oh.* Was someone going to attack her again? The door was closed. I looked up and down the hall. No one else in sight. I put my ear to the door. I heard a shuffling sound. I tried to imagine what might be going on inside. Something innocent, or could this be another attack?

What could I do? Should I try to find Benny? I waited. That might be too late. I listened again. I heard a faint moaning sound.

My heart rate shot into the dangerous range.

I grabbed the knob and thrust the door open.

Mrs. Dempsey rested in bed with a blood pressure cuff on her arm and a thermometer in her mouth. Ken Yamamoto held her wrist, looking at his watch. He turned from his watch toward me.

"Mr. Jacobson?"

Oops. "Sorry. Wrong room."

I shut the door and took off down the hall faster than you could say "idiot." I returned to the front of the building and plopped down in a chair, clenching and unclenching my fists. I had become obsessed with a dumb idea and violated someone's privacy. I smacked my forehead. What a jerk. Maybe Henry and Madeline were right in calling me that. I clenched my jaw at the recognition of what I had done. If there were a punching bag in front of me, I would have slammed my fist into it.

After my heart rate returned to normal, I looked around. Other than the one CNA at the desk, the place was deserted. I shivered even though it was a warm evening and the building wasn't overly air conditioned. The hairs on my exposed arms stood at attention like alert soldiers. I rubbed the sleeves of my Hawaiian shirt to send some warmth into my arms. What a nudnick I had turned into.

I tried to focus my thinking and told myself to push aside my mistake. Somewhere in this building lurked a killer. I took a deep breath and sniffed the sharp aroma of rubbing alcohol. As if in response, my right calf cramped.

I shot upright. All the cavorting around today had taken a toll on my aged body. I shook my right leg. The knot loosened. Then my left calf cramped. I hopped around and rubbed it. Anyone watching would have thought I had invented a new dance called the Jacobson Strut. My shoulders tightened. I put my hands on my hips and flexed my back.

After a minute of those weird calisthenics, my muscles relaxed.

I looked around. The CNA behind the counter remained occupied, speaking on the phone without a concern for my gyrations. I guessed she was used to old people doing strange native dances.

What to do? I could have moseyed back to my room to saw some Zs, but I was too keyed up. I'd never be able to fall asleep even though I was physically tired. I'd spend hours counting sinister men jumping over fences. Bummer.

Might as well stretch my legs a little more.

I made a pass through my home base, the beige hallway, and peeked into my room. Ralph was nestled in his bed, snoring. No worries of the day disturbed my roomie. He slept the sleep of the innocent and unperturbed. Not likely for me in the foreseeable future. Turning back into the hallway and taking a step, I almost fell over an electric wheelchair at my heels.

"Watch it, you old coot," a withered woman warned.

"Who you calling old, missy?" I countered.

She thumped her caved-in chest. "No one calls Alice Teng missy."

The name registered.

I chuckled. "I understand you needed to take your chariot into the repair shop after an accident today. Rumor has it you couldn't handle your vehicle. A little too much speed on the straightaway?"

"Dang inconsiderate driver. An incompetent pushed me off the road. I wish the other racers would take training classes. Too many amateurs on the course these days. Someone is going to get killed." She eyed me. "You don't have a set of wheels, but you want to race me to the lobby?"

"Sure." I figured I could beat a wheelchair.

"Ready, set, go!" She took off before I even positioned myself.

"Hey, wait. No fair." I loped after her, pumping my arms like Jesse Owens and caught her two rooms down the hallway. As I started to pass, she veered her wheelchair toward me and ran over my right foot.

I yelped in pain and hobbled to a stop.

Alice continued to the front of the building and pumped her right fist in the air three times "Victory! Kicked butt again."

After rubbing my foot and deciding I wouldn't need surgery, I limped to catch up with her.

I shook my right index finger at her. "Foul. Obstruction of a competitor. You should be disqualified and banned from the track for life."

"If you can't stand the heat, don't put your face into the tailpipe. Want to race back to my room?"

"No thanks. I don't want to risk my good foot."

"Wimp."

On that happy note, I gimped into the break room to eliminate the risk of any further damage from traffic accidents. I had the place to myself, so I plunked down on a chair to contemplate.

What would it be like coming to a nursing home with a legitimate need for nursing service, not my fake one? The muscles in my chest clenched. This would be the last bastion after giving up any remnants of independence. Apparently, I had once lived in a retirement home, but that was different—an independent living facility that had no attending nurses and that allowed people to take care of themselves. I'd hate to be at the point like Ralph, where I couldn't get in or out of bed without assistance. That would be a pisser. But I had to be realistic. If more of my body gave out, I might end up in a place like this for real. I shuddered. I hoped I could return to living with Marion very soon and have a number of happy years ahead sleeping next to my bride.

My bride. I visualized Marion's smiling face. She had been through a lot today. All because of what I had gotten into. She deserved better. Here she had signed on to be hitched to an old poop like me with a memory like a leaky boat and how did I treat her? I became involved in this sordid mess, and someone had taken my interference out on her.

I let out a deep sigh.

My foot had stopped aching. *Start thinking clearly.* With that self-admonishment, I reviewed all the happenings—the sexual attacks, the murder, the rock thrown at me, the pillow put over my face, the time spent locked in a storage room, an intruder in my room, the abduction of Marion. Who could have done this? I had suspected Ken Yamamoto, but it looked like someone else had stolen his actor's makeup and disguised himself. What other clues had I overlooked? With everything spinning in my head, out popped one thing I had ignored. I slapped my forehead. Another link I had missed.

I needed to test my hypothesis. One simple way of doing this. I looked around to make sure no one was in sight. I raced into the adjoining locker room. I checked for the name I wanted and located it. Opening the locker I found a pile of dirty clothes. I gritted my teeth and sorted through them. At the bottom I found the smoking gun—an almost empty tube of face makeup.

CHAPTER 33

I heard a voice and closed the locker. I needed to find a safe place to call Detective Chun. I left the locker room and entered the break room to find two female CNAs there.

One of them looked up at me. "What are you doing here, Mr. Jacobson?"

I shrugged. "I got lost."

"Do you need to be accompanied back to your room?"

"That's okay. I can find it." I slunk away before any more interrogation took place.

I needed to find a private place. I headed into the blue hallway, dark due to a ceiling light being out.

Someone ducked into the storage area at the end of the hall. I couldn't tell who it was. Should I go look? Not after my earlier encounter in Annabel Dempsey's room, and besides, I needed to speak with Detective Chun.

I came to one room with no nameplate on the wall. The door was open with a light on inside. I entered to find a bed with no linen. I looked around at the bare walls. Pacific Vista had room for one more decrepit soul. I shut the door and took out my cell phone to call Detective Chun.

When he answered, I said breathlessly, "I . . . I figured out a possible suspect."

"Stay calm, Mr. Jacobson."

I gulped in two lungs full of air. "I spoke with Annabel Dempsey after the sexual assault on her. She mentioned the attacker wore a sweatshirt."

"Yes, she gave me that same information."

"From what I read in my journal, I spoke with a member of the night cleaning crew named Dan Aukina. He wore a gray sweatshirt."

I heard what sounded like scribbling. "Interesting."

"It's even better than that. Earlier I spoke with Ken Yamamoto. He's missing some actor's face makeup that can lighten skin. I looked in Dan Aukina's locker a little while ago and found an almost empty tube of face makeup."

The pen scratching sounds became louder. "We'll have to check him out immediately. I'll contact Benny Makoku."

"I'll also mention it to Benny if I see him," I said.

"Don't approach Aukina if he's there tonight."

"I'll leave that up to you and Officer Makoku."

I closed my phone and stuffed it back in my pocket. Maybe these damned electronic gadgets were useful after all.

I sat there for a few minutes to let my heart rate return to normal. I had finally found a useful clue. The police could grill Dan Aukina and try to force a confession. Then I'd be able to get out of this place and carry on the rest of my life with Marion.

I stood and headed out the door as a figure disappeared into a room across the hall from the storage area. It was a man, and he looked older than the CNAs on duty here. In the dim light I discerned he was wearing a sweatshirt. My curiosity was piqued. Could this be Dan Aukina in disguise? I slammed my right fist into my left hand. He had stolen Ken Yamamoto's actor's makeup and was trying to look like an older haole guy. Although I had promised Detective Chun to stay away from Aukina, I tiptoed down the hall toward the room the figure had entered.

I listened at the closed door and heard a muffled groan. Was I overreacting? Had I let my imagination run wild? Had I once again made a faulty assumption? Maybe it was someone else getting their blood pressure taken, and the cuff was too tight. I squinted at the nameplate. This was Evelyn Newberry's room. I could go inside on the pretense that I was checking on "Mom."

I hesitated and listened again. I heard shuffling sounds and another groan. The man I had seen definitely didn't look like someone on the staff. I could go find Benny Makoku and ask him to check. That might take too long.

What to do?

A gasp came from inside the room.

I couldn't wait any longer. I clenched my teeth, grabbed the doorknob, and pushed the door open.

The lights were off. I saw the shape of a man hunched over a lump in bed. The covers were bouncing as if legs underneath were kicking.

"Hey, what's going on?" I shouted.

The man shot erect, his hands flying off the covers.

"Help!" came a plaintive cry from the bed.

The man raced to the window and bashed his hands against the curtains. Glass exploded behind the curtain. He leaped through the broken window.

It happened so quickly that I stood there paralyzed until my synapses sent the right signals.

I bolted to the window and thrust the curtains aside. A figure disappeared through the parking lot. Damn. I had been too late to identify the intruder.

I turned on the light.

Evelyn Newberry lay in bed, shaking.

"Are you all right?" I asked.

"Red, green," she mumbled. She put her hand to her forehead. "That man attacked me. He put his hand over my mouth and pawed me. Red, green."

I found the call button and pushed it. I stepped out in the hall as one of the CNAs I had seen in the break room earlier came striding down the hall. I greeted her at the door. "Evelyn Newberry has been attacked. The intruder escaped through the window. Where's Benny Makoku?"

"In the break room."

"I'll go get him." I pointed into the room. "You attend to Evelyn."

I jogged as fast as my old legs could carry me to the front of the building, glad no wheelchairs lined my path. Dashing into the break room, I spotted Benny sitting there eating a sandwich.

"Not the time to stuff your face, you young whippersnapper. Evelyn Newberry has been attacked. Follow me."

He dropped the sandwich and jumped up as I galloped away, heading back to Evelyn's room.

Benny caught up with me as we reached the scene of the crime. The nurse held Evelyn's shaky hand.

"He went out through the window, Benny," I said.

Benny stepped over to the curtains and pulled the cord to open them. He leaned over and extracted something.

I moved over beside him and saw what he had found. It was a torn piece of navy blue cloth with the word "Auburn" on it.

CHAPTER 34

Benny Makoku pulled out his cell phone and called Detective Chun. He spoke in too quiet a tone to be overheard. I stepped over to the bed next to Evelyn Newberry, who continued to mumble about red and green.

The attending CNA frowned. "Mrs. Newberry seems to be in a state of confusion after being attacked."

I scratched my head. "I don't know. There's something she's trying to tell us." I leaned over. "Mom, this is Junior."

She shook her head as if trying to dislodge lice.

I tried again. "Mom, won't you speak to your son, Junior?"

She squinted at me. "You're not Junior. You're some old man."

Oops, busted. So much for role playing in her universe.

"You're right. I'm Paul Jacobson. I'm another resident here in the Pacific Vista Nursing Home. We're all here to help you."

Her eyes darted around the room. "Someone came in my room. Don't let him in here again."

The CNA patted her hand. "We won't."

"May I please have a glass of water?" Evelyn asked.

The CNA went into the bathroom and returned in a moment with a paper cup.

Evelyn greedily gulped down the water.

"Is there anything else I can get for you, Mrs. Newberry?"

"Not right now."

Benny came over and stood by the bed. "Mrs. Newberry. Can you tell us what happened?"

Evelyn put her hands over her eyes. "It was horrible. I had almost fallen asleep. I heard someone come in my room. I thought it might be one of the nurses checking on me. When I opened my eyes, I saw a man I didn't recognize. He put his hand over my mouth and touched me . . ." She began to sob.

The CNA glared at Benny. "She doesn't need to go through this right now. I think you should let her rest."

Benny leveled an equally intense stare at the CNA. "I will in a moment. It's very important that we understand what took place so we can catch the man who did this and prevent another occurrence."

The CNA gave a resigned sigh. "All right. But not for very long."

Benny leaned closer to the bed. "Mrs. Newberry. I only need to discuss a few things with you. Please describe the man."

She sniffled and wiped her nose with the sleeve of her nightgown. "He . . . he had white hair. Not as old as me." She let out an unladylike burp. She put her hand to her mouth. "Excuse me."

"That's not a problem. Tell me more about the man."

"Haole guy. A beard and mustache."

I nudged Benny. "May I ask her a question?"

He straightened. "Go ahead."

I leaned closer. "You said red, green. Were you seeing numbers?"

"So bright. Red, green." She nodded her head slightly, her eyes closed, and she fell asleep.

Benny and I huddled in the corner of the room.

"We have another problem, Mr. Jacobson."

"What's that?"

Benny tapped his hand against the wall. "I discovered some discrepancies in the log system the staff is using to sign people in and out of the building. They haven't been very careful in making sure people always sign."

Uh-oh. "So some of the suspects earlier ruled out for not being in the building could have actually been here?"

"Exactly. We thought we had eliminated Dr. Burber and Fred Langley, but either could have come back in and left again without an indication in the log."

I slapped my forehead. Damn. "I saw both Burber and Langley here earlier this evening. One of them might have attacked Evelyn Newberry. All the things with Ken Yamamoto's actor's makeup might be completely off base."

"Unfortunately, that's a possibility."

My mind went into mental overload as I tried to figure who might be our real culprit. "And all of our original three suspects are here tonight. Have you found out which staff members were missing last night when Marion was abducted?" I asked.

"Yeah. I spoke on my cell phone with Detective Chun on that subject right before you came into the break room a little while ago. After checking with the night supervisors, I narrowed it down to three men: Chavis Tobias, Sal Polahi, and Dan Aukina."

"I've never come across the name Chavis Tobias," I said.

"He's a temp who fills in on the cleaning crew. He was scheduled last night but called in sick."

My pulse quickened. "Maybe we're getting somewhere after all with one of those people. I called Detective Chun earlier. Dan Aukina might be our guy. He wore a gray sweatshirt and Annabel Dempsey had identified her attacker as wearing a sweatshirt. He had that same sweatshirt on tonight when I saw him earlier. And I found a tube of actor's makeup in Dan's locker." I took a gulp of air. "And there's Fred Langley. He always wears a sweatshirt when he visits his mother . . ." I paused, realizing the fallacy of this line of thought. "But the fragment of sweatshirt on the window tonight was navy blue."

Dan Aukina topped my list for the most likely suspect, but my gut didn't fully agree. I had a little niggling feeling that I had overlooked a crucial clue. What had I missed? The gears started grinding. Thoughts and words from my journal clinked around my brain like dice in a cup. Then a series of weird connections came together. I gasped. "A few minutes ago I was convinced Dan Aukina committed the crimes. I think someone else put the tube of makeup in his locker as a diversion. You aren't going to believe this, but I just figured out who our perp is."

CHAPTER 35

Detective Chun strode into the room, his shoes clacking on the floor. His crumpled suit looked as if it had been stored in a shoebox overnight. "Did I hear Mr. Jacobson say he has figured out who's been committing the crimes around here?"

I waved. "Hello, Detective. It's good to see you on this fine evening. Yeah, I have an educated guess."

The CNA cleared her throat loudly. "If you gentlemen would go out in the hall, Mrs. Newberry can have some peaceful sleep. I'll stay with her."

Benny Makoku, Detective Chun, and I honored her request and stepped out of the room.

"It's probably just as well the CNA doesn't overhear what I have to say." I checked to make sure there wasn't anyone else in the hallway. "It's a strange set of circumstances and no sense having rumors start."

"Go ahead, Mr. Jacobson," Detective Chun said.

I took a deep breath and almost choked as an antiseptic aroma went up my nose. I pulled out a handkerchief and blew my nose into it. "Okay, here's the deal. Mrs. Newberry has synesthesia, a condition where she sees colors for numbers."

Both men stared at me as if I were some foreign species of invasive weed.

"Bear with me a moment. I have my short-term memory problem, and Evelyn Newberry has her own variation of unique mental wiring. Where you two and I might see the number three, she sees red, sometimes so brightly that she can't make out the digit itself."

"O—kay," Chun said.

"And for four she sees green," I continued. "She has been saying 'red, green' since I came into her room, repeating it over and over. I think she saw the number thirty-four, red for three and green for four."

Chun continued to give me his detective's questioning eye, above which he shot his eyebrow as high as his hairline.

I gulped in another breath, this time not choking on any unexpected aromas. "Through some friends of mine, I learned that thirty-four was the number on Bo Jackson's jersey when he played college football."

Chun clicked his tongue. "Thanks for the sports lesson. Where's this going, Mr. Jacobson?"

I put up my hand to hold off the skepticism stampede. "You'll see. Benny found a piece of cloth with the word 'Auburn' on it."

"That's right," Benny said. "It was torn off by a shard of glass when the perp went through the window."

I rubbed my hands together since we were getting closer to the punch line. "Bo Jackson was number thirty-four on the Auburn football team many years ago. I suspect the perp wore an Auburn sweatshirt with Bo Jackson's number thirty-four. Evelyn Newberry was telling us in her synesthete way that she had seen that number thirty-four."

Chun tapped his foot. "Okay, let's say I go along with this convoluted logic. How does this prove who the attacker was?"

I smiled. "Here's the interesting part. Some number of days ago two of the CNAs, Ken Yamamoto and Sal Polahi, helped me to the shower. We debated the greatest athlete of all time."

Chun glared at me. "And you remember this conversation, Mr. Jacobson?"

"No, but I wrote it in my journal, which I read very carefully this morning." I tapped my forehead. "And since I remember things fine during the day, what I read is fresh and locked in my temporary circuits. In the discussion on my trip to the shower, Sal Polahi took the position that Bo Jackson was the greatest athlete of all time. He's an avid Bo Jackson fan. I surmise that he wore an Auburn Bo Jackson sweatshirt with the number thirty-four tonight. Furthermore, I bet that Sal Polahi stole makeup from Ken Yamamoto and used it to disguise himself as an older haole man when he attacked women. Ken Yamamoto is missing two tubes of makeup. I found one in Dan Aukina's locker but that was a decoy. Sal Polahi used the other tube tonight in preparation for attacking Evelyn Newberry."

Benny grinned. "Very good, Mr. Jackson. It does make sense in a weird way. Sal Polahi worked here each of the nights women were attacked but wasn't on duty last night when Mrs. Jacobson was abducted."

"Let's check to see if we can find any sign of Sal Polahi here in the nursing home," Chun said. "Mr. Jacobson, I want you to wait by the front nurses' station."

I moseyed up to my assigned position while Benny and Detective Chun made the rounds through the nursing home. They rejoined me in fifteen minutes.

"We found Dan Aukina, who has been working all this time, but no sign of Sal Polahi," Benny said. "Sal didn't sign out and no one has seen him in the last half hour."

"I'll put out an APB and get a search warrant issued for his apartment." Chun pulled out his cell phone and made a call.

"Now while you gentlemen catch Sal Polahi, I'm going to my room."

I had had enough activity for one night and moseyed back to find Ralph awake.

"Paul, I fell asleep waiting for you, but just woke up. I have something important to tell you. Where have you been?"

"A lot's been happening. What's up with you?"

"I know who the intruder is!"

"The guy you heard sneaking into my room before?"

"That's the one. He came to help me right after you left. His name is Sal Polahi."

"That's the guy who attacked Evelyn Newberry. How did you identify him?"

Ralph patted his ears with both of his hands. "He introduced himself. I'd never met him before because I have a standing request for Ken Yamamoto to be the CNA to help me at night."

"Yeah, and I suspected Ken for a while, but Sal's our guy. Unfortunately, he escaped, but the police will nab him. Detective Chun will want to interview you. It will add one more piece of evidence to convict Sal when he's caught."

I galumphed off to find Detective Chun, and he followed me back to interview Ralph. After they spoke, I said to Chun, "You now have an ear witness account of who has been sneaking into my room. One of those times he retrieved a tube of actor's makeup he had previously accidently dropped on the floor."

After Chun left, Ralph wanted to get back to sleep, so I pulled the curtain and turned off the light on his side of the room. I sat on my bed thinking over the evening's events. I had finally done something useful in my assignment here to help the police identify the attacker. I still felt too keyed up to sleep. I heard footsteps in the hall, and Marion rushed into my room.

"I fell asleep and forgot to bring you your journal," Marion said.

I jumped off the bed and gave her a hug. "Am I glad to see you. We've had a whole wagonload of excitement this evening."

"What trouble have you been causing now?"

"Not me. I think I actually helped for a change. An intruder went into Evelyn Newberry's room a little while ago."

Marion put her hand to her cheek. "Oh, no. Is she all right?"

"Yep. Everything's copasetic. The bad guy jumped out the window. We think he's a CNA who works here named Sal Polahi."

"Have the police arrested him?"

"Not yet. He's on the run, but they'll nab him."

She tapped the spiral notebook in her hand. "You'll have a lot to write, if you can stay awake."

I arched my back to stretch it. "That won't be a problem. I'm too tense to go to sleep anyway."

Marion snuggled close against me. "Why don't you come back to the condo with me tonight?"

I gave her a kiss. "With an invitation like that, how can I refuse? Ralph won't miss me, and I think my mission has been accomplished at Pacific Vista. A little stroll in the night air will also do me a world of good."

We left the room, and at the front counter Marion signed me out. Before we stepped to the door, Detective Chun and Benny Makoku came out of the break room.

"I'll be spending the night at Marion's condo if you're looking for me," I said. "I'm taking a break from this joint."

"One thing first. Take a look at this picture of Sal Polahi. I pulled it out of his employment file." Benny handed me a photograph.

I waggled my eyebrows at Benny. "I didn't think you police types snooped in files without a search warrant."

"Hey, I am the night security guy here." Benny grinned. "I have a legitimate reason to open the file."

I regarded the picture, seeing a face with a blank expression. He had thick eyebrows, deep-set eyes, and dark hair. I tried to bring up a previous image of Sal. But as is always the case, *nada*.

Marion peered over my shoulder. "I've seen him around here

before. He's on night duty, if I recall."

"That's him," Benny said.

"I don't remember what he looks like, but for the moment I have him locked in my mind." I handed the photo back to Benny.

"I want to thank you for your assistance," Detective Chun said.

"Hey, all part of the service. I hope you have him behind bars soon."

"We're working on that," Chun said. "We'll get you checked out of Pacific Vista tomorrow, Mr. Jacobson."

I tipped an imaginary hat. "It's been a pleasure, and I'll catch up with you gentlemen in the morning."

After being buzzed out, we strolled along the sidewalk as a mild breeze danced through my remaining locks.

I squeezed Marion's hand. "It's been quite a week or so."

"With your undercover duties completed, we can schedule our trip back to the mainland," Marion said. "I'm anxious to see my daughter and grandson."

I looked up at the few stars visible through the ambient city light and passing clouds. "Yeah, I guess I'll have to leave Ralph on his lonesome. He'll eventually have to break in a new room-mate."

Off to the side I heard a rustling sound in the bushes. *Uh-oh.* I froze, my stomach as tight as a bongo drum.

A cat shot across our path. I let out a loud sigh. It wasn't even a black cat.

I wiped a drop of sweat off my forehead. "That's a relief."

Marion held my arm as we reached her building. I felt so lucky to have this woman who put up with me.

We climbed the stairs to her apartment. As she put the key in the lock, I heard a creaking sound behind us. I spun around to see a woman carrying a bag of groceries. Man, I was tense.

In the condo I drank a large glass of water. I didn't realize how thirsty I was after all the excitement. After documenting my adventures, I asked, "Do you have a toothbrush I can borrow?"

"There's an extra one in the medicine cabinet."

I scrubbed my pearly whites and went back into the bedroom.

Marion was already in bed with the covers pulled up to her chin.

"Oops," I said. "I didn't bring any pajamas."

Marion winked at me. "I don't think you'll need them tonight, hotshot."

"That sounds promising."

I dispensed with my clothes, stacking them neatly on a chair. I didn't want to make a mess because I wanted to be invited back again.

I hopped into bed and discovered a soft, warm female body pressed against mine. This was getting interesting.

A little-used part of my anatomy came to attention. Duly inspired, I launched into a more enticing form of undercover operation.

CHAPTER 36

The morning brought bright sunshine and a clear memory of the preceding day's events. The wonders of a sex-infused brain. So this was how normal people woke up in the morning. I'd have to do whatever I could to duplicate this experience. I stretched my arms, still feeling a tingle from the night before.

Marion opened one eye. "Aren't you going to sleep in?"

"Nah. I'm too chipper to stay in bed. The wide world awaits me." I hopped down to the floor and danced a jig.

Marion groaned. "Don't get carried away."

I leaned over and kissed her forehead before moseying into the kitchen to fix a cup of coffee and scarf a bagel.

"You want something to eat?" I called out.

"Not yet."

While I masticated, I reviewed the events of the previous day. I clenched my fists at the thought of Marion being abducted. Fortunately, Detective Chun found Marion unharmed. I unclenched my fists. Then entering Evelyn Newberry's room and seeing a man flee through the window. I was glad I had been able to piece together the clues to identify Sal Polahi as the perp. Now the police needed to catch the bastard.

By the time I had wiped the last crumb off my chin, Marion was up, padding around in her slippers and robe. I whistled. "Boy, you look good even in a baggy robe."

She pirouetted in front of me.

"What's on your agenda today?" I asked.

"Let's see. Since we'll soon be leaving the island, I need to do some last minute shopping."

"I thought that's what you've been doing while I've been held prisoner in the nursing home."

Marion rolled her eyes. "I've been to a few stores while you carried on your investigation, but I still need to find something for my grandson, Austin."

"He's a lucky kid with the special presents he gets from you."

"Of course. He's my only grandkid, same as Jennifer is your only one."

"Speaking of Jennifer, I'll have to give her a call later today to tell her the recent events."

"Jennifer likes hearing from you."

Marion gave me a peck on the cheek. "And what is on your agenda today, Mr. Jacobson?"

"I need to mosey over to the nursing home and collect my belongings. I'll also say goodbye to Ralph. I'm going to miss him."

"He's going to miss you as well. You two bonded. I know he enjoyed having you read to him."

"Maybe he can find another reader," I said.

Marion gave me another kiss. "But no one can replace you."

"Thanks for the vote of confidence. I'll also have to check in with Detective Chun to see if they've nabbed Sal Polahi."

A worried expression crossed Marion's face. "I sure hope so. I don't welcome the thought of him being on the loose."

A cold chill went down my spine. I shared her concern. It was spooky that he might be wandering around.

"When do you want to head back to the mainland?" I asked.

"I'm ready to go right away. I'll check with the airlines. We can probably get a flight out tomorrow night."

"Fine by me."

We both dressed. Marion reminded me to take my cell phone.

I turned it on and stuffed it in my pocket while Marion called for a cab.

Downstairs, I waited by the curb with her until the taxi pulled up.

"Happy shopping," I said. "I'm glad it's you and not me."

Marion smiled. "I know. We have a division of labor. I do the shopping and you take care of catching criminals."

After the cab drove away, I headed toward Pacific Vista.

A gentle trade wind ruffled a nearby palm tree. I imagined sitting in the shade, sipping a tall tropical drink while hula girls entertained me with an island dance. A red-headed cardinal hopping on the grass under a banyan tree pecked at the ground and turned its head from side to side. All was good in the universe.

A block along my jaunt, I heard the plunking of a ukulele from a nearby apartment. I had tried to learn the ukulele many years ago, back before my memory went on the fritz. In spite of remembering the chords, I couldn't get my fingers in the right place. Oh, well, I guessed I'd have to pass on becoming a world-renowned entertainer.

I turned the corner, and there a block ahead of me loomed the two-story building, home for the last week and a half of one Paul Jacobson. I wouldn't miss the place. Sure, I would miss Ralph and some of the local characters, but by tomorrow I wouldn't remember any of them anyway. Such a life when your memory goes down the drain every day.

I was within ten feet of the nursing home entrance when I heard a rustling sound off to my side. I thought it might be a cat or dog. Instead, a man jumped out of a hedge, brandishing a handgun.

I immediately recognized the face from the picture Benny Makoku had shown me last night—Sal Polahi.

He snarled at me. "You caused me trouble, you interfering

old goat. You and I are going for a little one-way ride."

I looked frantically around me. "No thank you. I think I'll just continue on to Pacific Vista."

I took a step toward the nursing home.

He lunged in front of me, barring my way. "I don't think so." He jammed the gun into my gut. "Get in the car at the curb."

My pulse raced, and my mouth went dry. I saw a gray Honda Civic parked next to me. I couldn't make a run for it, but I certainly didn't want to get in a car with this madman. A door slammed, and out of the nursing home and down the ramp charged Alice Teng in her electric wheelchair, followed by Evelyn Newberry.

Alice pumped her fist in the air and shouted, "Jailbreak! Evelyn found the release button behind the nurses' station."

Her wheelchair veered right toward Sal and me.

Sal looked over his shoulder but didn't react in time.

I saw my chance and dropped to the sidewalk, curling into a fetal position.

Alice plowed right into Sal, who fell over my body, and his head bashed into the Honda. The gun went flying out of his hand.

I stood up. Sal slumped to the sidewalk, unconscious.

"Sorry," Alice shouted as she continued past us.

Evelyn waved and shuffled away behind Alice.

Puna came running out the door. "Stop!" he shouted at the ladies.

"Don't worry about them," I said. "I need your assistance to make sure Sal Polahi doesn't get away."

Puna thundered to a stop next to Sal's sprawled form.

I picked up the gun, my hand shaking.

Sal groaned and tried to get up on his hands and knees.

"Don't move, slimeball!" I waved the gun at Sal.

Sal tried to crawl away like a crab. Puna dropped on him like a wrestler making a final takedown.

Sal let out a loud, "Oof!"

"Keep him there," I said. "I'm going to call nine-one-one."

I stuck the gun in my belt, pulled out the cell phone Detective Chun had given me, and punched in the three digits. "Send a police officer to the Pacific Vista Nursing Home. We've apprehended a fugitive named Sal Polahi. Notify Detective Chun."

While we waited, I watched Sal squirming under Puna's weight.

"Get off me," Sal moaned. "You're crushing my ribs."

"No way," Puna said. "Not after what you did to those women." He bounced up and down as if on a trampoline, causing Sal to groan.

"I'm going to be in big trouble for letting Alice and Evelyn get away," Puna said.

"Not to worry," I replied. "They'll be back for lunch. Besides, you're a hero for catching Sal Polahi."

Puna grinned, showing his gold tooth. "I only did the cleanup. The real heroes are Alice Teng and you for disarming him."

A cruiser pulled to the curb, and a police officer came over to where we congregated.

Puna stood and pulled Sal to his feet as if lifting a piece of balsa wood. He kept a good grip on Sal's collar.

"This is Sal Polahi, wanted for sexual assault and murder," I said. "You can take him off to the slammer and lock him up for life."

Sal looked wildly around. "Thank goodness you're here, Officer. These men attacked me. I've been assaulted. I want to press charges."

"I know who you are," the policeman said. "We've been looking for you. Hands behind your back."

Sal tried to squirm away, but Puna spun him around. The police officer grabbed Sal's arms and snapped on the cuffs.

"You'll hear from my lawyer," Sal shouted.

"I'll welcome the opportunity," the policeman said before leading Sal away and stuffing him in the backseat of the cruiser.

I held up a hand, and Puna gave me a high five.

"A pleasure working with you, Mr. Jacobson."

"Likewise. You might want to go check on Alice Teng and Evelyn Newberry. They shouldn't be too far away."

"Good idea." Puna galloped away.

An unmarked car screeched to the curb, and Detective Chun and Benny Makoku jumped out.

"What's going on?" Chun asked as he approached.

"Hi, guys." I waved. "You missed the excitement, but we have it under control."

CHAPTER 37

After I explained the details of the great electric wheelchair hit-and-run capture scenario, Detective Chun stood there with his mouth open, shaking his head as if he had been hit by a falling coconut.

Benny Makoku couldn't contain himself and broke out in laughter. He pounded Chun on the back. "Hey, doesn't matter how we got the guy in custody. Remember, it was your idea to have Mr. Jacobson go into the nursing home undercover."

Detective Chun regained his voice. "Yeah. I certainly didn't know what we were getting into."

"Cheer up," I said. "All it took was a bunch of old farts to catch that young thug, and he's where he belongs."

"You continue to prove that old people have very unique talents," Chun said. "I'll never think of a nursing home in the same way I used to."

"That's what we geezers and geezerettes do best. It's always fun to surprise you young kids. And now that I've completed my mission, I need to go inside to pack so my bride and I can return to the mainland."

Detective Chun gave a wan smile. "First, one more question. How did you recognize Sal Polahi?"

"My brain apparently has one overriding circuit. This morning I happened to remember things from yesterday. The picture that Officer Makoku showed me yesterday stuck in my feeble brain. I recognized the gun-brandishing Sal Polahi when he accosted me. And you really have Alice Teng to thank. She's the one who bopped Sal with her wheelchair. She saved my bacon and took care of Sal long enough for Puna Koloa to contain him. The staff and residents of Pacific Vista contributed to the successful capture."

Puna came running up. "I can't find Alice Teng and Evelyn Newberry. Have you seen them come back this way?"

"Those two women can be pretty slippery," I said. I turned toward Detective Chun. "May I be excused to help Puna track down the escapees?"

"Sure. We'll touch base again inside when you return."

"I went around the block but didn't spot them," Puna said. "Where could those two have disappeared to?"

"Shouldn't be too difficult to find them." I thought back to what I had read in my journal of the little jaunt around the neighborhood Evelyn and I had taken. "There's a park down the street. Let's check it out."

Puna and I took off, and when we reached the park, we spotted Evelyn sitting on a bench with Alice alongside in her wheelchair.

"Good morning, ladies," I said. "Are you enjoying the sunshine?"

Alice looked up. "Uh-oh, you brought the enforcer. You'll never take me alive." She thrust her wheelchair into gear, but Puna put a large shoe in front of the wheel, and she came to an abrupt, lurching halt.

"Whiplash," Alice shouted holding her neck. "Assault and battery. Citizen's arrest. I'm going to sue."

"Calm down, Mrs. Teng," Puna said. "You're fine. There are some cookies waiting for you back at Pacific Vista."

Her eyes grew wide. "Cookies? Do you have chocolate chip?"

"Nice fresh, soft cookies with melted chocolate." Puna licked his lips. "I hope they haven't all been eaten."

"Yum." Alice punched Puna on the arm. "Out of the way. Don't block me. I need to go get my snack."

Puna removed his foot and helped Evelyn to her feet. We headed back with Alice leading the way while shouting, "Let's get a move on. No time to delay."

Puna leaned over and whispered in my ear, "That's the one thing Mrs. Teng can't resist."

"Do you actually have some cookies for her?" I asked.

"I keep a batch in the cupboard for this type of emergency. I'll zap a few in the microwave for her."

Alice raced ahead of us but noticed we were lagging behind. She made a wheelie and came back. "Get a move on, you bozos. Cookies are waiting."

"I'm not as fast as you are, dear," Evelyn said. "I may have to get a hot rod like yours one of these days. It might come in handy when I want to break out again."

Alice grinned. "We're like Thelma and Louise. No one messes with us. We showed those yahoos, didn't we?"

"You certainly did," I said. "Alice, you helped catch the intruder who went into Evelyn's room last night."

"Hot damn." Alice came to a stop and spun her wheelchair to face us. "How'd I do that?"

"You ran into him and knocked him over," I said.

"I thought I hit a speed bump."

"Oh, you mean that guy who was blocking the sidewalk during the jailbreak," Evelyn said. "Good riddance."

"Hey, Evelyn," Alice said. "What say after cookies we bust out again?"

"I'm game."

"We can sneak past the guards and go on another fling."

"I'm going to put a boot on your wheelchair, Mrs. Teng," Puna said.

"You've got to catch me first." She shot off ahead of us.

When we reached the nursing home, Puna signed us in and escorted the ladies to the dining area for cookies. I sauntered along the beige hall toward my room. I was going to miss this place. Not.

"Paul, you're back," Ralph greeted me.

"Momentarily. I need to pack. The police nabbed Sal Polahi. Your hearing will be one of the pieces of evidence to convict him."

"No kidding? You going to tell me the whole story?"

"If you have the time."

"Paul, I have nothing but time."

I pulled up a chair and ran through the whole account of the encounter with Sal Polahi and his capture this morning.

"Quite an adventure." Ralph sighed. "It will be dull around here without you, Paul."

"I don't know. With people like Evelyn Newberry and Alice Teng, you should be adequately entertained."

An electric wheelchair raced into our room and ground to a stop. "Did I hear my name mentioned?"

"Hello, Alice," Ralph said.

"Hey, Ralphie. They have a big plate of chocolate chip cookies in the dining room. Want any?"

"Not right now."

"I'd eat more," Alice said, "but I'm stuffed."

"I'm going to miss your reading to me, Paul," Ralph said.

An idea occurred to me. "Alice, you have good eyesight. Do you by any chance read much?"

"All the time."

"I've been reading stories to Ralph. Now that I'm leaving the nursing home, would you be willing to read to him once in a while?"

She gave a wide, toothy smile. "Darn tootin'. When do we start?"

I retrieved my O. Henry short story collection and handed it to Alice. "You can pick out a story and read it to Ralph while I pack."

I found my suitcase in the closet and began to fold my Hawaiian shirts. In the background I heard Alice reading a story called "Sound and Fury." I didn't pay attention to it, but the title certainly captured the essence of Ralph and Alice.

Before I was done packing, Marion dashed into the room carrying two shopping bags. "I ran into Detective Chun in the lobby. He said the killer accosted you a little while ago. Are you all right?"

I shrugged. "I'm fine. He waved his gun at me, but Alice Teng here knocked him over with her electric wheelchair."

Marion put the bags down on the floor, placed her hands on her hips, and clicked her tongue. "Paul, what am I going to do with you? I can't leave you alone for two minutes without your getting in trouble."

"Actually it took approximately ten minutes."

Marion crossed her arms and tapped one shoe on the floor. "I expect the full story, Mr. Jacobson."

"Yes, ma'am." I again recited the account of the capture.

When Alice Teng finished reading to Ralph and closed the O. Henry book, Marion said to her, "Thank you for saving my husband, Mrs. Teng."

"It's Alice. Didn't even know I helped until afterwards. You never know what you're going to run into on these sidewalks."

"I need strong women to take care of me," I said.

Marion helped me finish packing, doing a much better job of neatly folding my clothes. Hey, I was merely a guy, what do you expect?

Detective Chun made the rounds, interviewing Alice Teng, Evelyn Newberry, and Puna Koloa before stopping to see Marion and me.

"I need you to come to police headquarters. Before you head back to the mainland, I'd like to do a video interview of everything that's happened."

"As long as you bribe me with malasadas."

We went with Detective Chun, and I starred in my own closed circuit television show. As promised, I had my pick of the best malasadas in the police department. I decided that the Honolulu Police Department had it hands down over any jurisdictions on the mainland. The others merely settled for donuts.

After completing the interview and patting my tummy from being duly stuffed to the gills, I sat with Marion while a friendly woman administrator took care of arranging our return reservations to Los Angeles, informing us of a confirmed flight the next night leaving at ten o'clock.

While we waited for a lift back to the nursing home, Marion suggested I call Jennifer. My granddaughter answered the phone and told me she had just returned home from school.

"Good timing. I want to tell you the outcome of my investigation."

"I bet you tracked down the bad guy, Grandpa."

"I helped. We cracked the case when the perp attacked the woman with synesthesia. And I had a lot of help from other people, including Henry and Madeline's discussion of Bo Jackson and my roommate's good hearing that helped eliminate another suspect. Then today I escaped being shot when a resident in her electric wheelchair bumped into the fugitive."

"You do lead an interesting life, Grandpa."

"I try to make each day count."

"I have another geezer joke for you, Grandpa."

I held the phone close to my ear. "Go for it."

"How can you tell a geezer has a good memory?"

"I don't know. That's not my area of expertise."

Jennifer cleared her throat. "He suddenly remembers where

he put his car keys ten years ago. Oops, Mom is calling. I need to go shopping for a new ski jacket."

After I finished the call, Marion said, "We have all tomorrow to enjoy Honolulu. Any ideas?"

I thought for a moment. "Let's see. Nothing to do with the ocean. We could tour the county jail or go skydiving." Then an idea occurred to me. "Okay. I know exactly what I want to do."

CHAPTER 38

Late the next afternoon we gathered in the dining room at the Pacific Vista Nursing Home. The tables had been cleared away except for one row that contained food and a large bowl of punch. Residents, staff, and guests helped themselves to all kinds of delectable puu puus including sushi, buffalo wings, fried calamari, veggies, fruit, miniature chocolate éclairs, and a huge plate of chocolate chip cookies. Colored balloons bobbed on the walls.

Puna Koloa stepped up to a lectern, grasped a microphone that became buried in one giant fist, and held his other hand above his head.

"*A—lo—ha!*" Puna shouted.

"*Aloha,*" came the response from the crowd.

"Good to see all the smiling faces." Puna added his own gigantic grin, light shining off his gold tooth.

"Puna rocks," Alice Teng shouted.

Puna waved to Alice. "We're gathered here today thanks to Paul Jacobson. He's been with us for less than two weeks and will be returning to the mainland tonight with his wife, Marion. He decided to put on this bash for all of you before he leaves."

A round of applause rippled through the room.

"Paul, come say a few words." Puna handed me the mic.

I breathed into the microphone, and a static scream came out of the speakers. Puna grabbed my hand and moved the mic farther from my mouth.

"Thanks, Puna. I wanted to get all of you together to say goodbye. Even though I've only lived here a short time, I've made some good friends, not that I'll remember them tomorrow with my short-term memory loss."

"But we'll remember you, jerk," Madeline yelled from the back of the room.

I smiled, glad that Madeline, Henry, and Meyer could attend the party on such short notice.

"As I was saying, maybe it's a good thing I can't remember anything from day to day. I'd like to thank several people in particular. First, my roommate, Ralph Hirata, who put up with me and taught me that hearing can overcome the loss of eyesight. Come up here, Ralph."

Puna pushed Ralph's wheelchair up to the front of the room.

"And if Alice Teng would join him."

Alice came charging out of the crowd in her electric wheelchair and performed a perfect three-hundred-sixty-degree wheelie.

"I'm willing my collection of O. Henry short stories to Ralph and Alice. Alice has agreed to read to Ralph."

Alice pumped her fist in the air three times. "And I can whip any of you yahoos in a race any time."

"I'm sure you can," I said. I handed the book to Ralph who waved to the onlookers with his shaky hand. "One more thing for you, Ralph. Here's a box of licorice, And, Alice, the big plate of chocolate chip cookies over there is especially for you."

"Yum." Alice put her wheelchair in gear and headed over to the goody table.

"Next. Evelyn Newberry. Please come forward."

Evelyn shuffled up to the lectern.

"As some of you know, Evelyn has the amazing ability to see colors for numbers. Her unique talent contributed to tracking down the man who had been causing problems around the nursing home. I have a quilt for her that has numbers on it. My wife helped me pick it out." I handed it to her.

"This is beautiful," Evelyn said. "It looks like a rainbow."

Benny Makoku stepped to the lectern and asked to speak. "As most of you know, we have a suspect under arrest, thanks to the efforts of Paul Jacobson. He agreed to help the police track down the perpetrator at risk to himself. I'd like to present him with a memento so he can remember his stay in the islands." Benny put a kukui lei over my neck. The black nuts shone with a bright luster.

"Okay," I said. "Everyone dive into the food."

Marion came up and admired the lei. "You can add this to your collection when we get home."

"Collection?"

"Yes. With your escapades, you've built up a considerable amount of memorabilia given to you by police officers all over the country. You have a butterfly collection from Detective Saito of the Kaneohe police, a picture of the Boulder County Jail from Colorado, a framed ticket from a fishing violation in Venice Beach, a whale figurine from our Alaskan cruise, an award last month from Detective Chun here in Honolulu, and now this kukui lei from Officer Makoku."

I scratched my head. "I'll be darned."

I moseyed over to the food table and noticed a woman with wild spiky hair looking wistfully at a plate of cheese. She saw me there and said, "I wish I could find some soap instead of cheese."

That clicked with what I had read in my journal. "You must be Louise Wilkins."

"The same."

"When you have a favorite food, nothing else will do." I reached in my pocket and pulled out a small wrapped bar of soap I had removed from Marion's condo that morning and handed it to her. "This is a present for you. Nibble on it, but don't eat it all in one sitting."

Officer Makoku pointed out Ken Yamamoto to me, and I went to shake his hand. "I'm sorry I suspected you of the crimes."

He grinned. "Hey, no problem, Mr. Jacobson."

"Sal Polahi really fooled us. I jumped to the conclusion that since you're an actor, you had disguised yourself."

"With my actor's makeup being used, it was a natural conclusion to reach. I'm going to get a lock for my storage bin from now on."

"Good idea."

I spotted a guy with an earring and a surfboard tattoo on the back of his right hand. I approached him and said, "Dan Aukina, I presume?"

"That's me, Mr. Jacobson."

I shook his hand. "I have to confess I suspected you at one time of the crimes committed by Sal Polahi. My apologies."

He laughed and leaned close to whisper in my ear. "It couldn't have been me. Most people don't know, but I'm not interested in women."

Puna performed a Hawaiian war chant, and, afterward, Madeline challenged him to an arm wrestling match. They cleared one of the food tables and set up chairs on either side. The combatants took their seats and locked wrists. Veins popped out of Puna's neck as he strained to move Madeline's hand. Madeline's face turned a shade of red and then purple. Both arms quivered, but no one gave in.

Finally, Benny intervened. "I'm ruling it a tie."

Puna and Madeline slumped into their chairs.

"First time I haven't won," Puna said.

"Same for me, and I've been arm wrestling for a good many more years than you have," Madeline replied.

"Maybe you're getting old," I said.

Madeline stuck her face an inch from mine. "Would you care to repeat that?"

"Maybe you're getting bold," I said.

"I don't care what anyone says about you, jerk, I like you." Madeline gave me a hug that knocked the wind out of my lungs.

I watched as Henry grazed, stuffing his face with one handful after another. It was amazing. For a little squirt, he sure put away the food. After popping a tomato in his mouth, he turned to see me staring at him.

He crinkled his nose. "Are you going to stand there, jerk, or are you going to eat some food?"

"I'm enjoying the sight of you decimating the local flora and fauna. I won't get any closer to the food because I don't want to risk losing one of my fingers."

After the eating frenzy had died down, Benny, Meyer, Henry, Madeline, Marion, and I accompanied Puna, who wheeled Ralph back to his room.

"Meyer, you'll have to come visit Ralph and listen to Alice Teng read stories now that she's taking over for me," I said.

"If I can convince Madeline to drive me here," Meyer replied.

Puna brought the wheelchair to a halt. "She'll have to do that so we can have an arm wrestling rematch and I can whip her good."

Madeline poked a solid finger into his beefy shoulder. "You and who else? In your dreams, pigmy boy. I'll take you on again any time, any place."

They stared at each other, and both broke into laughter. They hugged, and for a moment I imagined they might try to throw each other to the floor, but instead they released their grip.

"All right," I said. "There's a reason for all of you to get together again. I'm not going to miss this room, but I'll miss you, Ralph. You've been a good roommate."

"Likewise, Paul." Ralph let out a deep sigh. "There's only one thing. I wish I could find my Bronze Star."

"You lose it?" Madeline asked.

"Yeah," Ralph replied. "It was in my box of memorabilia but it disappeared."

I turned to Benny. "Did the police by any chance find it in Sal Polahi's apartment?"

Benny shook his head. "We uncovered the jewelry stolen from Linda Rodriguez and Annabel Dempsey but not Ralph's missing Bronze Star."

"Henry is good at finding things," Meyer said. "Have him take a look."

"I bet the jerk lost it," Henry said.

"I was showing Paul the medal when I last had it," Ralph said. "He put the box back in the closet, and some things fell out. He couldn't find it when he looked around on the floor."

"Let a professional take care of this." Henry marched to the closet, pulled open the door, and began rifling through the clothes. "Pissant probably didn't even look closely . . . yup, here it is. Fell in this jacket pocket."

Henry emerged from the closet holding the missing Bronze Star.

"Honeybunch is so observant." Madeline picked up Henry, squeezed him, and planted a kiss on the top of his bald head.

Henry let out a squeak.

"Honeybunch to the rescue." I squinted at the metal star and accompanying ribbon. "Mystery solved."

Detective Chun marched into the room. "Sorry I missed the party. I did want to stop by before you left, Mr. Jacobson."

"Do you have all the evidence you need to send that scumbag Sal Polahi away for life?" I asked.

"Yeah, we're in good shape. We found a torn sweatshirt with

Bo Jackson's number thirty-four on it. When confronted with the evidence, he spilled his guts."

"Good job," I said. "Any indication why he committed all these despicable acts?"

Chun sucked on his lip for a moment. "A strange tale. He confessed he planned to sell the jewelry so he could buy an expensive set of actor's makeup and props and not have to take Ken Yamamoto's any longer. He said he was sexually attracted to old women. That's why he took jobs in nursing homes. He indicated his interest reached a point where he played out his desires with Mrs. Rodriguez. He justified it by saying he provided excitement in her life."

"Including killing her?"

"Sal went back a second time to . . . ah . . . renew their intimacy. This time she threatened to scream. He says he didn't mean to kill her. He only tried to keep her quiet."

"Right. Like he tried to keep me quiet with a rock to my head and a pillow over my face."

"He figured he needed to scare you off."

"Including kidnapping Marion." Then the realization struck me. "It was lucky he didn't try to sexually assault her."

Chun's mouth twitched. "Sal said Marion was too young for him."

"Good thing. I'm glad she's not too young for me."

"Thanks again, Mr. Jacobson," Chun said. "Sure you wouldn't like to stay in Honolulu and help with other cases?"

"No thanks, Detective. I think I'll hightail it back to the really big island—the mainland—before I get in any more trouble."

ABOUT THE AUTHOR

Mike Befeler is author of five previous novels in the Paul Jacobson Geezer-Lit Mystery Series: *Retirement Homes Are Murder, Living with Your Kids Is Murder* (a finalist for The Lefty Award for best humorous mystery of 2009), *Senior Moments Are Murder, Cruising in Your Eighties Is Murder* (a finalist for The Lefty Award for best humorous mystery of 2012), and *Care Homes Are Murder.* He is also author of two paranormal mysteries, *The V V Agency* and *The Back Wing.* Mike is co-chair of the Boulder County Aging Advisory Council and is president of the Rocky Mountain Chapter of Mystery Writers of America. He grew up in Honolulu, Hawaii, and now lives in Boulder, Colorado, with his wife, Wendy.

If you are interested in having the author speak to your book club, contact Mike Befeler at mikebef@aol.com. His website is http://www.mikebefeler.com.